Love Vibes

Jen Davenport

For more information, or to book an event, contact :

authorjendavenport@gmail.com

https://authorjendavenport.com/

ISBN - Paperback: 978-1-955532-41-9
ISBN - Ebook : 9781955532402
First Edition: December 2024

1

Maddy

Ten pairs of eyes focused on Maddy as she held a carrot—dull, withered, and desperately limp—in the air. "This is not what you want to put the condom on."

The room filled with quiet chuckles and giggles as the carrot flopped back and forth in her hand. She'd learned carrots went limp if kept in a paper bag in the fridge. Perfect for the class demonstration.

Her class, Pervertibles 101, had all ages, shapes, personalities, and types of people. The idea of an intimacy enhancement class for adults had been risky, but her eighty-three-year-old nana said they'd never know if it worked if they didn't try.

Maddy grinned as she traded the carrot for a crisp, girthy cucumber and surveyed the room. She bit the inside of her cheek, hoping to stop her trembling lip—the first sign of her crowd-anxiety kicking in as she looked over the small classroom. More people than she'd expected signed up. So many, in fact, she'd scheduled four more classes in the next month and a half.

Pinks and Pearls, the erotic toy boutique her grandmother owned, was in no way struggling, but Maddy wanted a way to contribute without doing any sales work.

"This–"

"Makes a great toy," a lady with salt and peppered hair seated at the back of the room chimed in.

The room erupted in laughter and Maddy nodded. The response was unexpected, but not unwanted. Maddy's greatest fear had been a silent class where everyone stared at her with blank faces. Questions signaled they were paying attention and comfortable enough to get involved.

"Yes, it is. Not only can you use it to practice putting a condom on with your mouth, but it can also be used as an insertable." She paused to give everyone time to consider her words and take a few calming breaths of her own. "As long as you are careful."

People raised their hands, and the questions flowed. What else could they use around the house to spice things up in the bedroom? How did she recommend "being careful" when using food?

Maddy's lip quit trembling and beads of sweat no longer threatened to drip off her palms. The anxiety lessened with each new hand raised in the air.

"How bad does it hurt to get a spanking with a wooden spoon?" A lady not much younger than Maddy's thirty-five years asked with hesitation.

"I won't say it doesn't hurt. Expect some pain. Severity is dependent on the person and their tolerance. What I can tell you is a wooden spoon is more of a sting than a thud, which means it burns for a few seconds and then the pain starts to dissipate. A lot of people will tell you it's a good pain." Maddy winked. She hoped her openness and lack of judgment helped her participants realize no question was a stupid one.

Not that she had a lot of experience with spanking. That wasn't her thing, and it hadn't been her ex-wife's cup of tea. No, Natasha preferred to hurt Maddy in more inconspicuous ways, like telling her how ridiculous it was to think she could run a business. Maddy shook off the morose train of thoughts. It was not the time to bring up the past.

An hour later, pleased with the way the class went, Maddy flopped down onto her chair, the room empty, her table covered in the fruits, vegetables, and condoms they'd used for hands-on demonstrations. Exhausted from the energy she'd used to hide her hesitations and fears.

"Well, if the chatter outside means anything, I'd say you found your purpose."

The click-clack of cane and heels followed the compliment. Nana's grin stretched ear to ear. Lola Begay was best described as short and sassy with more than a little spice. She'd shrunk over the years to a little more than five feet tall, but that didn't change the way she commanded a room the moment she walked through the door.

"They seemed to have fun. I hope they learned something," Maddy pressed her palms into her eyes, attempting to stop the burn of exhaustion.

"Even better if they come back to buy things." Nana winked.

Maddy stood with a sigh then motioned for Nana to take her seat. When she'd come up with Pervertibles 101 as the first class she hadn't considered the possible impact on sales downstairs.

"I'm sorry," she said.

Her shoulders sagged. To think, her parents begged her to go into corporate America like them. They wanted her to build a reputable business from the ground up.

Despite having a degree in business, Maddy lacked business savvy. She'd tried to launch two businesses of her own. Neither of them lasted longer than a year, something her parents and ex-wife reminded her of often.

Business was an afterthought for Maddy. Growing up she'd wanted to explore public speaking, or teaching—a career where she spent time with people. Each dreaded semester brought more boring business courses. She stuck it out because that's what her parents wanted, and more than anything, Maddy wanted them to be proud of her.

Ten years later and a master's degree in business, she still hadn't achieved her goal of obtaining their approval. Nope. She was the misfit of the family. Failed entrepreneur. A flighty thirty-five-year-old child who ran off to Oregon to take care of her grandparents, which wasn't appreciated by her parents at all.

When she explained her plan to teach at Pinks and Pearls her parents laughed at her. They said she wouldn't keep the classes going long enough to see a true profit. If she kept missing the opportunities to boost sales for the shop through her classes, they'd be right.

"Whatever are you sorry for?" Nana's voice rose with the question.

"For not thinking of the financial side of things like an owner. I mean, I taught ten people how to have fun at home using kitchen utensils and vegetables. I didn't even consider suggesting they purchase toys from the store. There are four more classes scheduled like this one. Fifty potential customers, I'm teaching how to avoid the shop, not to come here."

Nana clicked her tongue. "You're wrong. You're making the shop money by bringing in fifty potential new customers. Not everyone who comes in buys something on their first visit. With this class you've taught them how to make the bedroom more fun, and you've given them ideas that they can run with. If even ten percent come back, then it's a win."

Maddy hated the struggle of missing foresight beyond the current moment. First, she failed to think about promotion, then she didn't consider the possibility her attendees would return later for more toys. She made a mental note for her future classes of how to improve their return on investment.

"Thank you, Nana." Maddy sighed. "On the plus side, they did pay to take the class so at least we got something there."

"Of course, my sweet girl. If they spend money downstairs, it's added revenue. You're charging them twenty dollars each. That's a thousand dollars we wouldn't have otherwise. I'm glad you gave this a shot. Pinks needs your ideas to continue growing. This town is too sexually repressed. It needs your education."

She couldn't help but laugh at Nana's observation.

"I don't know about that, but I do know I need to get downstairs and help with the last few hours of the day. You should head home. El will be here soon, I'll ask if she can drive you. There's no reason to stay all night."

Twenty minutes later Nana didn't argue when Maddy's best friend arrived and left with Elowen. People filled the shop.

Regular customers in the market for a new toy or way to spice things up, new customers with wide eyes and red cheeks as they meandered around the displays, and the younger ones who wanted a condom or two. They came in with their heads down, grabbed what they needed, paid, and left without a word.

After the door was locked and the open sign flipped off, sweat matted her hair from wiping down the counters, front-facing the products, and sweeping the hardwood floors. Maddy's feet ached from the stupid heels she'd worn, and what she wanted most was a drink at the bar next door.

A steady beat sounded from The Rustic Knob, a bar her grandfather opened at the same time as Pinks and Pearls. At the register, finishing the final count for the day, Maddy swayed her hips to the low hum of jazz floating through the back door where the two businesses connected. Papa built the cigar bar with a décor of well-worn leather and dark mahogany that matched Pinks and Pearls. Back when shops like Pinks were supposed to be underground, he'd told Nana the speakeasy would be a good way to hide the erotic toy boutique.

Maddy's back creaked when she leaned down to pick up the broom she'd dropped. When did she get old enough for her bones to be noisy? El sashayed through the back room with a wave. It was time to head next door for a nightcap with her best friend before going home.

"One of our last customers caused quite the scene tonight." Maddy slid onto a bar stool with her chin tucked to her chest.

The bartender, Jack, grabbed a cider from the cooler; popped the cap before handing it to her.

The Knob was a cigar bar with a selection of whiskey, rum, and brandy wasn't meant to serve a lot of beer. Jack kept cider for Maddy because she limited her intake of hard liquor and—well, there were perks to being Lola and Delbert's granddaughter.

El, on the other hand, preferred the selection of liquor. She accepted a glass of their finest bourbon on the rocks.

"What do you mean? Were they causing problems?"

"Oh no. Not at all. They...well, the wife asked me about one of the double-ended dongs. When I explained how they could use it, her husband fainted. I lost another sale."

"Girl, they asked how it worked. How were you supposed to know he couldn't handle the thought of pegging himself? They didn't want to know; they shouldn't have asked." El shrugged.

Maddy choked on her drink. Elowen patted her on the back.

"If I were any good at sales, I'd have used more of a filter. Maybe asked if they'd ever explored anal sex to get a reaction first. In to help the store, I've got to quit scaring customers away." Maddy leaned her elbows on the bar top.

A tap on her shoulder had Maddy spinning around to face a couple of men, one she recognized from her class. The other, well, Maddy spent more time than she should checking out the man closest to her and El. He stood tall; a dark shadow marked the outline of his jaw. She noticed the muscles of his forearms flex and relax as he drank from his bottle.

She didn't realize the other man was talking until El nudged her in the ribs.

Maddy cleared her throat. "I'm sorry. What was that?"

The man from class gave her a knowing smirk. Yeah, she'd been caught ogling his friend.

"Crash." He held his hand out for her to shake. "I wanted to stop by and thank you for your class today. I can't wait to try out some of your suggestions. Out of curiosity, do you think you could do a class about pegging with those cucumbers?"

The man next to him shook his head and walked to the other side of the bar. Elowen snorted and Maddy sat with her mouth gaping open, unsure how to respond.

"Umm, I'm not sure that's such a good idea. A lot of people have a bad reaction to pegging," Maddy said.

"Only because they don't know what it is. Isn't that your whole point in this adventure? To teach us how to be more open-minded and give us a safe place to talk about things we're curious about, but don't know how to bring it up? Or don't want someone to search our browser history and judge us?" Crash didn't hesitate to lay it all out there.

"A good argument." El snickered.

Maddy cast a glare in El's direction, but she didn't shy away or explode into flames.

"Crash?" Maddy asked.

"That's right. Got it from the guys on-site. What do you think?"

What was she supposed to say? The courses were designed to promote sex-positivity. The best recommendations sometimes came from the customers.

"I'll think about it. Maybe we can have a subject-specific class, and I can find a more knowledgeable presenter with experience in pegging."

Crash nodded. With a twinkle in his eyes, he smiled wide enough to show his teeth.

"Thank you. I enjoyed your presentation today. It's a great idea. Next time I'll drag that prude with me so he can learn a trick or two." Crash pointed his thumb over his shoulder at the other man.

"Sounds good." It had been a long day, and she was ready for the man to move on, even though she was grateful for his praise.

"You two ladies have a good evening. I'll leave you alone now." Crash offered a quick chin nod before heading toward his friend.

Maddy glanced to where the two men now sat. The man who wasn't Crash winked. She held her hand to her chest, but it did nothing for her racing pulse. With each passing second her body warmed a bit more. Maddy bet he had one of those voices that melted a woman's insides.

"You going to go talk to him?" El asked.

"What?" Maddy whipped around to face her best friend. "Why would you even ask that?"

El tossed her head back and laughed. "Don't think I didn't see him wink at you. That was an invitation if I've ever seen one."

"No. You're wrong. That was more like 'I'm sorry for my friend but thank you for not being rude to him.'" Maddy shook her head.

They sipped their drinks in silence. Maddy let the smooth jazz lull her into a near sleep. Out of the corner of her eye, she watched El trace circles around the bottom of her glass.

Even though the guy with Crash was hot and got her blood pumping, Maddy wasn't ready for a relationship. She hadn't been in one since her divorce a few years back. El and her nana kept encouraging Maddy to dip her toes in the water again, but Maddy didn't have the mental bandwidth for drama.

The rings of condensation on the bar held her attention. Crash and his friend were attractive. They'd gone to her class, so they weren't too sexually repressed, not that Maddy judged those who were. It made it easier knowing someone was open to sex. Maybe El and Lola were right, and she did need to re-enter the dating world. Being bisexual gave her plenty of options.

Maddy's skin prickled with anxiety. Any other night El would talk her ear off. It was one of the reasons she suggested going to the bar. Listening to El ramble on while sipping on a cold cider made for a great way to come down from a day of working.

"Back to the not-near-as-interesting conversation about you and the shop, Lola won't work forever. She's going to need you to take over and keep things going. This is your chance to learn." El broke the silence between them.

"Maybe it would be better for Nana to hire someone to replace me. I could fill in when needed but put my focus on the classes. There's no point in giving me the store. I'll scare too many people away." She took a drink then turned back to her friend. "I don't want to be a failure from the start. If I lost Pinks or The Knob, I'd die of guilt."

"Your grandmother wouldn't have let you start the classes if she didn't trust your judgment. What makes you a failure is if you let your pride or the ridiculous thoughts your ex-wife planted in your head override logic. Your grandmother knows this business like the back of her hand. She's willing to show you the ropes. Don't throw that back in her face by handing the store off to someone else. Take time. Figure it out. There's nothing wrong with that."

While Maddy appreciated the reprieve from her own thoughts, El's pep talk wasn't working to convince her that this business wouldn't crash and burn like the others.

"I've already blown it with two startups. Why should I think this would be any different? It's better to admit my weakness up front." Maddy didn't look at El.

El tossed back her drink without another word. The conversation stalled once more. Maddy leaned over the bar to grab a bowl of pretzels.

"Random question, why're you wearing those damn six-inch heels?" El asked.

With a groan, Maddy stuck her foot in the air and twisted her ankle from side to side.

"These? They were a mistake, and I didn't bring extra shoes. My goal was professionalism—so ridiculous."

Elowen reached forward and grabbed Maddy's ankle and pulled her leg across her lap. The skirt she wore made it so Maddy had to stretch both legs across her friends lap to keep her balance.

"What are you doing?" Maddy laughed as she tried to pull her legs back down, but Elowen draped her arm across to keep them still.

"You have a very cute dress on, but if you don't quit moving, you're going to show everyone what's under it." Elowen winked.

Heat raced up Maddy's neck to her cheeks.

"You'd like to know what I'm wearing under this petticoat wouldn't you?" Maddy ruffled the skirt of the gold plaid swing dress.

Elowen's fingers danced up Maddy's leg from her ankle to her knee.

"Mmm. I would, but it's better if we don't scandalize Jack like that." El chuckled.

Maddy leaned her head back and released a slow breath. Elowen gently lifted Maddy's legs off her lap and lowered them to the small bar around the lower half of the barstool.

"What was that all about?" Maddy asked.

Her friend shrugged. "You seemed to like Crash's friend. I noticed him checking you out, so I thought we'd give him a show."

What was Maddy supposed to say to that? She hadn't noticed anyone paying attention to them, much less the hot guy on the other side of the bar.

After a few minutes of awkward silence, their conversation returned to Pinks and Maddy's newest venture with the classes. Elowen offered her thoughts on potential topics. Eleven turned to midnight. and Jack made the last call.

"There's a new account you have to hear about." El started then paused. "It's a blind dating site. You choose your own blind date, get to know them, and when you're ready, meet them. They named it Blind Love. My tagline right now is 'Find emotional love not just physical.'"

Companies hired El to develop marketing plans for new products and once the initial contract expired, she moved onto the next one. She loved being able to pick and choose the projects rather than working for corporations and doing whatever they said.

"That sounds...frightening." Maddy winced and shook her body like she was covered in bugs.

There were many ways a blind dating site could go wrong. Catfishing was the least of her worries.

"Frightening?" El squeaked. "Why would you say that?"

"Seems like it could be a cesspool for weirdos that prey on people. Probably more women than men, but there's no reason to limit predatory people by gender." Maddy shrugged.

"That's fair. I've worked with these guys for a few months and helped them beef up security. There's no way to eliminate the risk, but at least they've taken some measures. It took me weeks to decide whether to sign the contract. One of the things I accepted was that no dating app is perfect. Even with pictures there are still catfish." El took Maddy's hands in her own. "I need your help. If I do well with this contract, it can turn into something long term."

Maddy stared at their linked hands. A jumble of thoughts fought for attention. Her heart wanted to try out the app and see if she was ready to date again. Her head wanted to try out the app to help her friend, but nothing more. Maddy needed to put her focus on figuring out a way for Nana to retire without losing the shop and bar.

"You said this is a blind dating app. How are there pictures?" Maddy needed to know a little more about the app.

"The idea is you get to know the person before you see their pictures. In fact, if you don't connect and never decide to meet, then the person won't know more than your basic information. Name, age, gender, likes and dislikes. Those kinds of things. If you agree to meet, then you'll see each other's pictures."

El made a strong case. Still, Maddy wasn't sure she wanted to say yes to helping. If her heart got involved, then she may end up worse than she started. Fear of falling in love was the worst kind of excuse for not helping a friend in need.

"I'll help. You wouldn't take on a project that was inherently unsafe. What do you need from me?"

El paced behind them. "Okay, I know you're crazy busy with the shop and the bar."

"You want me to try out the app so you can either use my testimonial or turn down a long-term contract if they offer it."

"Yes and no. I want you to try the app then give me feedback. Any long-term offers will hinge on success, but this is one part of the launch. There's no pressure. Second, Blind Love is willing to pay you a thousand dollars if you'll give us a review after a three-month trial."

"I'm not going to turn down the money. I already said I'd do it." Maddy rolled her eyes. "You knew I'd say yes."

El shook her hips back and forth and fist bumped the air. "Perfect. We need to—"

Maddy held up a finger. "Let's lay down some ground rules. One: You don't get a say in who I meet or don't meet. Two: If I match with someone, you promise not to get involved and turn it into more than a date or two. Third: I may not have plans to take over the shop and bar, but I won't let Nana down. She can't run things by herself. If this gets to be too much, I'll stop."

"Yes, yes. Of course, to all of them." She paused. "Except the last one, which your grandmother would veto. You worry too much, and Lola wants to see you happy." Elowen reached across Maddy to the bar and grabbed her phone.

Her foot bounced up and down on the floor as El downloaded the app so they could get the profile set up as soon as possible. Her fingers shook as she waited for El to put in the personal information. Maybe it wasn't a great idea to help. If signing up made her feel ready to throw up, then she didn't want to imagine how she'd react to meeting someone.

Had her ex-wife really done that much damage to her psyche? Maddy thought she'd gotten over the trauma, but maybe she was wrong.

"You know, I'm not sure this is such a good idea. Dating's fun, but these apps never work for me." Maddy laid her head on her arms.

El huffed. "It's a way for you to have a life. I'm your best friend, I know how much of a life you don't have."

"Right. You're my best friend and I'm doing this to help you." Maddy groaned when she caught a peek of the image El uploaded. "We're not using that picture of me on our canoe trip last year."

Her long black hair was an unruly mess since she'd left it down that day rather than pulling it up and the sunlight made gold starburst around her dark brown eyes. But she didn't have any makeup on, and she'd been too drunk to walk straight. Hence, the crooked sneer.

"Nope. Memories of being on a drunken boat, stuck in the middle of the river, are too much. Every time I look at it, I'm going to revert to the days of still trying to drink away the hurt from my divorce. It's embarrassing that I was hung up on Natasha two years after our split."

"Yes, you are. Without argument, too. You're using the cutest candid you've taken in the last year. These memories should be good ones. Happy ones you made with your ahhh-mazing new friend. Not sad ones over the disgusting woman who treated you less than you deserved." She clapped her hands.

As it turned out the pictures at the end were El's idea. Another attempt to keep the users as safe as possible given the intent of the app. Sure, it might end up in some heartbreak because people were jerks and would cancel the date once they saw pictures, but at least it might deter a catfish or two.

"Fine, let's finish setting me up on Blind Love." Maddy stuck out her tongue.

2

Ax rubbed his forehead and leaned against the wall next to the door of the trailer. He hadn't slept in a week thanks to crew drama. He swore men were bigger babies—and gossipers—than women most of the time. The night before, dreams of the woman from the sex class interrupted his sleep cycle and left him with a case of raging-hard-on the next morning. Her deep brown eyes and fiery gaze filled his dreams. No doubt her suggestions to spice up the bedroom would fuel his fantasies for a while.

When he moved to Podunk a year ago, he vowed not to get involved with a woman for at least two to three years. Ax wanted to enjoy being single after spending the last seven years tied down by either his ex-wife or his family. After learning some of Maddy's secrets, he wondered if maybe it was time to start looking to date again. He could dip his pinky toe in to test the waters, like his adopted grandfather suggested.

He pulled out his phone and searched for the app he'd overheard the women talking about the night before. Blind something. Once he found it, he downloaded it and started his profile.

Ax swiped to the left for a new profile. Since no one saw a picture until they agreed to meet, he had to decide based on their avatar and bio. The next one made him stand up straight. A unicorn with the middle finger as a horn avatar and a rainbow in the background made him laugh out loud.

He clicked on the Read More button to read her stats.

Name: Madelyn (Maddy) Begay

Age: Thirty-Five and a half

About Me: I'm bisexual, work in an erotic-toy boutique, and help my grandma with her cigar bar. If you have a problem with any of that, swipe left.

It was her. The woman of his dreams—literally.

The half made him chuckle. He hadn't met many women who would share not only their age, but their half age. The way she controlled the classroom combined with her excitement about sex, it didn't surprise him she was proud to share her age. A good thing, he was ten years her senior after all.

He closed his eyes to mentally recall the way she looked standing at the front of the room and then again at the bar. Sun kissed skin; wide, angular eyes; and what he'd guessed would have been smooth, black hair tied in a messy knot on top of her head.

Ax wouldn't have considered himself prudish, but he wasn't headed to the local store every weekend either. The subject matter of the class brought his lack of knowledge out into the open for everyone. If hadn't been for her diligence to make sure the class felt welcome, Ax would've left five minutes after it started.

The door banged against the wall as the guys came in for lunch. Right on time, too. His thoughts were taking a direction he didn't need during work hours. It was bad enough his dreams had him waking out of breath and sweating with his hand cramping.

"Ax, man, Crash is a dangerous bastard. The guy has a fucking cast on his arm and he's out there trying to run the damn splitter." Brett, one of the crew, started before he'd stepped into the trailer.

The rest of them filed into the trailer. Not for the first time, Ax was grateful the site manager purchased a larger trailer than some of the others they'd worked in. Fifteen loggers filled the space in no time. Ax hung back from everyone, scrolling through more profiles on the new app after swiping right for Maddy. If they matched, she could reach out and set up a time to meet. Or they'd chat first. He hoped for texting and then meeting. At least then he'd get to know her and maybe figure out a way not to drool when they were face-to-face again.

"Are you on a dating app?" Crash leaned against the counter next to Ax, his arms crossed over his chest. He nodded toward Ax's phone.

"Yeah." He didn't look at Crash, just continued flipping through profiles.

There weren't many good ones for him to stop and consider. In fact, there weren't that many people in the area at all—a surprise since people seemed to like dating apps.

"Didn't know you were looking for a relationship." Crash shoved a handful of chips in his mouth.

"I'm not. Thought I'd check it out to see what was available. Been awhile since I've had someone to warm my bed." Inwardly, Ax cringed. He never wanted to be one of those love 'em or leave 'em types like Crash.

The man was the first person he'd met when he moved to Podunk. On the outside, Crash came across like a real asshole. Ax knew better. He was loyal to his family, spent most of his time running around doing errands for his mom and sisters, and loved animals. His playboy persona was an act.

"That's a new one. What's it called?" Crash asked. "How did you find it?"

"Heard the ladies talking about it at the bar last night. Blind Love. You put your profile on here, if you find a match you see pictures after you agree to meet. The idea is that you match on personality before looks."

"Ahh now that makes more sense. You eavesdropped on a conversation and now you want to hook up with the teacher. Go get her." His friend elbowed him in the side. "Hot, knows her sex stuff, and I'd imagine she can take care of herself. Good looking friend, too. Maybe if you and the teacher hook up, then you can set me up with the friend."

"Didn't notice." Liar.

"Yeah. You're a lying piece of shit." Crash guffawed.

"Dean made me promise to get out more or he'd start setting me up with the ladies at the home. Said I'm worse than some of his neighbors when it comes to a social life." Ax punched Crash in his shoulder.

"The old man isn't wrong." Crash puffed out his chest. "Also, getting called out by your grandfather. That's sad, man."

Before lunch ended Ax's phone chimed with a new message notification. He clicked open the app and stared at the number one in the upper right corner of the message bubble.

He clicked the icon.

Maddy: Hey. I checked out your profile and thought we could maybe get to know each other. Sorry, this is awkward. I'm not sure what to say.

Ax read her message and laughed. He wasn't sure what to say either. The idea of an app to get to know people on personality was cool, but how was he supposed to take the next step? He could ask about her likes and dislikes but worried it might be too boring. He typed six different messages before deciding on a simple reply. Not to mention, he wasn't sure when to let her know they'd already met. Since she didn't know his name, she wouldn't find out unless they agreed to an in-person meeting. If he waited, would that be a deal breaker? Would she think he lied to her?

Ax: Hi. I hoped we'd connect. You sound like you know how to have fun. Maybe we can text until we're comfortable enough to meet.

It didn't take long for her to respond.

Maddy: That sounds good to me. Um, where do we start?

3

Maddy

Ax: Let's start with something easy. What made you start a profile? I mean, I know you're searching for friends, but why this way?

She read his question, and her heart stopped for a quick second. The idea of getting to know this man before seeing him brought an unexpected thrill into the mix. Her new mysterious potential partner. Her fingers moved across the screen.

Maddy: I did a favor for my best friend. She asked me to check it out, so here I am. What about you?

Well, that and she wanted to see if the grass was greener on the other side.

Maddy checked the time on her phone—eleven o'clock. She couldn't remember the last time she'd slept in late, even if it was Saturday. The notification she'd ignored the day before from the Blind Love app remained. She clicked it open.

After grabbing a shower Maddy headed to the kitchen for coffee. Sleeping in did nothing to stop her body from craving that first cup of coffee. On the way out of her room, Maddy swiped her phone off the nightstand. Her heart clenched a little when he hadn't replied yet.

Stupid. It's Saturday morning—almost afternoon.

The phone vibrated against her palm.

"Hey, sunshine. What's up?" Her best friend's voice sounded in her ear.

Maddy's body twinged with excitement. El had one of those phone voices that radio deejays craved. It was sweetness and sexy all in one. Maddy could listen to her talk about nothing. They might be nothing more than friends, but it didn't mean there wasn't a little attraction. More to the point, Maddy wasn't interested in acting on it.

"Just woke up. You have plans today?" Maddy asked.

"Nope. Was calling to see what you were doing. Want me to head over?" If El came over, then Maddy could tell her about the match.

El wanted Maddy to test the app. She'd even set up the profile, but it felt like more than a marketing ploy. For a reason Maddy couldn't name, the idea of talking to Ax without telling El first made her fidgety.

In true Elowen fashion, she showed up an hour and twenty minutes later than expected. Maddy wasn't complaining though. The extra time gave her a chance to binge one of her favorite comedies, which was how she ended up answering the door in her most comfortable pair of yoga pants, a black tank top, and her third mug of coffee.

El pinched her nose and squinted her eyes. "We have got to get you some new pants. Those have holes all over them."

El waved her hand through the air as she stepped over the threshold.

Maddy chuckled. "Yep, and we're not replacing them. They're my comfy pants."

Her apartment was tiny in comparison to El's cottage. A one-bedroom, one bathroom with a small living area and even smaller kitchen.

Maddy shut the door then turned toward the living room, knowing her friend would follow. She settled on the couch with her legs tucked under her while El took her preferred spot in the middle of the floor.

"Listen, there's something I have to tell you."

"What?"

Madelyn lowered her gaze to the floor and cleared her throat. "Umm. I connected with someone on Blind Love."

El rocketed off the floor, clapping her hands. A high-pitched squeal rang through the room and Maddy slammed her hands over her ears.

"El. Elowen. Stop. STOP." Madelyn shouted each word louder and louder.

Her best friend plopped down on the couch beside her and took Maddy's face in her hands before planting a kiss on her lips.

"Aww hell. I'm sorry." El turned away from Maddy and buried her head in her hands. "I don't know what came over me. That was a little inappropriate. I'm excited you found a match. Let's pretend I didn't do that. What are you going to do about the new guy?"

Maddy shook her head. "It's all good. It was innocent, nothing to worry about. How do you know it's a man?" she asked.

"Because women are never that quick to respond. A guy sees something he likes, and impulse swipes his finger to the right." El shrugged.

"Sometimes I worry about you. Of all people, you have the least amount of creativity when it comes to dating. Also, men aren't alone in being ready to jump in the bed. I've dated more women than men who wanted sex instead of a connection. The guys are the first ones who want a long-term relationship." Maddy chuckled.

She loved El for all her acceptance. Being bisexual, Maddy ran into more judgment than she'd like. Sometimes she was too queer and sometimes she wasn't queer enough. El accepted her for her and even rolled with Maddy's occasional flirting.

"Tell me about this new person."

"Today is the first time we talked. His name is—" Maddy pulled out her phone to see what his name was again. – "Ax. He's a forty-five-year-old lumberjack who moved to Podunk a year ago.

"He hasn't even responded to my latest message, which was almost three hours ago. For all I know, he's already moved on to someone else."

"That's not possible. He'd be stupid to pass up on the opportunity to meet you." El laid her arm across Maddy's shoulders.

Maddy rested her head on El's shoulders. "It scares me to date again, El. Natasha was my last relationship. Our divorce wasn't great and I'm still trying to understand the emotional damage she left. What if I freak out on this guy? Or he's like her. How am I even supposed to recognize the signs? Heck, before Nat, I didn't even know what gaslighting was. Emotional abuse wasn't something I ever thought would happen to me."

The fears spilled out of Maddy. She wanted to untangle her confused thoughts, not discuss her greatest fear when it came to dating.

"We're friends for a reason. I won't let anything happen to you. Natasha isn't here. You're going to talk to him, get to know him. If you like him, then you'll meet."

They sat in silence for the longest time.

"We need ice cream. Then you can help me come up with some more ideas for my classes and I can tell you about our low sales for the month."

The cling of bowls hitting the counter followed banging cabinet doors. Spoons landed in the bowl with a clink. Maddy pulled a pint of cinnamon snickerdoodle and coffee cashew—each a favorite from a local shop in Portland.

"Nana thinks our sales are low due to the customers waiting to see what happens now that I've been doing more around the shop. I, on the other hand, think our dwindling revenue is due to my inability to sell anything. Taking over Pinks or The Knob is out of the question."

With bowls in hand, Maddy returned to the living room. El held the ice cream while Maddy settled.

"Ahh, babe. Don't be too hard on yourself. Let's talk this through. You've got the classes. How do you feel about managing people?"

Her grimace made El laugh.

"I'm better at managing tarot cards than I am people." Maddy swallowed a heaping spoonful of ice cream. "El, this is pathetic. I'm thirty-five years old. We're talking like I graduated high school a week ago and am figuring out my path through adulthood. For chirp's sake I have a master's degree in business."

"Chirp's sake?"

Maddy flicked her hand in the air. "Words are boring. I need new ones."

Elowen smiled.

"Time for a movie?" Maddy asked, no longer wanting to dwell on her emotions.

"Yes."

They spent the remainder of the evening polishing off their pints while watching the latest romcom they'd waited to hit the streaming channel.

Maddy leaned back against the couch. It'd been a lazy Saturday spent at home. Maddy couldn't remember the last time she hadn't left the house all day. Sleep overtook her before the end of the movie.

The doorbell rang, shocking Maddy awake. Even though it was Maddy's place, El answered the door. On the floor was a rectangular brown box.

"Are you expecting a package?" El called into the living room.

"Nope. I get some toys delivered every once in a while, though." Maddy shook the box, which had a little weight to it.

No sound. No movement. Whatever was in there, they'd packed it well.

El followed Maddy into the kitchen where she grabbed a pair of scissors from the junk drawer. Maddy yawned. She pulled paper out of the box to reveal the contents inside. A glass dildo with a note from Pinks and Pearls top vendor—Sweet and Spicy Connections.

Dear Madelyn,

We hope you enjoy testing our latest glass toy, which will be available for the public in a month. We can't wait to read your review. Mark

"Looks like someone has a new toy to test tonight." El poked her elbow into Maddy's side.

"Mmm. Test, yes. Tonight, nope. I'm too tired." Maddy perked up then swirled around to face El, waving the glass dildo in the air. "You know what these are good for?"

El shook her head. Maddy went to the freezer and laid the dildo inside.

"Temperature play. You can do it by yourself. Freeze the glass or heat it up and then use it. The sensations are...mind-blowing."

"I never know what to expect when your eyes light up like a Las Vegas sign. Will you write a review for this one?" About six months ago El convinced Maddy to start writing reviews of the toys she tested.

She wrote them for most of her tests, but not all. One thing Maddy never did was write an undeserved bad review.

"You should share your reviews during your classes." El slung her purse over her shoulder.

"That's not a bad idea. I'll have to give it some more thought." Maddy winked.

"All right, I should head out. I'm subbing a yoga class tomorrow and it starts at eight. I need time to prepare and sleep."

Maddy leaned in for a hug. "You're an awesome friend. Thank you for reminding me my ex is no longer an influence in my life."

"I've got your back." El squeezed Maddy then let go.

4

Maddy

Maddy pulled into Nana's drive and headed inside to help her get out to the car so they could go to the shop together. Sundays were quiet since the shop wasn't open. Maddy liked to work at The Knob on Sunday.

"Morning," Maddy said as she pushed open the front door.

Nana smiled at her from the kitchen. A black crocheted tote with hot pink plastic handles hung from her left arm. As far as Maddy knew, Nana made the "Pinks" tote years ago and she kept all the important store information in it. No one touched the bag unless given permission—not even Maddy.

"Perfect timing." Nana greeted her. "Grab my cane and bring it to me, please. I thought I could make it over there, but my hip refuses to cooperate today."

"Of course."

A marble-like pearl handle with a collar of rhinestones connected the hand and shaft of the candy apple red carbon fiber cane. It packed a punch and doubled as a great defensive weapon in case Nana ever needed one. Not that anyone with an ounce of smarts would cross the woman.

"How are you doing?" Nana asked when Maddy handed her the walking cane.

"I'm a little confused, but I'll figure it out."

As Nana shuffled to the front door Maddy followed close behind, ready to catch her in case her hip gave out or she stumbled for whatever reason. Old, yes, but thin and frail Nana was not. Stubborn too. If she'd known Maddy walked a little behind and to the side to catch her, she'd make her granddaughter walk in front to prove a point.

"Confused about what?" Nana pointed to a duffle bag on the floor. "Take that with us. It has new merchandise. I got this thing called a merkin in there. It's a pubic wig. I don't know why on earth people would buy those things, but they're novelty items and should raise some eyebrows. It'd be easier to quit shaving." She shook her head. "Ridiculous what one can make money off of."

Maddy peeked into the bag, curious about the merkin. Orange, brown, and cheetah spotted tufts of fake hair rested on top. She shook her head.

"Nana, this is awful. El asked me to sign up for a dating app and I did."

"Well now that's a turn of events, isn't it." Her grandma patted her on the arm. "I'm aware of the novelty. It will make a great gag gift or be used by someone who needs one. Now let's get moving or we're going to be late. Jack knows we're coming, and he's got breakfast waiting for us. We can talk about this dating app on our way."

Maddy groaned. She didn't want to talk about the app or Ax. Then again, she shouldn't have brough it up if she didn't want to talk about it. Breakfast from Jack sounded good though.

"First, what made you agree to help Elowen?" Nana jumped into the topic of the morning before they were out of the driveway.

"This is the new app launch for the company she consults for right now. If I leave a review and provide a quote, then I get a thousand dollars. In less than twenty-four hours I matched with someone. I thought it was a good time to get back into the dating pool, but now I don't know if I'm ready."

Lola didn't say anything again until they pulled into the parking lot a few minutes later. When she didn't reach for the door handle, Maddy paused.

"My advice is to take everything slow. Don't drop this man because of your fears. Keep your options open and do not limit yourself to what most people think is normal." Nana did air quotes around "normal."

Maddy considered Lola's advice to keep her mind open. After breakfast from Jack, Maddy went to the office while Nana said she wanted to walk to the floor and talk to their bartender.

Twenty minutes later research for her introduction classes was done, and she'd moved on to planning the one-oh-two course. How to take it to the next level. She made a note on the piece of paper next to the keyboard: *Find out if there's a club or dungeon nearby with people who may volunteer to come teach a class or two.*

Maddy glanced at the spreadsheet in the background of the desktop. A red negative grabbed her attention. The same figure she'd stared at a lot over the last few weeks. They'd lost five hundred in sales last month. Nana didn't know about the specifics of the decline, and if Maddy could figure out a solution, her grandmother wouldn't know. The muscles in her jaw tightened and her stomach flip-flopped. She'd been given more responsibility, more time to run both businesses, and her accomplishments included losing shop revenue. She added another item to her list of reasons why it was bad to run a business. Not that she intentionally lost money, but her sales skills were abysmal and Maddy spent more time daydreaming about what could be rather than what needed to be done. Even though she knew it was a bad habit, she'd yet to figure out a way to stop.

Rather than trying to solve the problem, she set an alarm on her smart watch. It was time to stretch her legs, take a stroll around the store before settling back into the torture chair.

Nana chose that moment to walk into the office. Maddy lunged over the desk, yelping as she clicked her way out of the financials to keep Nana from accidentally finding out what happened.

The older woman chuckled and tapped the end of her cane on top of the desk.

"Young lady, you're not supposed to hurt yourself while sitting down. What are you covering up from your grandmother?"

Maddy huffed. "Nothing. I was about to walk around the store then forgot I didn't save the spreadsheets."

"Yes, of course. A great way for you to hyper-focus on a problem you can't solve."

Maddy had been careful to keep it from her. Her mouth opened and closed, then opened again.

"Well—" Maddy stopped.

"It's—" she tried again.

"The store—umm..."

"Oh, for heaven's sake, spit it out. We're down in sales. Somewhere around five or six hundred dollars if my math is right." Nana huffed. "Do not try and tell me this is why you wanted to start the sex-ed classes, either."

"How did you know?" Maddy asked.

The part about the classes wasn't true. In fact, it never crossed her mind to use the classes to make up for the loss. The classes were fun. She didn't have any other reasons that she'd pitched the idea.

"I don't need to inspect the books to know sales are down. I've done this long enough; a quick inventory perusal tells me what I need to know. Stock isn't as low as it should be if we maintained normal sales. There's a learning curve. Your fancy degree should have taught you that."

Nana sat in the chair across from the desk and rested her cane against the arm. Maddy slunk back down into the stack of bricks that was supposed to be her comfy seat.

"That's not the reason, Nana. I'm horrible at sales. You shouldn't have me on the floor at all. Ask El. Customers run away from me with nothing to buy. If you keep me around much longer, the whole place will go bankrupt."

"There's a drama queen whine if I've ever heard one." Lola shook her head. "Don't be that person, Madelyn. Your parents have drilled into your thick skull that you aren't good enough, but I'm telling you that you are. There may be other reasons like supply and demand, inflation, is there anything else affecting the sex market right now?"

Maddy let her head drop into her hands. Retail ebbed and flowed. Sex didn't. It always sold. At least that's what she'd learned. Porn was a billion-dollar industry. Even romance publishing was worth billions. Yet she couldn't figure out how to keep the sales up for a small-town boutique, with no competition in a fifty-mile radius.

"Madelyn, give yourself a break." Nana interrupted her lamenting.

"I know. I know," Maddy answered. "You and Papa did so much for this town with The Knob and Pinks. All I've wanted since I moved here was to help and do what I can to make sure your legacy lives on. You're eighty-three years old, Nana. It's not like you can do this forever. In fact, you deserve time to enjoy life."

Lola pulled Maddy's hand across the desk.

"Pay attention, Madelyn. I love this store and Jack's taken over the bar as his own. If you want the businesses, they're yours, but don't rush any decisions. We have capable managers who keep things going. I get to spend my days talking to people and making sex fun. My bucket list is complete. Rather than sit around the house and prepare to die, I've chosen to own two businesses, join a knitting club, and watch my granddaughter find her way. If I died tomorrow, I'd die happy."

5

Maddy

After spending the day with Nana, Maddy was ready for an evening of relaxation that included time spent soaking in her claw-foot bathtub. She lit some candles, turned on cello music from her favorite band, and grabbed the glass toy from Sweet and Spicy to test so she could write a review and post it to her blog. It wasn't a well-paying side gig but being a reviewer for several of the store's toy suppliers had its perks.

A smile turned up the corner of her lips as she slid into the tub. The water wrapped around her like a hug, soothing and relaxing. Maddy studied the dildo with a critical eye. When she tested toys it wasn't always about how quick she got off, but rather if it would exceed expectations.

This particular item was supposed to come in purple, blue, and clear glass. They'd sent the purple option. The description provided stated it was tempered for cold and heat, like she'd explained to El. It had a flat, round base at the bottom. The glass of the shaft was swirled to massage the inner walls. For extra pleasure, the dildo was curved to hit the g-spot every time.

Maddy fit her hand around the head then slid it down the shaft, using touch rather than sight to take in the smoothness of the glass, free of blemishes. She grinned at the possibilities and parted her lips for the next test. Maddy swirled her tongue around the shaft as she twisted it in and out of her mouth. Even though she was supposed to be thinking about the review, her thoughts drifted to Ax and how they could play. Would he be willing to use it on her? She wondered if he'd be more interested in playing with it cold or room temperature.

Her stomach fluttered. She bit the corner of her lip. It was time for the part everyone cared about. Maddy propped her feet on the edge of the tub, legs spread wide. She rubbed the head of the dildo up and down her outer lips, drawing out the pleasure. So far, she'd give the product four stars, one missing because she'd like a little more girth than what it had—sometimes using two hands to grip the toy wasn't a bother.

The glass surface rubbed over her clit with the ideal amount of pleasure. Maddy wiggled, making small waves in the tub that added to her increasing need. She eased the dildo deeper between her lips into the wetness of her arousal, circling it as she went. As promised, finding her g-spot wasn't difficult with the curvature. Maddy moved the toy in and out, speeding up with each pass. Her muscles clenched around the glass with her orgasm building.

"Holy mother of Moses." Maddy clenched her jaw.

She rolled her eyes. What a disaster. Headlines for her next blog post ran through her thoughts—a necessary distraction while the on-call gynecologist pulled pieces of glass from between her legs.

"Not for the Lighthearted." Or any woman with a vagina. *"A Shattering Climax"* Literally. *"Hot or Cold, the Glass Will Leave You Wanting..."* a cold compress and morphine.

"All right, ma'am. What's the problem?" The doctor's low, steady tone gave Maddy a focus other than the pain between her legs.

"A glass, well..." Tears streamed down her face. Maddy cleared her throat then stared at the bloodstained towel clutched between her legs. Piercing pain shot from her waist and up her back. The smallest move made her breath catch and her vision blur. "Glass dildo burst. Vagina. Blood." She sucked in a breath. "Glass inside of me."

"You could always sue them," Nana suggested.

"I'm with Lola. They should pay for what happened." El squeezed Maddy's hand.

Maddy groaned. "Sure. Let's sue the company that provides the majority of your store's revenue." Her words slurred from the pain medication. Little starbursts twinkled on the white walls.

Pretty.

"Pssh." Nana waved away Maddy's argument. "I can find another distributor. Your grandfather and I ran Pinks and Pearls together for forty years, we've had distributors come and go. These guys need to pay for the damage done to you."

Maddy clenched her jaw when the not-so-gentle doc prodded her clit. An unwanted jolt of pleasure followed the release of pressure when the glass slid from her flesh.

"Okay. Maybe if I need surgery we can sue." Damn pain meds weren't enough.

Maddy asked for more, but they told her no—something about needing to determine the severity of the damage before numbing away all the pain. It made no sense, but her brain refused to work, so she didn't question the supposed experts. Maddy clutched her fist around the metal bar of the hospital bed and counted back from ten. The top of a screw dug into the palm of her hand, redirecting the pain for a split second when the doctor moved to a gash in the crease of her thigh.

That's more like it. Bring on the hurt. For thirty seconds—long enough to take away the weird pleasure.

"On a scale of one to ten, what's the pain?" Her doctor asked as if Maddy was in any state to answer.

Maddy squeezed her eyes shut. "A nine."

Better than the one hundred when the paramedics had picked her up.

"All right. Now that I have a pretty good idea how bad it is, let's get that down to zero."

Something cold raced through her veins. A minute or five passed, she wasn't sure, before fog replaced the agony.

"It'll be at least—" Nana reached for the privacy cloth "—six months before you're ready for sex again. A monetary reward for pain and suffering is much deserved."

"Ma'am." The doctor raised his arm to block Nana. "I need you to stay back."

"El can you please take Nana to find a cup of coffee or something?"

The frown Maddy received in response didn't take away enough guilt for trying to kick her out of the room. Maddy still wanted her to go. Sure, it wasn't nice to kick the older woman out, but no matter how open she was about sex, sharing the moment with her grandmother wasn't on the top of Maddy's to-do list. Ever. As normal as it had become for Nana to read her blogs, she didn't like getting too personal with her grandmother, even if customers at Pinks referred to Nana as Midnight Sugar and Papa as Molten Spice.

Her grandmother patted her on the shoulder. "Yes, dear. No more embarrassment. We'll be back in an hour. If they're any good, they'll have you sewn up and on the mend."

Maddy sighed. "Thank you."

She closed her eyes, thinking it'd be easier to pretend she was there for a broken foot or something if she wasn't watching the doctor work.

The fog of the medicine clouded her vision once more but didn't keep her from noticing the curtain of the emergency room bay slide back and a man stepping inside her room.

"Brother, you gotta slow down on those backroads." The stranger spoke, studying a small Styrofoam cup.

"Get out," she screeched.

Reality came back to focus, and she remembered her legs were up in stirrups with the doctor's head tucked into the space between them. Her mouth fell open when she squinted and focused on his face.

The guy from the bar. In her dazed state, Maddy scrambled to cover herself, the tubes coming out of her arm hobbled her and a blast of pain rocketed through her hips.

He jerked to a stop and sloshed liquid down the front of his pants. "Shit. That hurts."

The man slapped the inside of his thigh. His discomfort at the coffee seeping into his jeans lessened her embarrassment and Maddy smirked at the wet spot marking where his drink spilled.

"Doctor, get him out of here." Maddy's whispered words slurred.

"Sir, you need to leave." The assisting nurse walked to the man and pushed him out of her partitioned area.

"I'm sorry, but we're going to have to take you to surgery right away," the doctor said as if he hadn't paid attention to anything that had happened.

"What. Surgery?" Her scrambled brain had to have misheard. "Why surgery?"

The room went black when Maddy's eyelids became too heavy to hold them open.

Soft lips pressed against her temple. The scent of El's strawberry lip gloss filled the space around them. "You'll be fine. I'll be here to nurse you back to health."

Maddy thought maybe she dreamed El talking to her before she was wheeled off to surgery.

6

Maddy

With El off doing her own thing for the day and Nana spending time with her crochet group, Maddy had time to think. Thanks to El, she hadn't been alone much over the last two weeks while she healed from surgery. Ax continued to message as well. Maddy hadn't told him about her accident, or surgery, and didn't plan to. If they decided to meet, she'd have to hold off on any physical stuff until the doctor removed the ordered abstinence.

It was easy to learn about people when talking about mundane things like favorite movies. His was Die Hard – or any Bruce Willis movie.

Favorite food. He liked home cooking.

Maddy didn't have a favorite food, which was not something Ax understood. He wanted to know how it was possible to not have something she always loved to eat. Her answer was easy. She liked almost everything and rarely turned down the chance to try something new.

They shared an appreciation for coffee and pizza. They laughed until they cried over stories of attending fundraiser dinners and impressing the money powers that be. Both of their families were in New York. His in the City and hers Upstate.

Maddy's thoughts drifted to Pinks and The Knob. She needed to start planning her future with the businesses. If she wanted to help continue her grandparents' legacy, she'd have to get creative. The classes were a start she needed to perfect. Thankfully, the doctor gave her the go ahead to teach the next day – her second Pervertibles 101 session.

From one breath to the next she'd go from making a list of course topics to touching her lips and imagining performing some moves on Ax—her own version of him—with her mouth. The more she learned about the man on the other side of her text messages, the more Maddy's interest grew.

By mid-Sunday afternoon her focus was so screwed up, she quit trying to figure out her life goals. She had a class to prepare for, which meant she needed out of the house. First, she had to gather her groceries. Carrots, cucumbers, cherries with the stems still on, a small bag of ice, and chopsticks.

This time she planned to take a few more items in case she had more adventurous students. Nana suggested getting some inexpensive toys from the shop that could be used with things around the house. Step two included making a list of shop items she wanted. The ice cubes would go well with one of their feather toys. The chopsticks would combine with a pair of fuzzy handcuffs. The thin, but sturdy sticks could produce a nice sting when used the right way. For the attendees who wanted to get deeper into bedroom play, they could use two chopsticks and small rubber bands to make nipple clamps. Fuzzy handcuffs would give the receiver a softer sensation to focus on.

In the short time she'd been at Pinks, Maddy learned a lot of people enjoyed sensual options. They preferred a blend of opposites. Like hot and cold or stinging and soft, concepts people could explore without feeling too taboo.

Maddy's opinion that it shouldn't matter what others thought was a hard sell. Even though what someone did behind closed doors was no one's business, if nothing else, she hoped her classes would help people become more open-minded about exploring sexual desires and identities. It wasn't as black and white as many made it out to be. The fluidity of sex was the most erotic aspect for Maddy.

She smiled. Planning had taken her mind off the frustration of life for at least fifteen minutes. A win. Her phone alerted her of a new message at the same time she sat her cat's food bowl on the floor

She held her breath while waiting for it to load.

Ax: This weekend has been hell. Please accept my apology for the lack of response. I had a surprise visit from my aunt, which meant I had to devote every waking moment to taking care of her. Aunt Caroline likes to be waited on hand and foot. For some reason, she expected me to live in a mansion. Not a cabin in the woods. I laughed hard enough my eyes leaked tears.

Maddy shivered. A cabin in the woods sounded scary in the most enjoyable way. His aunt sounded awful. She wanted to know more about Ax, but more intimately than text. Maybe it was time to meet in person.

Maddy: I know this is sooner than you expected since we started talking a few weeks ago, but what would you say to meeting? I mean, it may not be possible for whatever reason. And maybe face-to-face isn't where you want this to go.

She read her message. *You're rambling.* Maddy chided herself. Her finger hovered over the delete button.

"No big deal. Either give him a time and place or don't. But make a decision."

Maddy had a habit of talking to herself. That didn't stop her. Sometimes her pep talks worked. Others, like right then, she felt like a crazy cat woman. She took a deep breath and finished typing her message.

Maddy: I'll be at The Rustic Knob tonight around six. If you want to hang out with someone, I'd love to meet you. If not, well, maybe some other time.

After hitting send she reread the message. Cringeworthy.

"I'm losing my mind," she said.

His response came less than two minutes later.

Ax: Sounds good. It'll be nice to meet you in person.

He finished it off with a wide grin emoji.

They set a date. Her first ever friend date.

Maddy updated the app to show they'd set a meeting. A new option popped up on the bottom of the screen. Pictures. Maddy clicked the camera icon.

She sucked in a breath, choking on the sudden realization of who she'd connected with. Maddy's stomach knotted in doubt of her impulse decision to meet him. If he backed out, she'd be more than bummed. He had it all, good looks and personality—at least in texts.

Her phone vibrated as the clock ticked to five o'clock. She needed to be at the Knob in an hour, and she was nowhere near ready. Maddy spent the better part of the afternoon debating what to wear. Since it wasn't a date, she didn't want to dress too sexy and come across as trying too hard. Sweats and a T-shirt were lazy. Ax wouldn't appreciate laziness, although it wouldn't have been the first time she'd shown up at the bar in sweats. In a perfect world, she'd wear jeans and a cute top. Except Maddy didn't live in that world. She lived in the world of twenty-six-stitches-around-my-vagina and jeans were too rough.

With time winding down, she rolled the dice and landed on a color-blocked, salmon, white, and tan V-neck, floor-length T-shirt dress. Casual but not too much, since the temperature cooled at night, she decided to wear her light brown leather jacket. She finished off the outfit with her favorite tan booties.

A knock followed by El's command for her to open the door interrupted Maddy's prep. Even if she still needed to do her hair and makeup, she was grateful for the interruption. El would help make decisions—regardless of whether or not Maddy agreed.

"Hey, gorgeous." Maddy fluttered her lashes at her best friend.

They'd always flirted in that friend kind of way.

"What do you want and wowzer you're looking quite delectable today." El smacked her lips.

Her gaze swept from Maddy's face to her feet and back again. A tingle began in Maddy's stomach.

Maddy ran her hands down the front of her dress slowing over her hips.

"It's too much isn't it? I was aiming for cute casual, but I overdid it."

El held up both hands.

"Whoa. No way. You've succeeded at cute-casual, but why?"

"I'm meeting Ax tonight. This was the best I had that didn't send mixed signals." Maddy shrugged.

"Ooh. Who asked who?" The hint of excitement in her question thrilled Maddy. "Did you get to see a picture?"

Maddy gulped. She still didn't know how she felt about learning his identity.

"Yeah. I did."

"And?" El tossed her bag onto the couch before following Maddy into the bathroom.

"I asked him if he wanted to meet. He's the guy from the bar. The first night. You know, the one with the friend. They came to my class." Maddy chewed on her lip.

El gasped then broke into a coughing fit. "Sorry. That's surprising."

Maddy messed with her hair. First pulling it up then let it fall down her back. The same debate played through her thoughts as with her clothes. Too casual. Too obvious. El pushed Maddy's hands away.

"Pull it back like this." Elowen separated the front of Maddy's hair into two sections.

She put a hair tie in each before pulling them to the back and tying them together in a half-up ponytail. Then she pulled the hairs apart in a fish braid style. "It's cute, shows you care about yourself, but doesn't take forever."

"Thank you." Maddy turned her back to the mirror and glanced over her shoulder. "I love it."

"Good. Skip the makeup. You're beautiful without it."

Maddy checked. "I need to leave in about fifteen minutes. I want to get there before him. Jack doesn't know I'm coming or meeting a man there. The last thing I need is twenty questions. He called Nana the other day after I had a business meeting at the bar. She wanted all the details about my 'new gentleman.'"

"Lola and Jack do love to be in the middle of your life." El fidgeted with a few strands of Maddy's hair. "At least you know Ax is good-looking."

Loneliness often led El to Maddy's doorstep. A hint of trepidation tainted the air in the bathroom. Maddy wanted to ask what was up but was afraid of El's reaction. If her friend had a meltdown, then Maddy would cancel the date with Ax. The problem was she didn't want to. That made her one of the most inconsiderate people she knew.

"Tell me what's wrong, El."

"Nothing's wrong. It's...the app guys emailed me today. They've asked me to prepare a pitch for a long-term deal."

El picked at her nails.

"Why are you freaking out? This sounds like the opportunity you've been hoping for. Are you worried you won't have a pitch? Elowen, you're one of the most creative people I know. Those people would be idiots to pass you up."

Seconds later Maddy was spun around and wrapped in a hug.

"Thank you. You always know what to say. I'm going to blow them away." El backed up. She ran her hands down the front of her T-shirt. "Go meet Ax. I've got a presentation to plan."

7

Maddy

"Madelyn, it's Sunday evening. I hope you didn't come in to work. Lola gave explicit instructions not to let you." Jack greeted her with a lecture.

"Can't a girl come to the bar for a drink on Sunday night?" she asked with a wink.

"Nope. Not on a Sunday night when I know you've got that class to teach tomorrow." Jack shook his head. He mumbled something too low for Maddy to hear.

She started to slide onto a barstool but stopped at the last second. It wouldn't take long for the wooden seat to become uncomfortable. She leaned against the bar instead.

"Not here for work. Meeting someone tonight."

Jack's eyes grew wide. "Is he someone I know or would recognize?"

"Can't say for sure. I know he's been in here before, but I don't know if he's a regular."

Right on time, the front door opened, and Ax walked through. Maddy turned her back to the door. Her stomach fluttered worse than a real blind date. A thin layer of sweat formed on her palms.

"Ax, how's it going? Surprised to see you tonight." Jack reached for a snifter and ashtray.

He was a regular. Maddy squared her shoulders and took a couple of cleansing breaths. She would face him sooner or later. This had been her idea after all.

"Oomph." She turned right into a very solid, very nice T-shirt that stretched across Ax's chest and smelled of forest and musk. Maddy let herself dream, for a second, what it would be like to cuddle against him every night before bed and every morning before getting ready for work.

Calloused hands wrapped around her upper arms, steadying her. Then he pushed her back a couple of inches. Jack snickered from behind them.

"That's our girl, stumbling her way through everything," Jack said.

"Maddy." Ax's voice was as smooth as the Extra Old Brandy tucked behind all the other bottles on the top shelf of the bar.

A hint of cinnamon and a splash of sex. His voice was almost as nice as his chest. Sure, she'd seen him when Crash talked to her and El, but she hadn't taken the opportunity to appreciate how well he took care of himself.

Maddy's cheeks heated. Jack was the annoying uncle everyone loved and hated all at once. He was one of the most loyal people she knew and brutally honest. In his defense, he tried to soften the harsh reality with humor.

"Umm. Hi." Maddy offered her hand to shake.

Ax took her hand in his and kissed the top of her knuckles. With extreme willpower Maddy managed not to swoon like the women in her historical romance novels.

"Nice to meet you, officially." Ax reached around her for the glass Jack sat within his reach. "Just curious...why The Knob?"

Maddy followed his gaze and grinned when she noticed a glass of Coke on the bar for her. Alcohol free while on pain meds.

"Don't you know?" Jack asked. "Madelyn's going to run this place someday soon. Lola is her grandmother."

Ax's smirk made her knees knock together. Thanks to her body's reaction to his voice, the stitches wouldn't be the sole hinderance to her health.

"I'm going to help keep it going when Nana retires, but I'm not running it." She raised her eyebrow in Jack's direction.

"Want to sit?" he asked.

"Yes, please. If you don't mind, I'd like to go to the parlor." Maddy took her glass from the bar.

With a nod, Ax led them to the room at the back of the bar. It was her favorite spot. The original serving area still stood in the room. Once, it was guaranteed to be packed every weekend. Now, the thick hickory slab sat unused except for special occasions. They didn't have barstools or high-top tables. Instead, the area had been filled with plush, burgundy leather chairs and deep mauve micro suede love seats and settees. Ax went to a spot in the corner near the bar.

At the entrance hung a sign Maddy found at an estate sale. It read "That's what I do. I smoke cigars and I know things." Papa loved the sign and insisted she hang it above the parlor entry.

"You run this place." It was more a statement than a question.

Maddy hesitated with her reply.

"I help here and at Pinks and Pearls. Nana can't do as much as she used to, so I'm learning the ropes."

"Nice. Can't say I've spent much time next door, but I can imagine it's well-done, like this place."

She nodded. "Nana put a lot of love into the shop. The bar was Papa's baby. When he passed a couple of years ago, Jack stepped right into his shoes."

"That was Delbert, right? Jack has mentioned him a few times. When he talks about the previous owner his voice rings with respect and loyalty. I wish I'd had a chance to meet him."

Two years ago, she'd moved to Podunk at the end of her grandfather's life. Her heart swelled with Ax's praise. Since her parents refused to take her to Oregon to spend time with her grandparents, Maddy's memories of them were too few. Bar patron stories were her favorite. Nana had stories, but they weren't the same. She was his wife; the others were his friends, and their memories came from a different perspective.

The always-present ache in her chest from missing him grew stronger. Maddy knew she needed to change the subject, or she'd embarrass herself by crying.

"What's your real name?" Maddy's cheeks warmed. "I'm sorry. That's a personal question. You don't have to answer if don't want to."

"No need to apologize. My name is Easton. I prefer Ax, though." He sipped his drink. "Do you mind if I smoke?"

Ax held up a thick cigar. She recognized the band at the head–white with a red crown.

"Is that a nineteen eighty-eight?" she asked.

The Warped Serie Gran Reserva 1988 Robusto was a Nicaraguan cigar. Those new to cigars went straight for Cubans in her experience. Aficionados, however, knew Cubans weren't always the best. The 1988 with its blend of chocolate, coffee bean, and earthy flavors received one of the highest scores in an international taste test done last year.

"It is. You know your stuff." Ax settled back into his seat and pulled one foot up to rest on the other knee.

"My papa loved his cigars. That's why he opened The Rustic Knob. He wanted a place to smoke, drink, and unwind. If I'm going to keep his legacy going, then I need to learn as much as possible."

"Smart man." Ax grinned. "And woman.'"

The conversation flowed easy between them. Maddy settled back into her own seat. For a while they talked cigars and brandy with a few questions about each other thrown in.

"You're laid back, but there's an air of sophistication about you the natives around here are missing," she commented.

The Rustic Knob had plenty of business. Very few knew about the parlor, much less used it. But Ax was comfortable in the environment. He'd become regular enough Jack talked about her grandfather and knew his drink order. When she suggested the parlor room he hadn't hesitated. In many ways, Ax reminded her of Papa.

"You know how I said I was from New York? My ex-father-in-law gave me the cottage he owns out here when he passed three years ago. After finalizing my divorce, I figured Podunk was a good place to start over."

Oh. Her parents moved to upstate New York when she was seven. Maddy loved New York, but she'd always missed Nana and Papa. The few memories of Podunk drew her back when Papa got sick. Her parents refused to visit, saying her grandparents were fine on their own and didn't need the interruption.

"Do you like it here?" she asked.

Ax drew in a deep inhale. The smoke from his exhale wafted toward Maddy. She closed her eyes and savored the sweet hints of chocolate and bitter tones of coffee bean.

Papa chose Dominicans when given the chance. He preferred the thicker ones, robustos or gordos, sometimes Churchills. Said they were easier for him to hold.

"I like it here enough not to go back home."

She startled when Ax answered after drifting off into her own memories.

"Hmm. Are you planning to go back soon?" Maddy asked.

He shook his head without hesitation.

"New York City isn't for me. Mother forced the socialite lifestyle down my throat my entire life. No sooner did she stop, than my ex-wife took over. One of the few reasons I'd go back now is to support one of my mother's charities."

Maddy cringed at his use of mother. He hadn't completely let go of the socialite lifestyle if he still referred to his mom in such a formal way. Her ex-wife had thrived in that environment. It was one of the primary reasons their marriage ended. Well, that and the emotional abuse Maddy acknowledged—even though it took a while to accept the truth of what happened.

"We could make a relationship work."

The more they talked, the more she realized how much she wanted it to work. Three hours had passed, and it felt like minutes. Conversation came easy for them. They had a lot of the same interests. Not to mention, Ax was easy on the eyes.

No. That wasn't fair. He was handsome in that socialite turned rugged outdoorsman way. He had the short, scruffy beard with gray highlights and roughened hands many pined over – Maddy included.

"Oh, it could definitely work." He winked at her. "Kind of sounds like you're winding down for the night. Do you need to get home?"

"How did you get the nickname Ax? Are you in a biker gang and that's your weapon of choice?"

He tossed his head back and laughed a deep laugh that echoed throughout the room. Maddy stretched her legs onto the loveseat. The change in position helped alleviate some of the discomfort.

Leaving was the last thing she wanted to do, but it was what she needed. Sitting with him didn't break any of the doctor's rules except the pressure from sitting rather than lying down. The pain had morphed from annoying surges to a constant burning. Medication would help, but they made her too drowsy to even think about driving after taking them. Telling Ax about the incident was out of the question.

"That's got to be one of the best guesses I've heard." He wiped a hand across his eyes. "It's nothing that exciting. I'm the foreman at Weald Lumber. They call me Ax because I can swing an ax better than most of the guys on my crew even though I have the least amount of experience."

Well, he'd been right. The truth wasn't half as exciting as her imagination. Maddy contemplated ways to extend their time together. She could order another drink from Jack. Maybe invite him back to her place. *No.* He'd run for the hills. She ground her back teeth together when another burning pain shot up from her core.

"And Crash?" she ground out.

"That's right. He talked to you after your class." Ax studied her for a moment. His gaze shifted and he tilted his chin down. "No one knows how he got the name. Crash is newer to the crew, a mystery."

Maddy sipped her watered-down Coke. Ax had finished his second brandy a while ago. The lull in conversation gave her a chance to catch her breath, which had turned choppy. One topic they hadn't breached was past love lives. Ax mentioned an ex-wife, but Maddy didn't push for more. He didn't ask her if she had any exes.

"Do you have plans in a couple of weeks?" she asked, accepting defeat from the fight with her body. If she couldn't stay longer, at least she'd set up another date.

Ax rubbed his eyes.

"I don't have any plans. You want to do something?"

Maddy nodded.

"It may sound cheesy, but there's this place in the city where we can go throw axes. I'd suggest this upcoming weekend, except I've already committed to a few things."

She bit the inside of her lip. When she learned about Blades of Fury six months ago, she'd wanted to go. El was busy every time Maddy asked, and she didn't want to go alone.

"That's not cheesy at all. Sounds like fun. Set it up and let me know what time. I'll drive." He smiled.

Maddy sighed in relief.

He leaned over and kissed her cheek. She wanted more. Her heartbeat quickened. It was too soon.

"I'll walk you out." Ax offered his arm, which Maddy took.

"Thank you."

Jack waved at them as they pushed the door open. Maddy headed toward her pride a joy. A 1967 Pontiac GTO.

"I'm guessing you're in the purple beast." Ax chuckled.

"She's not a beast. That's a classic. I can't even—" Maddy gasped. "You insulted my baby."

Ax stumbled and sputtered. She tried to hold in her laugh but failed. He opened and closed his mouth like a fish out of water.

"I had no idea your car meant so much to you. I'll, um, have to keep it in mind for the future."

Maddy laughed again. The poor guy didn't know what to do. They stood beside her car. If he hadn't blocked the door handle, she would've climbed in. It was the most awkward part of the evening and the part with the lowest expectations—at least for her.

"I'll wait to hear from you about plans for ax throwing?" Ax fidgeted with his key ring.

"Yep." Maddy looked around trying to figure out how to tell him he was in the way without being rude.

"Oh. I didn't give you my number." Ax pulled his phone from his back pocket. "Give me your number and I'll send you a text."

They exchanged numbers. When Ax still didn't move out of the way she cleared her throat.

"You're, umm, kind of blocking my door." Maddy pointed at her car.

"Shit. Sorry about that. Next time kick me out of the way." He stepped to the side, giving her room to get in.

Maddy smiled before firing up the engine. After backing out she turned around to find Ax standing in the same spot.

"Right. That wasn't awkward at all," she mumbled to herself.

For once she hadn't been the one to make things weird.

8

Ax

Friday couldn't have come soon enough. Ax sipped his bourbon, then turned his lit, half-smoked, cigar between his fingers. The muted lighting and mix of The Rat Pack and Jazz in the parlor made it one of the calmer establishments in town. He didn't have to worry about headaches or temporary deafness. Instead, he did his best not to fall asleep in one of the soft, oversized leather chairs, worn-in but cared for, which he'd done more than once.

After meeting Maddy at the bar and spending the week texting back and forth he saw signs of her all over the place. A vintage cigar sign hung on a humidor. The small refrigerator behind the bar with her ciders. If he closed his eyes and focused his mind, he caught the hints of orange, musk, and hibiscus. A perfume of scents that reminded him of her confident femininity.

"You look like you could use a vacation." Jack set a fresh snifter in front of him. The guy had been the bartender since the place opened forty years earlier.

"Thanks. As nice as it'd be, it won't happen any time soon."

"Problems of the female type?"

He pulled a white towel from his back pocket to wipe down the table in front of them. Ax glanced at the phone resting on his thigh.

"Something like that." He took a long pull on his drink, welcoming the burn from the apple brandy.

Jack clicked his tongue. "You should call her. Get things out in the air. Makes life easier. Not that I mind you here two or three times a week."

No chance in hell would he call the *her* in question. Doing so would cause increased anxiety, not make things easier.

The screen on his phone lit up with another text notification. The sixth one in the last twenty minutes. If he didn't respond soon his mother would start calling.

Ax unlocked his phone and then clicked the green message icon. As soon as the picture of a recent headline loaded, he closed his eyes and sighed. He'd been divorced for almost a year and his mother continued to push him back to Daphne. He'd tried to be respectful in his attempts to tell her to back off, but nothing worked.

He opened his eyes to the bold, black letters that read "Senator Hopeful to Marry New York Socialite." His ex-wife's smile sat right beneath the words. Her hand, with a rock the size of New Jersey, rested on the man's chest.

"Sucker. She's going to take you for all you're worth and then some." Ax slammed the rest of his drink. No slow savor. "At least I won't have to keep making alimony payments."

As expected, his phone rang again before he closed out the text message.

"Yes, Mother."

"It's about time you answered. Did you get the picture I sent? Her happiness radiates off the page, doesn't it, son?"

He cringed. No. The picture was a perfect representation of the manipulative, conniving woman he divorced.

"Mother, I quit caring about Daphne before we signed the papers. Why do you insist on sending me this sh—crap?"

"You should reconsider. She still has feelings for you, Easton. When you come back in a few months, talk to her and she'll be your wife again. She said so herself."

He guffawed into the phone. "Oh yes, feelings so strong she turned down a proposal and diamond the size of the Grand Canyon."

Daphne had been the love of his life at one point. They were high school sweethearts who were supposed to grow old together and have lots of babies. After graduation they went their separate ways. He left for college to become a lawyer and follow his father's footsteps into politics. She wanted to find a man who would dote on her and give her all his attention. Ax wasn't that man. Fate, or rather his mother, pulled them back to each other ten years later.

Ax thought he'd found his happily ever after. As it turned out, his mother got her wishes, and he got an attention-seeking gold digger who wanted his family for their status. When he refused to bow at her feet and turn over his credit card every time she wanted a new bauble, she left.

The worst part, his mother still didn't believe him. Lecturing him about being a weak man who didn't even chase his wife was her favorite thing to do.

Tired of his mother's games, he considered hanging up on the nosy woman. The drama wore him out more than his job. He propped his head on his hand while she continued to ramble on about Daphne. His thoughts drifted to Maddy. Her long, black hair. Dark enough the sunlight streaked it blue. Her smile and how much fun she must have had on the river in the background of her picture on the app.

In college he and his friends had gone on a float trip for Spring Break one year. He thought about taking Maddy on a trip this summer. A tingle built in his chest at the idea of planning for the future with her.

"The Sutherland family doesn't break promises, Easton." His mom's admonishment rang in his thoughts.

That wasn't true. They didn't break promises that would merit some social standing or advancement. His dad didn't make partner of one of the largest law firms in the state without making and breaking promises.

Promises were the reason Podunk, Oregon called to Ax after the divorce.

He put her on speaker phone and opened the Blind Love app. Maddy had been a pleasant surprise. He'd made a fool of himself the night they met after failing the car test. His family was lawyers and politicians. Humanitarians. Not car gurus or get-your-hands-dirty kind of people.

The annual Weald Family Picnic was coming up. Maybe he'd ask her to join him. Ax shook his head. No, she'd never agree to that. They didn't even know each other...not by "normal" standards anyway. Crash would tell him he was crazy for bringing a woman he'd just met. Dean, his adopted grandfather, would pat him on the back and tell him "Good job going after it, son."

At eighty-eight years young, the man considered every woman a treasure worth far more than mere friendship. He'd said they were the key to happiness.

"Easton, are you ignoring me?" His mother's high-pitched squeal slammed his brain back into reality.

"Excuse me, are you Ax?" A tall, skinny woman who resembled a model on a yoga advertisement walked into the parlor. She had short, blond hair. Pretty, but not stop his heart gorgeous. He preferred Maddy's luscious, full curves. Her big, round eyes. The laugh lines at the corner of her lips.

Perfect was in the eye of the beholder. While he and Maddy had one official meeting, he could say with certainty, she was perfect for him.

"Gotta go, Mother. Talk to you soon." He hung up the phone and turned his full attention to the lady in front of him. "And you are?"

She stuck out her hand to Ax. "Elowen. Maddy's best friend and the reason you two met."

Ax took a drink before he said something rude. Her certainty that she was the reason he and Maddy met made him smile. Something about a woman who owned her actions made him pay closer attention.

"How do you figure?" he asked.

"I set up her Blind Love profile. She agreed to test it for me since I need testimonials for the marketing campaign. I'm a marketing consultant and working for Blind Love right now."

"Oh. Then I should thank you." The woman looked familiar, but he wasn't able to figure out why.

Elowen smiled.

His eyes burned with exhaustion. It'd been too long since he'd had a good night's sleep. Maddy had mentioned El, they were friends—which meant he needed to play nice and not tell her to bug off.

The woman procured the leather chair next to him. She flicked a finger in the air toward Jack back at the bar.

"What's your choice?" she asked.

It took a second for Ax to figure out what she meant. El nodded toward his drink.

"Mm. Apple bourbon. How do you know who I am?" He glanced at his phone, but so far his mother hadn't called back.

Surprising.

"Maddy showed me your profile. I saw you sitting back here and figured I'd introduce myself. I was here the night your friend Crash introduced himself. You, on the other hand, scurried away."

"You sure that's all?" He hadn't intended to call her out, but his patience was thin thanks to the day's events.

Her laughter sounded like the bells they put on reindeer during the holidays. He smiled despite trying to maintain a reasonable emotional distance.

"Nope. I like your honesty. Maddy likes you, so I was curious who the man was that caught her attention. She hasn't dated since I've known her. Jack called and told me you were here."

Ax raised an eyebrow at Jack, who chose that moment to set a glass of amber liquid in front of El.

A woman after his own heart. No froufrou drinks for her.

"Traitor," he grumbled. "Do I pass your inspection?" he asked.

"You'll do, I suppose." She gave him the once over, with a grin. "Yeah, I can see why she likes you."

Ax paused in sipping his drink to study the woman next to him. She didn't look him in the eyes when she spoke, focused tracing her finger around the rim of her glass. No longer straight-backed, her shoulders rolled forward. Pink tinted her cheeks enough to make them appear sun kissed.

"A little shallow don't you think?" Ax shifted, uncomfortable with the way she'd appraised his looks. He recoiled realizing how he must have made other women feel when he'd done the same thing—not that often, but often enough.

"Maybe, but we don't know each other. What else am I supposed to judge you on?" She shrugged.

"You could talk to me, take the chance to know me first." The words didn't make sense as he spoke them. He'd been the one to ask if he met her expectations. "Look, I'm sorry. I must sound like an asshole right now. My mom is driving me crazy and I'm taking it out on you. Can we start over?"

As he glanced to his right the door separating the bar from the retail store opened. A woman about Madelyn's height tugged something over her shoulder, a purse or bag of some sort, before turning to face them. She turned, and his breath caught.

Madelyn was the best-looking, not-a-pinup, pinup model he'd met. She wore a pair of ankle-length, black pants that sat high on her hips. It would've taken a miracle not to stare at the way they framed her curvy butt. He curled his fingers around his glass. The red and white polka dot shirt tucked in close to her waist, the short sleeves brought his attention to her toned arms. He wanted to take in every inch of her body, but she showed very little skin. A tease of the best kind. Ax wondered if she had any idea how tempting she was.

"Hey, Ax. What are you doing here?" she asked while sauntering, in a pair of white tennis shoes nonetheless, his way.

"Rough day at work. I stopped by for some downtime. Didn't go the way I'd hoped given a call from my mother. On the upside, I met Elowen." He gave a chin nod to her friend, hoping the move was casual enough not to ruffle feathers.

He'd been in one too many fights with his ex-wife over jealousy. One of her favorite accusations was that he flirted with her friends.

"I don't get along with my mom either. In fact, my parents placed bets on how long it would take for me to fail at living away from home and making a life of my own."

Maddy hugged Elowen then gave her a quick kiss on her cheek.

Ax twisted around to face Maddy.

"That sounds awful. Can I ask you a question?" he asked.

Elowen watched the exchange, no doubt cataloging their body language the same way Ax did hers.

"Sure, but it's been kind of a long day, and I need to sit." Madelyn nudged El over to share the oversized chair with her friend. "Scootch a mooch, gorgeous."

"What's your question?" she asked.

Ax finished off his drink before setting it on the table once more. That had to be last call, or he wouldn't have been able to drive home.

"What's it like running a sex shop?"

All three of them cringed. Elowen spit out her drink.

"Way to dive right in. You're not a smart one," Elowen snipped.

Maddy chuckled.

"Be nice." She chided El before turning to him. "First, it's not a sex shop. We're an erotic toy boutique and I teach sex education courses for adults. It's like any other job. We have customers and we sell our inventory. It's no different than going to a retail shop to buy clothes." Madelyn shrugged. "Are you going to tell me you've never gone to buy toys for the bedroom?"

"Nope. I mean, I've been in a toy shop before, but it was to buy a gag gift for a friend's bachelor party. Cherry flavored condoms or something stu—" Ax caught himself before finishing the sentence. One insult a night was bad enough. Two would have been pressing his luck. "I mean, it was a novelty item, whatever it was."

"We have those too. Mostly, the people who come in for that are like you. They don't want to be there for longer than necessary."

Next time he attended a class he'd have to go downstairs and check out the store.

"Fun fact, Nana and Papa chose the location because they could put the entrance on the back, off the street. People can park at The Knob and walk to Pinks without being seen. If someone recognizes their car, they think they stopped at the bar." She winked at him.

"Now they've got a lock on a huge property that keeps other businesses from building right on top of them," Elowen added.

"What are your plans when you take over? Will you keep them both the same?" Ax asked.

"I'm not sure if I'm going to take over, if I'm honest. Even if I did make changes, I would never sell the businesses. These are my grandparents' legacies. As far as I'm concerned, my kids can have them when I retire—if I have kids." She ran her fingers through her hair, pulling it into a ponytail and letting it drop.

"What Maddy failed to mention was why she's not sure she wants to take over. For whatever misguided reason, she doesn't think she can do it." Elowen smirked while Maddy glared daggers into her.

He enjoyed the banter between the two women. They were a solid pair. He imagined getting to know El and becoming friends with her. The three of them making jokes. El accepting him as Maddy's partner. He shook the image out of his thoughts. It was too soon for thinking about the future. Ax still wasn't sure what he wanted with the whole dating thing.

The app was supposed to be a way to dip his toe in the water—not a way to insta-connect with someone.

"You two have known each other awhile? Do you finish each other's sentences?" As tired as he was, there were many questions he wanted to ask.

In New York, he'd never had a friend like Crash or El. His acquaintances were arranged for how they could help him or his family advance.

"Two years and nope. Maddy never knows what she's going to say until the words are out of her mouth. The harder I try to get a grasp on the way her mind thinks, the more I fail." El rolled her eyes.

Envy at the connection between them hit Ax square in the chest. If he wanted to get to know Maddy better, he'd have to work around her best friend. Too bad he'd already screwed things up with their introduction. She hadn't had a chance to answer whether they could start over. The potential disappointment if she said no hit him square in the gut.

"Why wouldn't you want to take over the businesses?" he asked.

Nothing about the woman sitting across from him said incompetent. Jack had full confidence in her abilities. Maddy was layers of fun and seriousness and much more. Ax wanted to spend to peel back every single one of them.

"Me and management don't get along well. I started my first business when I was twenty, not even out of college yet. It failed within a year." Madelyn fingers danced across her phone as she talked.

"You were young. Why didn't your parents help? They're CEOs, right?" Ax watched the women.

The way El draped her arm across Maddy's shoulders, situated herself in front of the other woman, and studied his every move, screamed of protectiveness. If he pushed too hard, she'd draw first blood in retaliation.

"Oh, they helped. Loaned me money. Told me if I wanted to make it in business, starting my own from the ground up would be too difficult. My mom told me to find a company I wanted to run, get in at a low-level, and work my way to the top. They intended for me to follow in her footsteps."

El played with Maddy's hair and Ax wished it was his fingers running through her locks. He chided himself. Jealousy would not get him far in his bid to date Maddy. One way or another he needed to reign in his emotions.

"You've never told me what kind of business you started," El said.

Maddy cleared her throat. "A clothing boutique. Back then, I thought I had the perfect idea. I'd specialize in plus size offerings with eclectic styles—clothes I liked to wear. To start off I sold my inventory from an online storefront. In the first six months, I paid off my parents and cleared twenty-grand in profit month over month. Being young and stupid, I opened a brick-and-mortar store front against Mom and Dad's advice."

"You love clothes, but sales aren't your thing. Neither is marketing." El chuckled.

A flash of pain passed through Maddy's eyes. Ax glared at El.

"You don't need sales and marketing to have a successful business. More importantly, you need to recognize your areas of weakness and identify someone who is better than you." He directed his explanation to El.

When Maddy offered a silent "thank you" he grinned. Talking to the women made him forget about his mother and the drama she continued to stir. Maddy brightened his evening.

"Right. That's where things started going downhill. I knew I wasn't good at selling, but I figured my social media presence would've been enough for the marketing. After hiring a couple of salespeople, the store should've taken off. When it didn't, Mom and Dad refused to help. They said I needed to learn a lesson. Being stubborn and convinced I knew everything; I didn't change anything. Within fifteen months of opening the web-front store I had to shut everything down."

The air around the three of them thickened. A twinge of distress laced Maddy's story. Ax knew the feeling of defeat and disappointing his family. Very few knew he'd failed the bar exam the first time he took it. After a month of intense studying, he took the test again and passed it by a handful of points. Being a lawyer wasn't his calling, but it was his destiny according to his parents. Instinct was to ask more questions or give advice on how she could've been successful.

El's phone buzzed, saving anyone from having to say something else. She jumped out of her chair, grabbed her bag, and kissed Maddy on the cheek.

"I need to go. It's the pitch I told you about," El said.

Maddy nodded. "No worries. I need to get out of here, too."

Before leaving, El said to him, "It was nice to meet you, Ax. I accept your apology for being an asshole and forgive you. You've made up for it taking an interest in Maddy."

"Not sure what that's about, and I'm not going to ask. Just remember, I'm the one he met first." Maddy winked then blew him a kiss with her free hand.

Ax acted like he caught her kiss and tucked it away, then took her hand in his to stop her from leaving.

"El, I look forward to getting to know you." Ax leaned in to whisper to Maddy, "Any chance you can stick around for just a second?"

"I've got a minute, what's up?" she asked.

He waited for El to leave. "I just wanted to say, you're not a failure. We don't know each other that well, but I want you to know that I'm going to make it my personal mission to show you how smart and business savvy you are."

Maddy stood in front of him, her eyes wide and glistening. He didn't want to make her cry. Ax kissed her on the cheek. "Good night. I'll call you tomorrow."

9

Maddy

Maddy slammed her hand on the alarm. Even if she couldn't go to work, she didn't want to get out of her routine. With a groan, she rolled out of bed, put on some jogging pants and a sweatshirt, then at six-fifteen in the morning shuffled to the living room for yoga to get the blood flowing. It should've been a run, but the doctor said no. Something about the friction causing problems with the stitches.

"Stupid explosion. I will never touch another glass toy again," she mumbled.

Maybe Nana was right about suing the company. Maddy sent them an email a couple of days after she got home from the hospital explaining what had happened, but they never responded. Nor did they comment on her blog post, which she sent a link to. During yoga she considered the ramifications of not doing anything. The incident never should've happened.

If she didn't make her problems more public, the company would continue to sell the toy. At the very least she needed to report what had happened to someone. *But who?* As far as she knew, there wasn't a regulatory agency for sex toys. A blog post was good for her opinions, but they brushed it off. They didn't have to promote her review.

There was one option left that would force them to make a change. A lawsuit.

After she finished her morning extreme low-impact workout, she called Nana.

"Well good morning, dear. I hear you had a rather entertaining evening. Since you're calling me at seven o'clock the morning after, I can assume your new gentleman did not stay the night."

Maddy groaned. Nana hadn't said a word about her seeing Ax a few days before, but she had something to say about the new vendor Maddy met the night before.

"First, what's the point of anyone staying over if I'm still practicing doctor-ordered abstinence? Second, my *gentleman* as you called him, was Paul. He's the sales manager for Rock N' Knockin' Adult Novelty Items."

"Since you aren't going to share details, why am I graced with a call from my favorite granddaughter?"

Maddy scoffed. Favorite. More like only granddaughter. The older woman was far too chipper in the morning.

"I need a lawyer," Maddy dove right in before Lola steered her off-topic again.

"Whyever, would you need a lawyer? Did something happen at the shop? Jack would have told me if there was an incident at The Knob." Nana turned all business. The sweet tone replaced with a stern, matter-of-fact question.

"You told me to sue Sweet and Spicy Connections. I'm taking your advice. If I don't do something, this could happen to someone else."

"Well, thank the good lord for showing you reason. Mabel from my knitting group has a son who's a lawyer. I'll get his information for you."

Knitting group. Maddy chuckled. *Yeah, right.* Nana referred to her group of eighty-something-year-old ladies who sat around doing shots of tequila and drinking beer while "knitting" tchotchkes like watermelon pasties with tassels or booby koozies—a knitted can or bottle holder with boobs on the front. The first time they showed her the booby koozie, the women laughed hard enough she feared they'd have heart attacks.

The group of five got together once a week. As a joke, Maddy helped them start a website to sell their items. To her surprise, they sold quite a bit of inventory. Now, for the holidays, they put some on display at the store as well.

"Do you know what area of law he specializes in?" she asked.

That should've been the first thing Maddy asked since she'd need a civil litigation attorney.

"Nope. That doesn't matter. Mabel says he's the best. I'm certain he'll help you. Maybe he can be your new gentleman since you insist last night was work-related." Nana tsked.

Lately, groaning had become second nature when talking to Nana. The woman's regular reminders included her eggs drying up, so she pushed Maddy toward finding someone to keep her bed warm—as Nana put it. But the older woman had to deem any potential partners worthy enough.

Her thoughts drifted back to last Friday with Ax at The Knob. Her desire to see him already grew with each passing day, which was not something she'd admit out loud. As she sat next to El that night, Maddy's insides melted imagining what it would be like to be wrapped up in his arms. To wake up spooned against him, she was the little spoon, his woodsy scent a blanket of comfort.

They shared a few more pleasantries before ending the call. Nana promised to call Mabel right away and then pass on the lawyer's number. As the hours ticked by, Maddy began to doubt her lawsuit decision. What if he laughed at the idea that she wanted to sue them?

The toy didn't come with a warning label, but that didn't mean she'd have a legitimate case. The company could argue that anyone who used a glass toy accepted the risk.

Later that afternoon her phone chimed with a text notification.

Ax: How's your day?

Her heart fluttered seeing his name on the screen. Then she remembered he was a lawyer in New York and wondered if he'd be open to offering a little advice.

Maddy: Boring. Hypothetically speaking, if you were injured while testing a product would you sue the company that sent it to you?

A new notification chimed seconds after the delivery indicator popped up.

Ax: That depends. Is the company requesting the product test the same one that manufactures and sells?

Maddy: Yep. One in the same.

Ax: Then hell yes. They'd pay for all my medical bills, any time off work, and mental anguish—if my lawyer recommended it.

Compensation for time off hadn't occurred to her, but the extra money would help. Lawsuits could take time, Maddy knew that, but once all was said and done, if she got behind, the money awarded would help her catch up. The thousand dollars from Blind Love wouldn't touch the medical bills she'd receive.

Maddy: Good advice. My grandmother would agree with you.

After hitting send she tossed her phone on the couch cushion next to her. The TV played in the background. She picked up her phone again and started another message to Ax.

Maddy: Coke or Pepsi?
Ax: Neither. Water, liquor, or iced tea.

She smiled at his quick response. Elowen was her usual go-to for meaningless conversation to pass the time, but she was busy. Maddy was thankful for someone else to have a meaningless discussion with.

Maddy: Coffee?
Ax: Black. No sugar. No cream. No syrups.
Maddy: Working today?
Ax: Yep. It's paperwork day. You?

All she'd been able to do at Pinks was paperwork.

Maddy: Paperwork. The second worst activity at any job. I took a sick day.

More like an undetermined number of sick days. Ax didn't need to know the details about her broken vagina or forced abstinence.

Ax: How about a game of twenty questions?

She appreciated his creativity. Maddy grinned as she typed.

Maddy: I haven't played that since I was a kid. I'm in.

Ax: Two rules. 1. Every question must be different. If I ask you your favorite show, your next question can't be about my favorite show. 2. No personal questions. Before you say everything is personal, I mean things like family, dating history, employment, and stuff like that.

In response, she sent a thinking head emoji. The sudden disappointment from his rule about nothing personal surprised Maddy.

The little speech dots popped up on the screen. Before he had a chance to ask if she was too scared, Maddy said okay.

Ax: Question 1 – Have you ever gone to the zoo by yourself?

A question she had to think about. Even though it had been forever since she'd gone to the zoo, Maddy was pretty sure she'd never gone alone.

Maddy: No. I've never been by myself. Now that you mention it, I may have to do that soon. Why the zoo? Most people who ask about doing things solo ask about the movie theater.

Ax: I'm not a fan of theaters. They're dark and dirty. If I had my preference, I'd have my own personal screening room. Pretentious, I know. The zoo, on the other hand, is fresh air and I love watching animals. Does that make me weird?

She laughed out loud. The man had no idea what the qualifications for weird were if he thought his love of watching animals gave him the designation.

Maddy: If that's weird then I'm well-above average on that scale. My turn. Do you prefer pens or pencils?

The answer to pens or pencils could teach someone a lot about a person. If they preferred pencils, they were prone to making changes. People who chose pens had more confidence or were surer in what they needed to write, at least that was her experience.

Around question ten Nana called with the lawyer's number. She and Ax spent the rest of the day going back and forth. More and more time passed between answers, but his responses continued to be full sentences, not single words that indicated he might be losing interest.

Maddy: Question 20 – Can you walk and chew gum at the same time?

She hit send then tucked herself into bed. After turning off the lights, she realized she'd forgotten to call the lawyer. Maddy set an alarm for the next day as a reminder.

10

Maddy

Maddy: Do you want to get together *on Saturday?*

She sent the message off to Ax while sitting in the doctor's waiting room. They hadn't seen each other for a week and Elowen went quiet while she prepared for her pitch with the app company. Maddy missed her people.

> *Ax: I'm sorry. My boss reminded me today that our company picnic is in a couple of weeks. As the foreman, I'm kind of required to help with the planning and we've had an emergency, so I have to work this weekend.*

Passed over, again. It wasn't Ax's fault he had to go to a company picnic, but the letdown wasn't any easier to digest.

Maddy: That's okay. I can get some things done around the house. Maybe we can meet up on Sunday? Brunch or hang out at the bar if you're more comfortable there.

"Madelyn?" The medical assistant poked her head out from behind the door.

Hopefully, the doctor would say she could go back to work. It'd be another few weeks before the stitches dissolved, so she wasn't expecting much in the pleasure department.

Her phone dinged with a message. Before the assistant shut the door after completing the vitals, Maddy was already checking the text.

> *Ax: I have a question, but it'd be better to talk in person.*

The doctor walked in, offering a much-needed distraction. She didn't know how long it would be before they could talk in person. If Maddy had too much time to think, the black hole she'd find herself in would be too deep to climb out.

"How are you healing?" Dr. Harris asked.

"Not too bad. If I sit too long in one position, or I move around too much everything starts to burn, but other than that, I'm good."

He nodded and scribbled something in the chart.

"All right. Let's see the surgery site."

Dr. Harris left the room while she cleaned up and redressed. Considering his silence throughout the check-up and afterward she had a pretty good idea whatever he'd say when he came back wasn't going to be positive. It took less than five minutes for him to return.

"I have good and bad news."

Maddy shifted on the uncomfortable exam bed. Her hands rested in her lap, and she crossed one foot over the other, then uncrossed them after a shock of pain shot through her groin.

"Hit me with both."

"You're healing well, but not as fast as I'd hoped. You're going to need to keep the activity restrictions for at least two more weeks. I'll let you go to work for no more than five hours a day and you can go every day to get out of the house. But I'm serious about not doing too much. With all the slicing and dicing you experienced there's a good chance you won't even realize it if you reinjure yourself. That's one of the unfortunate things about the location of your injury."

One. Right. One of a hundred. She hadn't figured out anything fortunate about the whole situation. With more restricted activity she was glad she'd made the call to the lawyer and moved forward with the lawsuit.

"At least I can go back to work part-time. How long before sex? I'm not used to this forced abstinence. If not sex, then self-pleasure?"

"It's been a month since your surgery. Let's get you back in here in two weeks and check those stitches. If everything heals like it should, I'll clear you for work and intimate relations, but I'm not making any promises, Madelyn."

She nodded. Two more weeks. Playing by the rules was much easier if she had a deadline. Maddy would send all the good vibes into the universe.

What a perfect Tuesday.

After the doctor's appointment, Maddy headed to Pinks to pick up Nana. She'd have to fill her in on Dr. Harris's decision. At least the drive would give her more time to think about Ax. A thousand possibilities of what he wanted to ask whirled through her thoughts. Did he want to ask about the picnic? Or their relationship?

To stop the spiral she found herself in, Maddy pulled up his number to call.

"Hey," he answered on the second ring.

"Umm. Hi. I, uh, I wasn't sure if you'd answer." Maddy's hand shook.

Starting the conversation was harder than she'd expected.

"I shouldn't, but your name came up on Caller ID and I wanted to talk to you. Is everything okay?"

"Yeah. You said you had a question for me. I guess I got a little worried."

"Right. I didn't mean to make you worry. The party planner bailed last minute. If I got some exposure for The Knob is there any chance you'd be willing to help out with the organization and planning? As much as I'd like to say Pinks, I'm not sure the company would approve."

Help him plan the company picnic. A smile snuck up on her. Spending time with Ax was what she wanted, it shouldn't matter whether it was eating sandwiches with his coworkers or a date with the two of them.

"Wow," she whispered.

It would be good for the bar if they had free marketing. Party planning wasn't a bullet point on her resume, but if the company was willing, she wouldn't turn down the offer.

"That's a yes?" he asked.

"You said it's in two weeks?"

"Yeah. I know it's super short notice. Stan's desperate. I don't mean to ask you as a last resort. You're the one person I know with the contacts to make it happen. Guess the cat's out of the bag as to how long my list of friends is—or isn't as the case may be."

"Yes. I'll do it. We can spend more time together and I can get some advertising for The Knob. I know a few people around town, but El is the marketing guru. As long as you're okay with it, I can bring her in on it if needed."

"Of course. I'm happy to help too, more if it means we're spending more time together. Not to sound obsessive or overbearing, but my days are always better when I get to see or talk to you."

Flutters started in her chest and worked down to her stomach. His confession made her feel less clingy. She'd never experienced this constant need to be near someone like she was with Ax. Maybe the day wasn't a complete wash after all.

"I could stop by tomorrow to meet Stan; find out what needs to be done?"

"Perfect. I'll tell him to expect you in the morning. If I'm around, I'll make sure to say hi. Do you know where Weald Lumber is?"

Maddy had seen the signs on her way out of town but never stopped. As she recalled, the office was nothing more than a trailer.

"Yeah, I think so. Where do I go once I'm there?"

"Hold on." Ax's muffled voice came through the phone, but she couldn't understand what he was saying.

A few other male voices joined in on his conversation. Maddy waited in her car for him to come back. Nana climbed in the front seat.

"Hey," Maddy whispered.

She'd meant to go in and help Lola get everything out to the car, but her grandmother was too quick.

"Everything okay?" Nana asked.

"Yeah. I called Ax, but he had to talk to some of his guys."

"Maddy?" Ax came back to the phone.

"I'm here. You were going to tell me where to go once I get there."

"Right. At the end of the gravel drive is a trailer. Go inside and ask for Stan. There's always one of us in there and we can get him for you. I hate to cut it short, but I've got to go check on one of the sites. If our schedules work out, I'll see you tomorrow. If not, I'll talk to you soon."

Maddy disconnected the call.

"I like him." Nana smoothed out the bag lying on her lap. "He likes you too. Tell me again how you met. Where are you going?"

"Well, we met on this app El is working on. She wanted me to try it out and I matched with him." Maddy kept that part of the question short. "Anyway, he asked if I could help organize their company picnic. In return, I get some free advertising for The Knob. He didn't think they'd be too keen on promoting Pinks and Pearls."

Nana's scratchy laughter filled the car.

"This man has it bad for you. How long have you known each other?"

Maddy thought back through the mental calendar in her head. Some days it felt like she'd known him forever. Their connection had been instant and easy.

"We've been talking for a little more than a month. Jack and El met him at The Knob last week."

"And he's already asking you to plan his company picnic with the benefit of promoting your bar. Yeah, he's doing whatever he can to get you there. I expect to meet him soon if he's already passed the best friend and uncle test."

What did I get myself into? Maddy wasn't known for moving quickly. She and Natasha dated for three years before deciding to get married.

"It was a mistake. I'll call him back and tell him never mind."

Nana smacked Maddy's thigh.

"No, you will not. This is a chance to introduce new people to our businesses. I expect you to go and have fun, and I want all the juicy details when you get home. Also, not being able to actively promote Pinks doesn't mean you can't tell some of the wives about your classes. I'm sure they'd be intrigued to know more. Think about how they may react when you offer to schedule a private class for Weald wives if enough are interested."

Maddy grinned. That was a suggestion she could go along with.

"Nana, can I ask you a question?" She began the drive home.

"Of course, sweetheart. Anything."

Her sweaty palms slid around the leather wrap of her steering wheel. Maddy chewed on her lip.

"Have you considered setting up a website for online ordering and shipping? Lots of places offer the service and even if you didn't want to sell regular merchandise, we could put your koozies and tassels on there. Provide a calendar for class sign-ups and accept pre-registrations."

The strained chuckle echoed in the car. Maddy backed out at the last second from the question she really wanted to ask. Everything with Ax was happening so quick, Maddy wasn't sure if it was normal. If anyone could give her decent advice, it'd be Lola. While chiding herself for letting fear get the best of her, she patted herself on the back for coming up with a fantabulous suggestion off the cuff.

Lola tapped her fingers on the bag.

"A website is a good idea. Selling merchandise is outside of my realm of expertise. Who would manage that? Do you know how to set it up or would we need to hire someone else? Maybe Elowen would be willing. Yes, that would work. There are a lot of questions with this proposal. Let's sit down and talk it out before I make a decision."

Maddy nodded. Coming up with ideas wasn't as hard as running a business. A solution for how she could stay connected with the businesses but not run them took root in her thoughts. Like Nana said, there were a lot of questions she'd have to work out before even thinking about voicing the idea. For the first time since the subject of retirement came up and Maddy taking over she wasn't afraid of letting her grandmother down.

11

AX

"She been here yet?" Ax stuck his head in the office where Stan spent most of his days.

His boss shook his head. "No. Same answer as the one I gave you five minutes ago. You got a thing for this one?"

"Nope." Yes. He wasn't ready to admit his feelings for Maddy. That led to questions, not just from the guys, but himself too. Like why he wasn't ready to date a month ago and now the idea of forever kept popping up at random times. "I know she'll be great at getting the picnic organized."

Maybe. He had no idea if she had any skills in party planning. There were still a lot of things he didn't know about Maddy, but he wanted to learn more. Ax wanted to ask all the questions. What did she do outside of the shop and bar? What was her family like? Did she have any siblings? Did she like board games?

Could she teach him more ways to add variety in the bedroom? Maddy was far more worldly when it came to relationships, sex, and everything in between. Ax thought he was experienced, but after meeting her he could admit to knowing pretty much nothing beyond vanilla, missionary-style sex in heterosexual relationships. In other words, boring.

She brought a spice he had no idea he was missing.

His thoughts drifted to the last time he'd seen her. Long black hair. Deep brown eyes he could get lost in, to be drawn back to earth by her scratchy yet sensual voice. Curves that fit against him like they were made for each other. Ax wanted her with him, tucked into his side with his arm draped over her shoulder. Protective. Close. Secure.

A knock on the trailer door pulled him out of the memory.

"Who in the hell knocks at a mill site? This isn't some fancy corporate office building." The older man pulled open the door to reveal Maddy, dressed in a black and white checked dress with a band of cherries at the top and along the upper edge of each of the pockets. She'd tied a red scarf in her hair with a knot at the top while the sides framed her face.

The style furthered his appreciation for covering up rather than baring everything for all to see.

"Umm. Hi. I'm Madelyn Begay and I'm supposed to find Stan?" Her voice rose in a question at the end.

Ax stepped into view from Stan's side. "Hey. You found us."

"Yeah. Your directions were helpful. I'm pretty sure I've passed by this place more than once."

An awkward air of silence hung around them as they stood at the entrance of the trailer.

"Right. Come on, let's go to my office where I can catch you up on what I have—not much—and what I need—a lot." Stan turned away from them.

Maddy giggled. She followed through the narrow trailer to his office. Ax paused as Stan opened the door. He tried to imagine what it might look like from her perspective.

The faux wood paneling had seen better days. One wall still had a hole from the time Crash put his fist through it after the boss took him off a job. It smelled of musty sweat and dirt. Ax wrinkled his nose and made a mental note to get an air freshener. The carpet wasn't carpet. More like a piece of scrap someone found on the side of the road. That hadn't bothered him before since they didn't need anything fancy considering they came in and out with dirt and mud all over their boots.

"Ax, get a couple of chairs from the tables." Stan focused on Maddy. "Sorry, we don't tend to use the office for anything more than paperwork. Since we use it one at a time there's no need to bother with extra chairs."

She smiled and nodded as though she understood. Even to Ax it didn't make sense, because it wasn't the whole truth. More than once he'd had conferences in the office with his crew rather than reprimand them in front of everyone.

Once all three of them huddled around the desk, Stan pulled out a white folder with Weald printed in blue and outlined in gold on the outside. He slid the top piece of paper out of the pocket on the left.

"Here's the checklist my wife made for me after our other planner bailed. There are a couple of boxes checked. Everything that's blank will need to be purchased. I'm happy to let you use my company card."

"You don't know me. What if I decide to take the card and ditch town?" she asked.

"You own that bar, The Rustic Knob, right?"

She nodded. "Yes, but—"

Stan held up two fingers.

"I go in there enough to hear more gossip than I want. You run that place like a bar should be run. They're lucky to have you." Stan tapped the tip of his finger on the desk.

Ax studied Maddy while she read the list. Her lips moved in time with her finger as it slid across the page. He knew what Stan still needed to do; he'd gone over the checklist that morning.

"There's a lot on here. You said the picnic is two weeks from Saturday?" she asked.

Stan nodded.

"Yeah, short notice. My wife told me the company would bail, but I didn't listen. She makes an effort to say 'I told you so' at least once a day now."

Ax groaned. His boss wasn't good at listening to anyone, least of all his wife when it meant he was wrong.

"Stan, how do you expect her to get all of this done. She still has a job," Ax cut in.

It wasn't fair given he'd asked for her help, but his brain refused to shut up. Maddy straightened her shoulders. Yeah, he'd put his foot in his mouth. After having a mother like his, Ax should've known better than to insinuate she couldn't manage the project better than anyone else.

"No. Planning the picnic will be easy. There are local places we can visit. It's going to take some compromise on your end though. If I'm doing this, it's my way, not yours. The checklist will be helpful, but a few items aren't feasible given the time frame." She bit the corner of her lip and tapped her pencil against the paper.

Ax licked his lips. He wanted to taste her mouth. Kiss away any discomfort from the bite. His mind buzzed with ideas, none of which were appropriate to act on in front of his boss—or in public.

"The caterer will be hard. Since you're having it at the park in the middle of town would you be okay with a few food trucks instead? If we do that, they wouldn't be exclusive to Weald employees and families, but I can try to negotiate a discount."

"Whatever we need for this to happen. Food trucks would be great. It's either that or we have a potluck." Stan grimaced.

Ax wasn't keen on a potluck either, but sometimes sacrifices had to be made when time was short.

"What if we do a dessert potluck? That would minimize the number of trucks she'd have to find. Desserts are easy, right?" Ax turned to Madelyn.

She nodded.

"That's a great idea. I'll need help. To get what you need in the limited amount of time, it's going to take footwork."

Stan waved a hand through the air in Ax's direction.

"Take him. I can manage the guys for the next couple of days. If you're more comfortable, he can keep the card too."

That earned Ax and Stan a smile. Ax wanted more of those directed his way. Later he'd thank Stan for letting him tag along. Besides taking orders, Ax wasn't any good at party planning.

"Perfect. A friend of mine, Elowen Turner, will help too. She's a marketing consultant and has contacts I'm sure she'll share." Madelyn stood. She tucked the checklist into her purse and held her hand out to Stan. "I look forward to working with you. This will be beneficial for both of us."

Ax's boss crooked his upper lip—the best smile he could give.

"More for me. Trust me, this picnic is an annual tradition. The families have some high expectations. If you pull this off, I'll be forever grateful."

They shook hands and the three of them left the office. Ax walked her to her car.

"Thank you. You have no idea how much it means to all of us that you're willing to jump in and take over." He chewed on the inside of his cheek to keep from stealing the kiss he'd spent the last half-hour imagining.

The glisten of lip gloss mesmerized him.

"This gives me something to do since the doctor says I still can't go back to work full time."

Ax tilted his head to the side.

"Doctor? Are you okay?" he asked.

She diverted her gaze to the ground. "Umm yeah. It's no big deal. Thank *you*, by the way."

"For what?"

"For giving me the chance. This'll be good for The Knob and Pinks." He opened his mouth, but she shook her head. "I know, I know. No direct advertising of Pinks and Pearls. This may be rude, but is there any pay included?"

He grimaced. She thought it was rude to ask for compensation for her work. Weald was better than that. Shame weighed on his shoulders for not making sure to mention it before the meeting concluded.

"I'll be honest, this was a selfish request. Please don't apologize for asking about pay. I'll make sure you're compensated. Stan will prefer a flat fee, is that okay?"

"I figured, and I'm okay with it."

Despite a growing desire to spend more time with her, Ax held back. They were still in the getting to know you phase. Even though it'd been a month, they hadn't gone on an official date, beyond meeting each other.

Ax could admit using the Blind Love app to remove the immediate physical attraction deepened his feelings. Now that he knew Maddy on a more personal level, he didn't want to jump right into bed.

12

Maddy

*Maddy: **Need your help!** Ax asked me to pull together a last-minute company picnic and I said yes. You're the marketing expert. Any chance you can help us out today?*

El: Can't help this morning, but maybe this afternoon. I'll let you know.

Maddy looked at her phone again. The twentieth time in the last three hours. Her lower lip stuck out in a pout. Childish. Yep. Maddy's body thrummed with excitement. Her stomach flip-flopped with nerves. Planning the Weald party was an opportunity for Maddy. A personal test to see if she could do more than teach sex classes to adults.

More than anything, she wanted to talk to her best friend—who didn't have time for her.

El: Lunch?

The chime of the incoming notification startled Maddy. She reached across the desk for her phone.

Maddy: "When did you want to get together?"
El: "Now. My stress is off the charts, and I need food."

The reply alert rang seconds later.

Maddy: "Sounds good to me. Meet you at The Diner?"
El: "Nope. I want Thai. Lunch is on me. Be there in fifteen."

The restaurant was a small, nondescript place in the middle of a strip mall at the end of town. The hostess sat them at one of the few empty tables, right in the center of the room.

"What's the latest on your broken lady parts?" El asked when Maddy sat across from her.

"Doc says it's taking longer than expected to heal, at least the inside cuts. I can't help thinking if I'd not had surgery life would be normal again. Anyway, two more weeks and he says I should be okay."

Water flew from El's lips, which landed on Maddy's cheek.

"I'm sorry. Normal and you do not go together."

"Gee thanks." Maddy flung her hand into the air to shake off the small drops of water.

"Don't go all snowflake on me. You're going to own a sex toy shop soon. Normal for you would not be a good thing."

A twinkle softened El's gaze. Maddy threw a small piece of bread across the table.

"Snowflake? Maybe a muddy one who knows how to have fun. By the way, I learned new ways to play with electricity today."

El scratched her forehead where the bread landed.

"Play with electricity? I'm going to need more."

They ordered their lunch and Maddy cleared the area in front of her. El was about to get a lesson in a new-to-her kind of sex play. The pure pleasure in learning and teaching about new things came out in Maddy's frantic hand movements. Her best friend and grandmother loved to tease her about how animated she became.

"There are these things called tens units. A lot of physical therapists use them, but there are ways to play with them safely in the bedroom. E-stimulation is the technical name. The machines don't cost a lot, and you don't need a prescription or anything to buy them." Maddy pulled up some pictures on her phone to show El before continuing.

"Okay, they're little sticky pads. Wouldn't the charge hurt you?" El asked.

Maddy shook her head. "Nope. It's not strong enough. Although, they do recommend not putting them above your heart."

"Makes sense." El took a piece of bread from the bowl in the center of the table.

"Another way to incorporate electrical play is with an electric wand, like what they sell for facial treatments. The sensations are different even though they both use electricity. One of my vendors demonstrated them on me." Maddy gestured wildly. She smiled, remembering the warm tingle the wand left behind on her skin as he rubbed it back and forth. "They were fun. Tomorrow I'm going to sit down with Nana and talk to her about an exclusive sale to class participants first before adding them to our regular inventory. Also, I was thinking about offering discounts on specific products to those who attend our classes."

Maddy rested her hands in front of her and took a deep breath. Her best friend didn't say anything. El's gaze floated from Maddy's face to the table and back again. A couple of times she started to say something then stopped with a shake of her head. Maddy knew El didn't always know what to say when it came to unfamiliar inventory. That was okay with Maddy. She'd rather have silence than criticism.

Her thoughts drifted to Ax. Would he judge her for her excitement over sex toys? Signing up for the app wasn't some grand plan to find a forever partner. Despite their growing attraction, Maddy wouldn't hesitate to dump him if he couldn't accept her as is. Her ex-wife did all she could to mold Maddy into a respectable, successful woman—at least Nat's definition of one. Now, Maddy was determined to forge her own path. Whoever chose to stick it out forever with her would need to be willing to support, not lead.

"That's incredible. You've taken these classes seriously. I'm proud of you. Lola must be too. She and Delbert set up the store and bar and you're going to make them even better. All the changes will boost the store's sales."

The warm touch of embarrassment rose up Maddy's neck to her cheeks. How to accept compliments without turning a dusty rose color was on her bucket list of items to learn before she died.

"The ready-made boxes are a major moneymaker after each class, which are still going strong. Nana and I agreed to add a third-level class to focus on kinkier bedroom ideas. This electric stuff could fall in-between. If we go along with the riskier topics, we'll limit the class size to five or six and they'd have to sign a disclosure."

El's eyes grew wide. "Are you into that stuff? I never would have guessed you to be interested in super kinky bedroom fun."

"No. I'm not, but I know some people who are, so we've invited them to come in. It's not like we're pulling out the whips and chains, but those who've attended the first two classes want more."

Soft kink could be fun. Maddy encouraged it when she talked to class attendees if they had more questions or wanted to explore further. She classified most of her information as a simple way to spice it up behind closed doors. Despite never venturing into the depths of kink, it intrigued her.

"If it means profit for Pinks, then I don't want to be the one to turn them away. Besides, if we bring people in, they can direct attendees on where to go if they want more. This is a trial run, nothing set in stone."

Images of lying on the bed with a blindfold, knowing that Ax stood over her with a feather or one of the leather paddles they sold flashed through Maddy's thoughts. The imagined anticipation of not knowing what would happen next had her core flooding with excitement. She wiggled in her chair. A sly smile turned up the corner of her lip. Maddy straightened her back and squared her shoulders.

"You okay?" El cocked her eyebrow.

"Sure. Peachy. Stitches in my vagina keep me from feeling any pleasure and if my body reacts to anything, then I get sharp pains in my crotch as a reminder that I'm on doctor-ordered orgasm denial for at least two more weeks. Yeah, life's grand."

Elowen tossed her head back and laughed loud enough the whole restaurant turned to see what happened. Maddy's attempt to shoot daggers with her gaze made El laugh harder.

"You'll heal soon enough, then I'm pretty sure Ax will make you forget the last six weeks and remind you how good it can feel."

"I hate you." Maddy took a long drink of cold water.

"Love you too, babe. Now stop with the whining and tell me about whatever it is you need my help with?"

Once their food arrived, they took a few minutes to eat and enjoy. Maddy told El about the picnic and how Ax asked her to help plan. She also told her about the marketing opportunities—subtle for Pinks and obvious for The Knob.

"What do I get out of helping you?" El asked. "I met with the Blind Love developers today to pitch my long-term strategy. If they call me tomorrow, I may not have the time to help."

The sour taste of a threat hit the back of Maddy's throat. She furrowed her brows. "El, don't try to throw out veiled threats. If you don't want to help, then say so. But please, don't treat me like I'm too naïve to miss the fact that your decision hinges on personal benefit."

El whipped her head up to look Maddy in the eyes. Tears threatened to fall from the corner of El's eyes. She swiped the back of her hand across her cheeks.

"What happened today?" Maddy asked.

Guilt for going on the defensive settled in Maddy's chest. She rubbed the twinge away. El may have had a bad day, but Maddy didn't do anything to deserve the snippiness. Regret, guilt, and an unnecessary apology were the tools she used to keep her ex-wife happy. They were used as manipulation. Maddy refused to let that happen again.

"Everything. I fell in the mud. They shortened my presentation. If the sky could've fallen, I swear today would've been the day. That doesn't mean I should take it out on you. I'm sorry."

Maddy reached across the table and took El's hand in hers. "You're forgiven. I'm sorry the pitch didn't go the way you'd hoped. Doesn't change the fact that they'd be crazy not to choose your proposal. The app is good. Your launch is even better."

"Thank you." El smiled. "I think I needed to hear that I hadn't crashed and burned. Of course, I'll help with the picnic."

"Good. Now, tell me all the good things about your pitch while we finish lunch. This should be a celebration. You've made it through a stressful morning, and I get to spend time with Ax planning an entire Saturday with him."

13

Maddy

Twelve seventeen. Ax had agreed to meet her in the food truck parking lot at twelve fifteen on Thursday afternoon. Stan assured her he would give Ax time away from the site.

"Hey, I'm sorry I'm late."

Maddy sucked in a breath. A lock of brown hair fell over his eyes. Without thinking she brushed it out of the way then stepped back. She shivered when his fingers caressed her arm, Maddy cleared her throat.

"It's okay. We better get moving if we're going to get this list completed. I need you to help me choose which trucks to secure. It's best if we sample the food."

"I'm starving. Where do we start?" He rubbed his hands together and turned in a circle.

His question triggered dirty thoughts. Maddy decided to push him a little to see how he dealt with her sometimes off-the-wall and over-the-top juvenile responses.

"We start in the bedroom with me spread eagle on the bed." She laughed at his furrowed brow.

"I'd be stupid to turn that offer down." Ax grabbed her hand and tugged her toward his truck. "Let's go."

"Mmm I like a man who knows what he wants. Unfortunately, I can't. Doctor's orders. I apologize now for the unintentional blue balls." Maddy kissed him on the cheek as a consolation prize.

"I'd like to know more about this doctor you keep referring to and why he or she has anything to do with you leaving me with a case of blue balls—later. For now, let's go taste some food." He winked and guided her to the trucks, still holding her hand.

Maddy smiled. Hand holding was the best way to connect in her opinion. Innocent, yes, but she loved how it made her feel desired. A demonstration they wanted to keep her close.

Fifteen different trucks filled the lot. Everything from tacos to gyros and even an Indian food truck. They were known for their chicken tikka masala—one of Maddy's favorites. Since there wasn't time to debate, considering a few of them likely had bookings for the weekend, they planned to try all of the trucks that afternoon.

Maddy chose a round table in the middle of the lot and waited for Ax. He joined a few minutes later with plates balanced on his forearms. She laughed while helping set everything down.

He cut a pulled pork sandwich in half, handed one piece to her then took a bite out of his.

"This is incredible," he said after wiping barbecue off his mouth and hands.

"Wait until you try some of the others," Maddy replied.

While they taste-tested Ax checked his phone every couple of minutes. Even though he never texted or took a call, Maddy found the constant pull of his attention annoying.

"I'm sorry. I'm being rude, I'm not always on my phone this much, but my mother insists on bringing me into unnecessary drama."

"Is there anything you want to talk about? Maybe I can help you," she offered.

"She won't stay out of my business. I recently—if you can call a year ago recent—left a bad situation, and she won't let go."

Maddy related to his situation. Not with pity but understanding, although she wasn't ready to divulge her past.

"Parents mean well, even if they don't show it. Mine never see each other or me. They haven't come for a visit since I left upstate two years ago."

He shook his head. "Same as mine. Dad wizened up, though, and told Mother she had to choose work or him. Mom says she didn't give it a single thought. Then again, being a stay-at-home mom meant she did what she wanted, when she wanted. We still had cooks and house cleaners."

"Our families were similar as far as working too much." Maddy checked the time. They had too much left to do. If they wanted to chit chat, it had to be while walking around town. "We should choose and move on to the next item on the list."

Ax decided against the usual picks like tacos and hamburgers and went with a few of the rarer options.

"All right. With the lunch rush over, I'll go talk to them and try to make some arrangements."

He nodded and shoved another forkful of food in his mouth. Maddy cleared her mess then left him alone. Twenty minutes later she had agreements with three main course trucks and an ice cream vendor. They'd proposed a dessert potluck, but Maddy couldn't resist the nostalgia of the age-old melody playing from the speaker on top of the truck. When she returned to the table Ax finished off his last plate of food.

"What's the verdict?" he asked.

"I got all of them. You're a slow eater." She grinned.

"Yep. I like to savor my food. These places are amazing and perfect for the picnic. I appreciate a new experience given I've never eaten from a food truck. Much better than a caterer."

She grabbed his empty plates and carried them to the trash.

"You ready?" she asked.

"Sure, and thanks for clearing my stuff. You didn't have to do that." Ax moved in the direction of the parking area, but she grabbed his arm and turned him toward the sidewalk.

"You're welcome. It's no big deal. My mom taught me it was my responsibility to clear the table after a meal—whether it be for me or my partner. I guess it's a habit now."

Maddy guided them to a local retail shop with a lightness in her step. One of her favorite memories of downtown was with her grandfather before he passed. They'd had ice cream, bought some gifts for Lola, and spent most of the day laughing at each other's antics. Being with Ax came easy like breathing. After the stress and pain she'd dealt with the last few weeks, the reprieve was welcomed.

"What are we doing here," Ax asked. "I don't remember anything like this on Stan's list."

"Not exactly. He wants a silent auction. I figured we could hit up some of the Main Street shops and the downtown area to get local items. While we may not end up with expensive stuff, it'll mean more being from around here. There's no note about what the proceeds go to, but I'm hoping he keeps them local."

"They go to a Weald family in need during the holidays, nominated and chosen by leadership."

Maddy's jaw dropped. That was the last thing she expected a corporation like Weald to do. They were a national company. In her experience, those were the worst about taking care of employees. It was one of the reasons she hated the businesses her parents ran. The Boards cared more about their own pockets. Maddy never wanted to be in that situation.

"Then it's even more important we get local shops to donate." She pulled open the door, smiling at the chime of the bell.

As they made their way from store to store, Ax led the conversations. One of the hardware stores negotiated a deal to donate a tool chest full of tools. Weald paid for the tools and the hardware store supplied the toolbox. It was free advertising, and they were more than happy to know that the money raised stayed local.

By three o'clock they rounded up everything for the silent auction. There were two dozen other things to do. All the walking resulted in jabs of pain between her legs.

"You all right?" Ax asked at one point.

"I'll be fine. We need to make a few more stops before we call it a day." She'd unsuccessfully tried to cover her winces with smiles.

If she didn't get off her feet sooner rather than later, she wouldn't be able to go into Pinks the next day. As far as the picnic, she could do half of the list over the phone.

"At least let me get my truck. I don't know where you want to go next, but we can drive."

She nodded. That would buy her another hour. While he went to his truck, she rested on a bench, contemplating the day they'd had. Her ex-wife would've demanded they hire someone to do the planning, all the while griping about how unprofessional it was to wait until the last minute.

Ax hadn't complained once. He'd jumped in when needed and accepted the fact that his boss was the one who dropped the ball.

"What's next?" he asked as soon as she climbed onto the seat.

"We need to get equipment for games. I'm thinking volleyball, maybe set up some horseshoes and cornhole. There's a store in Scappoose that should have what we need."

She had plans for tug-of-war too, but that would be a surprise for everyone. Maddy had some tricks up her sleeves for an adult versus kids round.

"Sounds good. I don't know what cornhole is, but I'm sure it's fun."

"How do you not know what cornhole is?" Of course, she hadn't known either until she moved to Podunk. "It's nothing difficult. There are two boards each with a hole at the top. You set them twenty-seven feet apart and toss bean bags at the holes to score points. There's a rulebook and everything. I don't know the official rules, but it's still fun—especially when alcohol is involved."

"You'll have to show me how to play during the picnic." The wink he tossed her made her body tingle.

"It's a deal," she answered.

The store wasn't more than twenty minutes away, but the silence in the truck made her fidget. She couldn't put her finger on the reason why other than he was still more or less a stranger to her. There was one way to fix that.

"Tell me the best memory you have from growing up," she said.

He tapped a rhythm on the steering wheel. Maddy hoped he wouldn't ask her the same question. Her best memories weren't from growing up, they were from the last two years since moving to Podunk.

"That's a hard one. Most of them involve my mom yelling at me to sit up straight and mind my manners."

She laughed. Maddy knew those orders far better than she'd have liked.

"I have the same ones. As soon as I asked the question, I regretted it because I didn't want you to ask me the same thing."

"Ahh, we have that in common as well. I guess if I must pick, one of my favorites is my sixth birthday. The birthday itself wasn't anything special, but my younger brother got in trouble for spilling red juice all over the sitting room carpet. That was the room we weren't allowed in. I dared him to sneak in, even told him it would be the best birthday gift ever. After he stepped onto the carpet without getting caught, he threw his hands in the air and spilled the drink everywhere. I had the entire afternoon by myself to do whatever I wanted since they were busy yelling at him."

"Wow. Umm. How do I respond to that? You were an evil older brother." she asked.

Ax chuckled. The deep rumble of his voice filled the cab of his truck and her entire body warmed. Maddy rubbed away the goosebumps on her arms. He was dangerous for her arousal, very dangerous.

"There's not a good way to respond." He reached across the bench seat and laced their fingers together.

Maddy grinned. Twice in one day. The callouses on his hand scratched her fingers, a gentle reminder he wasn't the smooth lawyer his parents wanted him to be, but a hardworking outdoorsman. Maddy gave a silent thanks that she met him after he left the socialite life.

"It's funny that one of your best memories was possible because your brother got in trouble."

"Do you have any brothers or sisters?" he asked.

Maddy shook her head. "Mom and Dad hadn't planned to have me. There was no way they would have a second child. In fact, Mom told me once that as soon as I was born, she went and had surgery to prevent having any more kids."

"Ouch. That's harsh."

"Some would say it is. Others would say at least they didn't bring another kid into the world they didn't want." She shrugged. "I guess it's all about perspective."

"Fair enough." Ax pulled into a parking spot at the front of the store.

Maddy broke their connection to pull the strap of her purse over her shoulder.

"If you want to come in you can, but I'd understand if you'd rather wait out here. All I'm going to do is rent the equipment and set up for them to bring it to the park."

He unbuckled his seat belt and reached for the handle. "I'll come in that way if you need the card, you won't have to make another trip out."

They handled the plans for games and then drove back to Podunk. On the way home Maddy thought about her memories and his. She'd often wondered what it would have been like to have siblings but realized she was okay being an only child. If his happiest memory was a time his brother got in trouble, she wasn't sure siblings would've been worth it.

He pulled up next to her car and put the truck into park.

"Thanks again for your help," he said.

Maddy wasn't quite ready to leave. She'd enjoyed spending the day with him.

"This was fun. I'm happy to help. It's like I'm giving back to the community as well."

"You're a good woman, Maddy. If your skills with running a business are half as good as your party planning, then the shops will never struggle."

Her cheeks flushed. They climbed out of the truck and met at the front.

"Thanks." Maddy stared at the ground. With the toe of her shoe she ground a bit of dirt into the concrete. "I know this is coming from left field, but would you ever be open to being my guinea pig for some of my class prep?"

Ax sputtered. Her intention was to put him on the spot. Over time she'd learned people's reactions were more authentic when they didn't know what was coming. He closed the distance between them, slipping his hands around her waist to pull her in close. His breath tickled against her neck.

"That sounds like a lot of fun," he whispered. "Are you sure you want me to be your test subject though? Compared to you, I might as well be a virgin. No matter what you say, I'll tell you it's great."

With a nod, Maddy released a long, slow breath. She swore his lips brushed her cheek before he leaned on the hood of his truck.

Their connection went beyond physical, and the fact that he called her bluff made him that much more attractive.

"I need someone who doesn't know everything. That way, if I get too winded or too technical, if you fall asleep, or the ideas don't get you curious to know more, then you can tell me. In this instance, less is more."

The last time Maddy was gifted a smile like Ax's she'd graduated with her MBA. Not even on her wedding day did Natasha make her feel like she'd been handed the whole world to protect.

"Count me in. Let me know when you need me." Ax glanced at his watch. "I guess I should go."

Maddy lifted onto her toes and draped her arms over his shoulders.

"I appreciate you, Ax." She kissed the stubble on his jaw before stepping back. "Give me a few days to make some more calls and finalize plans. I'll check in with you later in the week."

Maddy didn't watch him pull out of the lot. She did think about how much she wished he could've taken her home.

14

Ax

Rather than sleep in until Saturday afternoon, he'd woken up early, made an actual breakfast instead of frozen waffles and yogurt, and now he was about to sit in on his second class about sex and sex toys. Maddy's request for him to help her prepare put a skip in his step. That was one reason he'd decided to go to the class. If he was going to be any help, he needed a better idea of what the classes were like.

To the left of the door, a paper sign read "Pervertibles 102." The soft din of voices floated into the hallway. He was in the right place. Ax glanced around the door to check whether Maddy had arrived yet. When he was certain she hadn't, he eased into the room and stood along the back wall. His gaze landed on a chair in the corner, hidden enough to watch, but she wouldn't notice him right away.

The second reason he was there—he wanted to see Maddy. Her daily text updates were the extent of their conversation over the past week. Professional. Distant. To make matters worse, Stan threw a new project in his lap on Monday with a Thursday deadline. For the first time, Ax canceled his night on the town with his adopted grand-father.

While fretting over her, Brett, one of his crew members, suggested going to her next class.

He glanced at his watch, five minutes until it began. Most of the chairs had been reserved or taken by couples, groups, and a few singles. Ax counted twenty people in the room. Each group spread out to keep from sitting on top of each other.

A bang preceded the entrance of a big, black square entering through the door. Maddy followed, pushing the square. She shuffled her tennis shoes over the linoleum. The cream pencil skirt she wore did amazing things for her curves. Every bone in his body urged him to get up, offer help, but then he'd be discovered.

It wasn't that he didn't want her to know he was there. More like, he didn't want Maddy to think him a stalker or creep.

"Here, let me help you," one of the other attendees offered.

"Thank you, Roger. I wore the wrong clothes to lug around a massage table." Maddy chuckled.

Roger took over, lifting the table off the floor and carrying it to the front of the room. Maddy straightened the gray cropped sweatshirt she wore and moved a strand of hair off her face.

"Hmm. I wonder why you didn't offer," a soft, feminine voice said.

Ax jerked his gaze to the woman standing next to him with her arms crossed over her chest. Green eyes scrutinized him. The charged air around them had Ax pulling at the collar on his shirt to help him breathe.

"Do you come to her classes often?" he asked.

"Nope. She's been busy and I wanted to see her. How about you?" El took the empty seat in Ax's left.

He leaned back in his hair with his legs stretched out.

Ax lifted his chin toward Maddy. "She doesn't know I'm here."

"Did you sign the sheet when you registered?" she asked.

"Nope. Convinced the guy downstairs not to add my name in order to keep it a secret."

Elowen smirked. "She hates surprises, you know."

"I didn't but thank you for sharing."

He couldn't take his eyes off El. Each time they'd shared the same space the mood tensed. He wondered if he was the problem.

Maddy stepped up to the middle of the room.

"Good afternoon, everyone. I'm glad you decided to come back for the second class." Her brown eyes sparkled.

He loved the dimple in her left cheek. While they'd worked on getting donations for the silent auction, he'd noticed the dimple was more pronounced based on her level of happiness. At the front of the class, she held their attention, and the depression was as deep as he'd seen.

Being professional, Maddy didn't pause as she made a quick sweep of the room and noticed him. El received a chin tilt when she waved at her best friend.

"Last time we discussed food items that can spice things up at home. Cucumbers, strawberries, eggplant, and grapefruits. In a few of the other intro classes, we talked about incorporating things like ice to play around with temperature sensations. This time we'll go a little further with your exploration and I'll show you ways to have fun with a massage table."

A few of the students chuckled. Ax's mind went wild with possibilities. One of the older ladies up front raised her hand.

"Are you sure it's safe to use a table like that? We'd have to call the ambulance if my Henry and I tried one of your tricks and it broke, sending me to the floor."

Maddy shook her head. To her credit, she didn't laugh or give any indication that the woman's question was unreasonable.

"These are quite sturdy. If you're worried about falling, then I'd recommend getting a more expensive one with metal legs. They can be harder to move around, but if you have a room to set it up permanently, then you'll be fine. In fact, I can come over and help if you'd prefer."

The woman who asked had to be nearing eighty. Ax squirmed at unwanted mental images of Ax's grandparents having sex. Maddy was one hell of a teacher to make that kind of offer.

"She's incredible with her hands. If you want an excuse for her to touch you, ask for a quick shoulder massage. They're heaven." El winked.

Ax's mind conjured images of Maddy's hands skating over his body, lighting up nerve endings from head to toe. He wanted to experience her touch, her tricks. He cleared his throat and shook his head. If his daydream went much further, he'd need a clean pair of pants.

"You know we're getting to know each other, right?" Ax asked.

Elowen nodded. "Yep."

"And how do you feel about that?" he asked.

"Excited. She deserves to have a little fun. It's been too long." With tight lips, El turned her attention toward the front of the room.

"For anyone interested, you can get these online for as little as seventy dollars and have them delivered to your home. The more expensive models can cost upward of three hundred dollars. Before we get too much further, would anyone like to share something they've tried and liked, or didn't like, from our first lesson?"

Ax didn't expect anyone to talk about their sex life. Then again, they paid to attend a class that gave tips and tricks to spice it up, who was he to judge.

"I have to say, we were quite pleased with the DIY bundle you offered downstairs. Jules loved the fuzzy handcuffs." One of the youngest men in the room spoke up.

He'd spiked his hair, and his jeans were ripped in very strategic ways. The kid paid at least a hundred dollars for someone else to rip them for him. *Ridiculous.*

"That's fantastic. I'm glad you enjoyed the bundle. We're considering doing more of those, so if any of you have suggestions, please let me know."

A few others shared their experiences. After each story there were nods and murmurs of agreement. Some said they tried a few things, but nothing worked for them. They'd come to the class for more tips. Ax listened in awe. Maddy took every comment and anecdote to heart. She maintained eye contact with each speaker, never interrupted, or told them what they did wrong. A few times she suggested they talk to her after class, and she'd give them suggestions how to change their approach.

For her part, her class was just that...a class. Not some juvenile sex lesson or a game.

"All right, then let's get started. I'm sure most of you have a few ideas for how to use this table. One of my favorites doesn't involve intercourse at all."

Maddy's voice hitched when she said intercourse and their gazes connected.

Ax's dick twitched. The stutter in her words sent his control careening back into dangerous territory.

"Umm okay." Maddy cleared her throat a couple of times. "I love using wax as foreplay. We sell candles that will not burn you the way a scented candle from the candle store can. We have UV candles, primary colors, and liquid metals like silver and gold. They are soy and paraffin wax to keep the burn point low. You can light them, then drip the wax up and down the body. There are also wax cubes that you can place in a melting pot for artistic wax play. For the purpose of this class, I recommend staying simple and doing drips while using a shower curtain on the floor for cleanup."

Hands shot into the air. Ax took a second to adjust in his seat. The relieved groan came out a little louder than he'd planned.

"One last option, for those who want to dive into the world of kink. If you're up for altering your table, you can attach rings for bondage. These work well with rope or carbineer clips. I would not recommend a massage table for heavy bondage. Keep it light, and you'll be fine."

Candles. Belts to strap someone to the table while tickling with feathers, and rings for bondage. Incredible. The single use Ax knew for a massage table was a massage with sex at the end—boring compared to Maddy's imagination.

"Listen—" He faced El as soon as the class ended.

El held up her hand to stop him.

"I won't give you the 'hurt my bestie and I'll kill you speech.' I like you. She likes you. Be nice. Have fun. That will ensure I get a good review from her for Blind Love, and we all leave happy."

Ax waited in his corner until the room emptied out, pondering El's departing speech. He didn't want to borrow trouble, but El's comment about good reviews rubbed him the wrong way. Maddy told him why she signed up for the app. He didn't think she'd continue seeing him if she wasn't enjoying their time together. Why did her best friend care more about the success of the app than Maddy's happiness?

Maddy took time to answer questions or offer more demonstration. Couples waited patiently for her attention.

"Umm, hi." Maddy's cheeks turned a deep shade of pink as he approached her.

"Hey." Ax smiled

Maddy packed up her table then sat in a rolling chair and twirled around. During class she'd been focused. He witnessed a transition from determined to relaxed and carefree. Two sides to the same woman.

"What did you think?" She continued to twirl in the chair.

"I learned a lot. Where do you get these ideas?"

"Personal experience, websites, you know...research."

Ax tossed his head back and laughed. "You say that like everyone researches this kind of stuff."

"They should. There's nothing to be ashamed of when it comes to sex. Life is too short not to have fun. Sex can get boring after a while if you do the same thing over and over."

When he thought about her observation, Ax realized she was right.

"The way you view things with such openness. It's inspiring."

"No, it's not. There's nothing special about me. I tell people about things I like."

He made a note of her reluctance to accept a compliment.

"Want to go get some coffee?" Ax asked.

Maddy checked her watch. "Umm. Sure, that sounds like fun."

"Great. Can I help you carry the table downstairs? I'm not sure if you need to tell anyone you'll be back or grab anything. Coffee's on me. We can go to the shop a couple of blocks from here."

"That would be great, if you don't mind carrying it, I mean. I'll grab my purse and let Cameron know the class is over." Maddy gathered the other items she brought in for show and tell.

Ax reached around her, careful not to brush his hand against the sliver of skin peeking out from under her sweater. He had to resist scaring her away with his need for more than a fly-by romance.

"I'll follow you," he called out when she left the room.

Maddy led them down the stairs to a hallway that stretched along what he assumed was the back of the shop.

"You can put that in the office." She pointed toward a light brown door at the end of the hall.

"Any specific place?" he asked.

"Nope. Set it out of the way. I'll take it home later."

She pushed it open to let him in. They returned the way they came, passed the original door, then down the opposite direction.

On the right side was an arched doorway. A heavy bronze curtain hung from the top of the arch. She tugged the fabric back before stepping inside the store.

The few stores he'd shopped in weren't inviting at all. Dingy white walls. Dirty tiled floor. Some reeked of patchouli, his least favorite smell. Maddy's place was clean with dark wood furniture and gold accents. A light floral scent he couldn't place wafted through the air. It was pleasant, relaxing.

"Wow. This is not what I thought it would be."

Maddy beamed. She wiggled her whole body in excitement. *Damn cute.* Ax wanted to be the one to make her that happy all the time.

"Good. I wanted the décor to surprise people."

"This is your work?" he asked while turning in a circle, taking everything in.

The woman's level of talent exceeded his expectations. Interior design. Teaching adults without any sign of discomfort, no matter the question. Running a bar. Planning events. He wondered if there was anything she couldn't do.

"With the help of an interior designer. I gave her the ideas and she worked magic."

She walked across the floor to an alcove. A round table with a clear top and a starry night underneath the glass sat in the middle of the space. It had two chairs on one side and a cushioned bench seat on the other.

"What's this? A place to sit and chat about toys?"

"Once a month I give free tarot readings. This is my spot. It's tucked away for privacy, so clients don't have to worry about what's going on around them."

Tarot. He'd heard of it but didn't know what it was.

"That's like telling them their future, right?"

Maddy scoffed. "Tarot isn't an exact answer; the cards help guide you in making decisions for yourself. It's not a simple black and white event. There are different spreads, and it depends on whether it's an open reading or a question reading. An infinite number of variables. It would take me days to explain."

Ax nodded. "Sounds like it. You enjoy doing them?"

Once more she lit up; not as much as when he complimented her on the design, but the passion for reading cards couldn't be missed.

"Yes, I do. The practice helps me focus as much as those I do the readings for. When I'm having a rough time, they give me the building blocks I need for finding my way through life."

He flipped through a deck she'd left on the table that morning. "Do you sell these?"

Maddy laughed. "The yellow planet and stars on the back of the cards don't scream witchcraft, which puts customers at ease." She searched through the deck, setting specific cards on the table. "Ray guns instead of swords. Specimen tubes replaced the Cups. Disks like the rings of a planet for the pentacles. My favorite...dick-shaped probes instead of wands. Appropriate for the shop, all things considered."

Ax studied the cards. Aliens and planets to give someone advice. If he stuck around with Maddy there was no end to things she'd teach him.

"We sell tarot." She pointed to the glass case in the middle of the store that surrounded the register. "But not that particular deck. I special ordered it for the shop."

Ax reached for Maddy's hand, satisfied when she didn't pull away.

15

Maddy

The walk from the store to the coffee house was quiet—not un-comfortable. Maddy let Ax guide them, closing her eyes for a few seconds to enjoy the heat of the sun on her skin. When she did talk, she asked a few questions about Weald.

Ax stood at the entrance of the shop, studying her, but didn't say anything. It was unsettling in a sexy kind of way. He winked as he walked inside once again setting Maddy off balance.

Maddy studied her nails on her free hand, cataloging each chip in the polish.

They stood at the counter, still holding hands. "What do you drink?"

"I'll take an iced vanilla latte please." Even though the coffee shop was small, they had a variety of local beans and knew how to make a good drink.

"Oh good, something I can order," he mumbled.

Maddy grinned. There were plenty of people with orders that took five minutes to place. Those type of people were the ones her parents associated with. The better-than-everyone-else people who demanded goats' milk instead of whatever milk the shop offered. Her ex-wife.

"Here you go." Ax stopped her from spiraling down a dark hole with thoughts of Natasha.

"Oh. Thank you. Sorry, I spaced for a minute." Maddy offered a weak smile.

"It's okay. You pick the seat."

She chose a two-seater near a window. Unable to ignore the pain of being on her feet, Maddy gained a new appreciation for padded chairs. Increasing her hours had been more difficult than she'd expected.

"How's your drink?" Ax asked after they sat down.

"It's good. How's yours?"

He chuckled. "It's black. Dark as they have. I love it. This is one of my favorite places to get coffee. If they were open earlier than six a.m. I'd be here every morning."

"You know you can buy their coffee, right? To save time at home have them grind it to your preference."

"Nope. It's not as good. I did try, before you ask, and it wasn't the same. Maybe it's the water they use. Or it's all psychological. Either way, I prefer fresh from here."

"I get that. There are some ice cream places that I'm the same way. Oh, and pie from The Diner. I've tried to make my own, but they never taste as good."

"What's your favorite?" he asked before taking another sip of his drink.

"Hmm." She took a minute to act like she had to contemplate an answer. "Peach a la mode."

"Vanilla or vanilla bean ice cream?"

"Vanilla bean?" Maddy had never heard of anything other than vanilla.

Sure, vanilla ice cream came from the vanilla bean, but there had to be another ingredient or something that made them different. Why else would he have separated them?

"Vanilla is made with the flavoring. Vanilla bean is made with the actual beans. The easiest way to notice the difference is the little black spots in vanilla bean ice cream. I once took a trip to Dallas. They have an ice cream whose claim to fame is vanilla bean. One of these days I'm going to get some for you to try. It was damn good."

He licked his lips, sending a surge of desire straight to Maddy's core. Hopefully, she'd get an update on the lawsuit soon. Nana was right, she deserved compensation for their faulty toy.

"That sounds delicious. Have you had the peach pie at The Diner?"

Ax shook his head. "Nope. My favorite is the chocolate cream pie, but the marionberry comes in a close second."

"Mmm. That marionberry is a good one. I can't say I've ever had the chocolate cream. Ready for a confession?"

"Always."

Maddy leaned into him, lowering her voice as if she had something serious to tell him.

"I don't like chocolate."

She sat back and waited for his reaction.

"There's not much typical about you. The fact you don't like chocolate doesn't surprise me."

"Thank you, I think."

"My turn."

With the straw of her drink touching the edge of her lips, Maddy waited for his confession.

"Tell me about Pinks. Do you like working there?"

Maddy sat silent for the longest time. No one had asked her point blank if she liked working at Pinks. She and El talked about her dislike of sales in general, but not the actual job.

"That's a good question. In the past I had a couple of businesses. While I understand the job, it's not my favorite." Maddy stared at the top of her cup.

"You told me about the clothing shop, but not a second one. What was that?" he asked.

Heat rose in her cheeks. "It's embarrassing. By the way, you still haven't confessed anything."

Ax peeled her fingers from around her cup. He held her hand in his, running his thumb along the inside of her palm. She sucked in a breath. Their eyes connected and no matter how much her mind told her not to drown in his mismatched eyes, she didn't look away.

"I had no idea you could do those things with wax you talked about in the class today. Tell me more about your entrepreneurial experience."

Maddy wanted to talk about anything other than her own failures.

"Can't we talk about you instead?" she asked.

Ax laughed and shook his head. "Nope. Right now, we're talking about you."

He lifted her hand to his lips and pressed a soft kiss against her skin before releasing her. No one had ever said something so nice to Maddy. Natasha never cared what she had to say. Her parents never had time. She cleared her throat, trying to release the lump forming.

The first time Maddy became a business owner she'd been excited to share with Natasha. It took less than ten minutes for the other woman to begin listing the ways the business would fail before she ever got it off the ground.

"My second business was a bookstore with a reading nook and serve-yourself coffee bar. We sold used books and new books. There was even a sitting area with a fireplace and recommended books already on the side tables for customers to try before they bought. Upstairs I'd planned to have a writer's loft where artists could rent a space for the day, or hours, at a time."

Ax whistled. "That sounds like a great opportunity. What happened?"

"Nothing. I bailed within six months; fear took over. My ex-wife convinced me it was a money pit. She didn't think there would be enough interest to have the space for rent and I tried to offer a large selection of romance books. Natasha despised romance, saying they weren't real books. Me being stupid at the time, believed her—on the money side of things. I love the romance genre. As far as I'm concerned, those are the best authors to read."

The failure turned her down a path that proved to be impossible to steer away from. When Nana liked the sex ed classes, Maddy procrastinated for months before doing any real planning. Even after a few classes, she wasn't convinced the success would last, which was why she needed a backup that wasn't Pinks or The Knob like party planning. The last thing she'd do was run those into bankruptcy.

"You won't take over Pinks when your grandmother retires?"

Maddy shrugged.

"Still a maybe. Nana and I haven't discussed her retirement or me taking over. Since Nana can't work as much, I started helping when I could. After these classes and then planning the picnic this last week, I've accepted that sales doesn't make my heart happy."

"That makes sense." He took a drink of his coffee.

"Do you like being a logger? What did you do in New York?" She shifted in her chair.

"I'm not sure like is the right word. I prefer the outdoors to a stuffy office, that's for damn sure. I worked with my family in New York."

Ax moved around the table to her right side and draped his arm across her back to pull her closer to him. Maddy laid her head on his shoulder and sighed. It had been a long day. Being surrounded by his scent ramped up her desire to spend more time together. She wanted to cuddle on the couch. One night lay against his chest with her legs stretched out and her cat snuggled between them.

She'd had plenty of fantasies with Ax as the lead character but kept the idea of anything real from taking root. It was a risky move, but Maddy wanted to take the leap.

"Are you okay? I've noticed you've been moving around a lot and wincing like you're hurt."

She nodded. "I'm fine."

"Any chance this is connected to the evil abstinence doctor?"

Coffee shot out from Maddy's lips. Ax grabbed a couple of napkins. He handed one to her and wiped down the table with another.

"Yes and thank you. I can't believe I spit my drink everywhere. Evil abstinence doctor is the most appropriate title." She cleaned up the coffee. Before getting into the story, Maddy sent up a wish that he wouldn't run screaming from the building when he found out her vagina was recovering from a terrible disaster.

"Do you remember a couple of months ago ending up in the wrong hospital room and spilling coffee on your pants?"

He nodded.

"It was my room you ended up in. By the way, did the coffee leave a mark?"

His shoulders shook with laughter.

"Nope."

"Why were you there?" More than anything, Maddy wanted to buy herself a little more time.

"Crash wrecked his bike and called me to pick him up."

Maddy nodded.

"He earned his name, huh?" she asked.

Ax laughed again. The deep rumble vibrated all the way to her toes. Maddy's insides clenched causing a sharp pain between her legs. Tears pricked the corner of her eyes.

"Yes, yes he did. You look like you're about to fall asleep. Let's get you back to the office so you can go home."

"What's your schedule like this week?" He was right about her going home, but Maddy didn't want to leave without setting up a date with him.

They gathered their drinks and cleaned up the table. Ax took her hand in his to lead them out of the shop.

"Clear. As usual."

"Don't you have family or other friends that you go out with?" She didn't have a lot of room to talk. Nana and El were the people she spent time with, but at least she had them.

"The guys from work like to drink or play pool. I'm too old for a bunch of nights drinking. Once or twice a week I might go to The Knob. Oh, and darts on Thursday with my adopted grandfather." His voice softened.

"Adopted?"

"Yeah. It's funny. Weald makes all of us put in community service time. We have to give at least two days a quarter to a charity or help out around the community. Shortly after I moved here, I spent the day helping the local senior housing complex. That's where I met Dean."

Maddy laid her hand on his arm. The more time she spent with him, the more she found herself needing to touch him. Be next to him. "That's incredible. Not that you all give back to the community, but that you've connected with him. Too many of our local seniors are alone without family in the area. Nana talks about them all the time."

Ax nodded. "Weald gives us two days off to donate our time. This is the first company I've worked for that cared as much as they do, which was one of the reasons I chose them. A company that cares about the community must care about its employees. And they do."

She didn't have enough time with him before they made it back to Pinks. Ax followed her to the office, still chatting about Dean and the kinds of things he helped the elderly gentleman with. It was a lot like her relationship with Nana. Dean was the true definition of an adopted grandpa.

"Do you have any time this upcoming week for us to finalize the picnic plans? El and I are available on Friday. I know it's the day before the event, but we don't have much to do other than go over everything and make sure you don't think we need to make changes."

"You're not going to tell me what you were doing in the hospital?"

She swallowed—twice—but the dryness in her throat didn't go away. Maddy took a minute to sit at the desk and rearrange some papers.

"A glass dildo exploded while I was using it."

"Holy hell." His instantaneous response didn't surprise her at all. It was no different than what she would have said in his shoes.

"Yeah. Pretty much."

"Please tell me you're getting them to pay for everything. How could a company put such a dangerous item on the shelves?"

Maddy rubbed the bridge of her nose. She'd asked the same question a thousand times.

"Glass toys are not uncommon. A lot of companies make them and many, many people love to play with them. However, this company failed to temper the glass, or whatever it's called to make it harder. As a result, the slight—very slight—force of me using it caused an explosion. I don't understand the logistics of it all, but that's the explanation they gave me. My lawyer says it's a cop out. They don't want to admit the truth, which is that they don't know what they're doing. To answer your other question, yes, I'm suing them."

"Good. As for your question about the picnic, I'll talk to Stan and see if I can get the day, or at least part of the day, off. He should give it to me for helping bail his ass out of the jam. Let's plan on meeting at the bar and I'll text if I can't make it."

Maddy nodded. Without hesitation, she stepped up and wrapped her arms around his waist. When he didn't pull away, she tucked her head into his shoulder. Ax lifted her chin with two fingers. Maddy bit her lip. This was what she wanted—and didn't want. He lowered his mouth toward hers. Every muscle in her body tensed in anticipation. Their lips touched and her knees buckled. Ax tightened his hold around her waist and held her up.

She'd wanted this. Waited. As much as she enjoyed being pressed against Ax, there was hesitation in his touch. Not that he wasn't a good kisser, but Maddy wanted more.

Ax pulled back. His eyes spoke volumes, but he didn't say anything. Didn't ask what he'd done wrong. With a nod, he kissed her on the cheek then left.

Every moment they'd shared built up to the next one. Why did that kiss leave her wanting more?

16

Ax

The week flew by without any extra time. What little free time he had was spent in his head. Their kiss wreaked havoc on his emotions. He'd screwed up with such grandeur he had yet to find a way to recover.

Ax recalled the memory for the millionth time. Her lips molded to his like they were meant for each other. Perfect—until it wasn't. The dreamy haze he'd hoped to see wasn't there. She didn't whimper or beg for more—not that he'd have expected that from Maddy. No, if she'd wanted more, she would've taken it. But she hadn't and it was his fault.

Friday morning arrived and Ax couldn't wait to spend the day, or part of the day, with Maddy and El. This was his chance to make things right. Maybe she'd let him try again. Not that it would be any better. The wall he'd erected as he pressed his lips to hers, still stood and he had no idea what to do to bring it down. He'd texted Maddy the day before confirming they were still on to meet at the bar and finalize the picnic plans. On his way, he stopped to pick up breakfast for the three of them.

Maddy, gorgeous as ever, opened the door to the bar wearing a simple dress with a short-sleeved plaid shirt hanging loose over it. The black lace-up sandals she wore showed off her legs better than any pair of short shorts. Those laces framing her muscular legs would star in his fantasies that night. Even the long necklace nestled against her chest didn't appeal to him the way the shoes did.

Ax tried to adjust himself without getting caught before gathering up the food and climbing out of his truck. The plastic to-go containers wobbled in his hands. If he wasn't careful, his gift of eggs, bacon, and waffles wouldn't make it past the front door.

"Good morning. Let me help you with those." She took two of the platters out of his hands. "El's in the parlor."

Maddy kissed him on the cheek.

"Good morning, beautiful." He wrapped his free arm around her waist to lead them back to El. "How's your morning?"

"I get to spend it with you, I'd say the day is kicking off with a bang—it'd be better if we were banging in bed, but this will do."

Ax floundered for a response. Maddy laughed. There wasn't any awkwardness between them like he'd expected. Her sex jokes lifted a weight off his shoulders. Their first kiss flopped, but he hadn't ruined whatever they were building between them.

"Too early for that," El called out to them.

After putting down his food containers and Maddy's hands were empty, he pulled her in for a hug, needing her arms around his waist and the comfort of her soft body pressed against his.

"My brain isn't awake, leaving me without retorts. It's not fair."

Maddy blew raspberries. She sat in the empty armchair. Ax took the open seat on the couch next to El.

"Not my fault you two lack my level of wits. Hope you don't mind coffee and apple juice for breakfast. I wasn't sure if you were the type to drink coffee with your meal, so I got both." She glanced at the food.

Ax grinned. "Both are good. I'm not picky when it comes to breakfast beverages. Food is a different story." Ax pushed El's hand away when she reached for the to go container with extra bacon. "That one's mine."

"What makes it different?" El asked.

"The extra bacon. Don't even try to steal mine if you don't want a fight."

El batted her eyelashes and snuggled up close to him. "Now we both know you'd never fight a lady. Besides, sharing the extra slices of deliciousness would win you some brownie points with your girl over there. Don't you want that?"

"Neither of you play fair." As hard as he tried to glare at El, he failed. The woman's puppy dog eyes were too hard to resist. "Let's make a deal. I'll split the extra yummy strips of gloriousness with you if you team up with me to beat Maddy in at least one of the picnic games tomorrow."

"Deal." She held out her hand for him to shake.

Ax glanced over at Maddy. She winked and smiled at him.

"Good luck," she said.

Maddy placed their drinks on the table. Ax handed out the food and split his bacon with El as promised.

"How were both of your weeks?" he asked, not ready to dive into the planning.

If they got through everything too fast, he'd have to figure out a way to spend more time with Maddy and not make El feel dismissed—she was Maddy's best friend. He didn't want to alienate her.

"Not bad." Maddy took a bite of food then continued. "I limited scared customers to three this week. That counts as a win for me."

His brow furrowed. "What do you mean you scared them?"

"Maddy lacks finesse when it comes to selling things like double-ended dildos and merkins. People aren't quite ready for her blunt explanation," El jumped in before Maddy had a chance to answer.

"I made a guy's knees wobble, and he almost passed out when I explained how he and wife could use a double-ended dildo for anal play."

"Does that constitute an applaud? As much as I'm going to regret this, what is a merkin? Is it a Halloween costume? Toupee? What do you do with it?"

El shook her head. "Yeah, you should've skipped that question."

"It's a pubic wig. We have red, brown, and leopard print. There's also a landing strip if you don't want the full bush." He was impressed Maddy got the explanation out with a straight face.

"Please tell me you don't let people try it before they buy it." The horror in the possibility made his jaw clench.

"No, besides being against health codes, that's a whole lot of area I do not want to explore."

They ate their breakfast in companionable silence. Every once and a while El would snatch a piece of bacon from either Maddy or Ax then they'd all laugh. Half an hour passed and El rose from the couch.

"The guys at Blind Love have some questions about our current campaign. I'm going to the office for the meeting and then I'll be back. You two talk about the picnic. Maddy already knows what I've got working for tomorrow. She can fill you in." El wiggled her fingers in the air as she walked out of the parlor.

Silence filled the space between them. The big gray elephant he'd expected, entered the room almost as soon as El left. If he didn't apologize or offer some explanation for the last time they were together the unease in his gut would ruin breakfast.

"Everything is ready for tomorrow?" he asked Maddy.

She nodded. "Yeah. You and I did most of the leg work a couple of weeks ago. Random side note, I'm glad you got the day off today. If we wanted to spend the day together, we could."

"That sounds like a great idea." Ax moved to the end of the couch to be closer to Maddy. "If you're up for it we could go throw some axes."

"El's been working on some marketing items for Pinks and The Knob. Before you freak out over Pinks, everything is G-rated. She's a genius when it comes to creative, covert marketing. Also, we've put together a basket of goodies for the silent auction."

"You didn't have to do that. There aren't enough words to express our gratitude for you helping us out of the bind. Stan is still fuming over the planner quitting like she did."

Maddy took a bite of the last piece of bacon. "Why did she quit? I've been meaning to ask."

Ax shrugged. He'd asked Stan the same question without any results.

"Stan won't tell me. She's his niece. From what I understand, she's coordinated the picnic for the last four years."

Maddy dipped her finger in syrup then licked it clean. Ax wanted to be the one to taste her with syrup dripping down her finger. His pants tightened enough he had to shift on the couch to relieve some pressure.

"Hmm. You like that?" She teased before dipping her finger back in the syrup.

Ax lunged forward, grabbed her wrist, and devoured her finger. He should've been embarrassed by the lack of restraint. Instead, he was proud that he'd taken the leap—literally—and gone after what he wanted.

"You two were supposed to be talking about the picnic. Not sharing breakfast condiments." Rather than sit next to Ax again, El stood at Maddy's side, smirking.

Maddy laughed. Ax fell against the back of the couch.

"Or you could join us and try the syrup, too. Maddy has a very delectable finger." Ax smirked. He hadn't meant to flirt, but when Maddy didn't glare at him and El didn't lecture him for stepping over the line, he rolled with the joke.

"I've been cleared by the doctor, but I don't think Jack wants to come in this morning and find the three of us christening his couch." Maddy winked at them.

"He might find you two on the couch, but I have to go. The Blind Love guys need me to come talk about the launch and how things are progressing." El looked at Maddy. "Do you think you'll be ready for that testimonial soon? The next phase of the project starts in a couple of weeks, and we'd like to start using quotes in the marketing."

In the same moment Ax tried to breathe a sigh of relief and sucked in a gust of air. A coughing attack had him doubled over trying to catch his breath.

"Are you okay?" Maddy rubbed circles over his back.

Ax sat up. He pressed his hand to his chest and took a couple of deep breaths. "Yeah, sorry about that. Choked on air."

Maddy and El shook their heads.

"What do you think, Maddy?" El asked again.

She looked at Ax then El and back at him again. He wondered what was going through her thoughts. Did she want to wait and see how things went before committing? Was she ready to say it was a flop? Or a win? He didn't understand the sudden nervousness brewing.

A minute passed. Then two. The women stared each other down. Their eyebrows raising and lowering like they were having a silent conversation. Maddy sighed.

"I know you want the quote, and I agreed to give you one. Ax and I are going out this afternoon. Let me think about it and get back to you. It wouldn't be fair to you, the company, or me and Ax if I placated you with a good review. I want it to be honest."

El crossed her hands over her chest. "All right. Let me know. Y'all have fun this afternoon."

With El gone, Ax and Maddy cleaned up the meal.

"Since you're cleared from the doctor, you ready to get physical and throw some axes?" he asked.

She tapped her chin. "I don't think I can throw you, but I'm willing to give it a try."

Her sense of humor was quirky. He loved it.

17

Ax

Blades of Fury was different than he'd expected. Maddy made reservations before they left Podunk, so the attendant walked them to their lane as soon as they arrived. The place was set up like a bowling alley with eight lanes. Each one had a wall of welded wire fencing on either side. A pit of wood chips filled a square area at the end of the lane and a giant target with gouges taken out from the axes hung mounted to the wall. The rest of the floor of the lane was putting green turf.

"All right, have either of you thrown an axe before?" Todd, the coach they'd been assigned, asked.

"Not me, but he's a logger." Maddy pointed her thumb in Ax's direction.

"Throwing a competition axe is a bit different than swinging one to cut down a tree. There are a couple of ways you can hold the axe. I recommend starting with a two-handed stance. Set yourself up about twelve feet from the target. To aim, you'll line up your hands with the point on the target you're aiming for. If you want the bullseye, you set up in the middle of the target."

"Why wouldn't we want the bullseye?" Maddy asked.

Ax was curious as well.

"There are games you can play rather than just throwing at the board. Some of them require you to hit other areas of the target to receive points."

She nodded. The coach picked up with the explanation again.

"Once you've got your spot and you're twelve feet back, stand with your dominant foot in front of you and your other behind.

You'll bring the axe over your head as if throwing a soccer ball, then bring your hands forward and release the axe at eye level."

They stayed behind the yellow caution line while the coach demonstrated how to throw. Ax mimicked his movements.

"Who wants to try first?" he asked.

Ax volunteered. He wanted to test the truth about the difference in throwing versus swinging.

"This shouldn't be too hard. I know you said it's different, but how different could it be?" Ax tried to keep his cockiness to a minimum, but this was his livelihood.

He followed the step-by-step directions, smiling when the axe sailed toward the target. A bullseye for sure. Except, the axe didn't stick. Hell, it didn't even hit the large circle. The damn thing bounced off the outer edge of the floor and landed in the pile of wood chips.

Todd was right, throwing was different than swinging.

"Let's make a few adjustments."

Ax adjusted his stance, then practiced pulling the axe over his head and the follow-through. Each of his next three throws improved.

"I think it's time for Maddy to try," he said after the fourth one stuck where he aimed.

Maddy stepped up, put one foot in front of the other with precision, pulled her arms over her head and let the axe fly. It hit dead center.

"I did it." Maddy jumped up and down.

"Lucky throw." Ax grinned.

She stuck her tongue out at him. Ax groaned. He wanted to yank her to him and kiss that sassy mouth.

"Jealous?" Maddy winked.

Ax gave up resisting the urge to touch her. He wrapped his fingers around her wrist to pull her into his chest. "Yes. Care to share some tips?"

"Ahh grasshopper, you want to learn from the master. Then watch you must do." Maddy threw again. She missed the bullseye, but still did better than Ax.

When she returned to the edge of the lane, she dropped the axe in the little box and curtsied to him and Todd.

"Was that a challenge?" Ax bowed. "I accept."

Todd's eyes lit up when Maddy laughed. Ax slid her against his side. *Back off. She's mine.*

"Yoda and Kung Fu don't go together at all." Ax didn't resist the urge to kiss the curve of her shoulder.

She shrugged. "Sure, they do. You need to use your imagination."

Todd and Ax shook their heads. Their coach showed them where to find directions for games and left them. Ax located the drink menu.

"Want something?" he asked the ladies.

"You order. Surprise us. I want to throw some more." Maddy bounced on her toes. She couldn't wait to get the axe back in her hands.

It didn't take long to place an order for French fries, fried mushrooms, and drinks.

"Let's play a game." Maddy picked up the gamebook and flipped through a few pages. "How about this. It's called cricket. We each hit the numbers one through six three times. The first one to get all the numbers wins."

He read the directions. It seemed simple enough, but given his troubles with accuracy, he wasn't sure who would win.

"Sounds good. After that, we should play Axes. We each get one throw. The one with the lowest score in the round gets a letter. Whoever spells a-x-e-s first loses," he suggested.

"I like that plan." Maddy stepped up to the line.

"Wait. Let's up the stakes of the game."

Maddy's brows furrowed. She waited a couple of seconds before nodding. "How?"

"Whoever wins gets to ask three questions and the loser has to answer without hesitation." Ax leaned back against the table.

His cheeks flushed as Maddy stared him down. Ax had never struggled with emotions and his masculinity, but right then he was out of his element. She invaded every thought in his head. Every emotion in his heart. Yet, he still managed to erect a wall between them when it came to intimacy.

"What if I win all the games we play? The lane is ours for an hour. It could be a long night." Maddy smirked.

He didn't think she'd win everything, but Ax was almost certain he'd have a lot of questions to answer. That was okay with him.

"Then that's the way the ball rolls. Dig as deep as you want." He stood taller and crossed his arms over his chest.

"How personal is personal?" she asked.

Ax settled onto a stool before crooking his finger toward Maddy. She slid one foot in front of the other, then the next. He wasn't sure if she was flirting or truly worried about getting close to him again.

"Nothing is off-limits, and we promise tomorrow will not be awkward."

He leaned in, watching for a sign she didn't want him close. When Maddy leaned her head to the side, he backed off. Ax lowered his chin to his chest. They could touch in a casual, flirty way, but it seemed Maddy wasn't ready for him to get close again. He didn't blame her. Ax needed help figuring out what happened. He wasn't sure who would offer the best advice, Crash or Dean. Asking El was off the table since he suspected she'd take everything right back to Maddy.

"I'm going to wipe the floor with you." Maddy turned around, wiggling her butt the few steps it took to get back to the lane. "First game is cricket. You've got to hit all six numbers first to win."

"Hmm. I think I'll take first throw." Ax tapped Maddy on the butt when he passed by her to step into the lane. He snatched the axe from the box.

Ax hit the outside ring for number one. Maddy followed suit with a one as well. Over the next twenty minutes they went back and forth, sometimes missing, most of the time not. In the end, Maddy won. Ax managed to score one, four, and two, but struggled with the rest—especially the bullseye. Maddy's fist shot into the air on her final throw.

"I win. I get three questions." Maddy danced in front of their table.

"Yes, you do. Bring 'em on. Oh, and congratulations." He smiled.

"If you had to purchase one new item from the store, what would it be and why?"

Maddy's question surprised him. They'd agreed to personal topics. While her question was interesting, he hadn't expected something so...surface.

Since Ax hadn't looked around Pinks, he didn't have a clue how to answer. Instead, he tried to recall items he'd seen online.

"Okay, I don't know if the store sells them or not, if they don't I think you should consider getting a few. They're expensive and cumbersome." Ax wrung his hands together.

"Spit it out already," Maddy said.

"I want one of those things you plug in and sit on it. There are fake dicks that you can attach to it and maybe other things. I'm not sure. I saw a video once where the girl sat on like this fifteen-inch rubber cock." Ax blurted out the answer. The woman would change her mind about dating him if he kept showing his ignorance.

Maddy licked her fingers after dipping a fry into a cup of ranch dressing and taking a bite. His mouth watered with the urge to taste her.

"Mmm. A good choice. I haven't used one, but they're called Sybians. Tried to talk Nana into adding them. She thinks they are too expensive. Now that we have a new vendor maybe I can revisit the idea." Maddy turned her smirk on Ax.

"How do they work? Do you sit it on the floor?" he asked.

"You can. I've seen some people put it on a massage table, or a spanking bench. Others put it on the bed." Maddy talked about the machine like it was another item in their inventory.

Sex wasn't embarrassing to Ax. He'd had plenty of it, enjoyed it, joked with Crash about it. Talking out in the open like it was a regular, every day conversation was new, though. It would take him some time to adjust.

"And the attachments." He pointed to a picture he'd pulled up on his phone. At least he recognized what they could be used for. "People use all of these?"

"Yep." She popped the p. "Can you imagine how much fun that would be to tease and torture someone? It comes with a remote you could use to control it while I ride it, or if you're adventurous, you could take a turn."

Ax pulled back at the idea. Maddy laughed.

"I think maybe I'll pass on taking a turn." He cringed. Even though he was willing to try new things, that wasn't on his list at all for the moment.

"All right, sexy logger beast. Next question."

"Hit me," he said.

"Why did you make our kiss awkward? I thought we had something going, but when you kissed me last week there was a spark of connection and then nothing."

Words stuck to the roof of Ax's mouth. This was a question he wasn't prepared to answer. Maddy wasn't wrong about her observation. Moving to Oregon had been less scary than looking deep inside his emotions and answering question. Yet, he wanted to try again, know what it would feel like to do more than kiss.

"Every free moment I've had since kissing you I've asked myself the same question. I won't deny what you're saying, but I don't have an answer. The connection between us is real. More than anything, I wanted to kiss you—I want to kiss you again." She started to say something, but he shook his head. "Don't worry, unless you consent and I can figure my shit out, I won't."

Maddy nodded. "We'll get past that one day at a time. I appreciate you being honest with me. You're the first person I've had real feelings for in close to five years. If you're not ready to take it to the next level and want to stay flirtatious friends, I can deal with that. The time may be best for both of us."

He appreciated her candor. Maddy knew who she was. Accepted others weren't like her and didn't judge them for their differences. Like her, he hadn't had feelings for anyone in a long time—even before the divorce finalized. Maybe time was all they needed, his instinct didn't agree, but Ax wasn't ready to look further yet.

"Anything else?" she asked.

There was, but he wasn't sure how to put everything into words that made sense. To give himself time, he went to the lane, grabbed an axe, and took a throw. Then three more before coming back.

"I'm not good at feelings and emotions. Kind of like the sex stuff, my family didn't talk about those things. If we were angry, we yelled at each other then left with things unresolved. If we were happy, we celebrated alone. My dad told me if I wanted to be a real man, I couldn't show anyone my inner feelings. My mother used emotion to manipulate everyone into doing what she wanted."

Ax sat at the high-top table. In all of his forty-five years, he'd shared his feelings twice. Once when he stood at the altar with Daphne and the second time when he handed her the papers to end their marriage. If he was going to be enough for the woman in front of him, he had to open up at some point.

"Emotions are hard." Maddy took his hand in hers. "You and I have a lot in common when it comes to how we were raised. I didn't realize how much until right now."

The woman leaned in and planted a loud, wet kiss on his cheek. Ax threw his head back and laughed. This was the best date he'd been on in a long while.

18

Maddy

"Do you regret getting married?" Maddy pointed the axe at him. It was her last question, and she wanted to find out a little more about the man's history after his reveal about emotions and sex.

"No. I don't regret it at all. While I feel like an idiot more days than not, I wouldn't change anything. Being with Daphne helped me wake up to what was happening around me. For forty-three years I let my parents decide my life. They wanted me to be a lawyer, so I went to law school. Mother wanted me to marry well, so I married Daphne. If her gold-digging ways hadn't made me open up to the reality my life had become, then I'd be well on my way to campaigning for some local office."

"I don't regret mine either. Natasha was a bitch. She emotionally abused me, but I learned about myself because of her. I'm not the woman she made me think I was. If I changed anything, it would be that my parents stepped in sooner and helped me see the damage. In their defense, I didn't show the truth when I was out with people. The hurt inside festered until I couldn't stand it anymore. That's when I got out."

"It's not my turn, but I'm going to ask a question." Ax pat the stool in front of him for her to sit.

"Yes?" One of her favorite songs came over the speakers above them and she mouthed the words.

"Why did you marry Natasha? From what you've said, she mistreated you for a long time. I've always wondered what could've made you take that step." Ax took a bite of food.

"The truth is embarrassing. Cringeworthy." Maddy grabbed the menu off the table.

Her mood shifted from fun-loving to closed-off. Out of habit, her shoulders rolled forward. She studied the menu like it was written in a foreign language. Maddy signaled their server and placed an order for fried pickles. They had plenty of food on the table, but she wasn't ready to talk about her wedding mistake.

"I married a woman because my mother told me to. I'm forty-five years old. You want to talk cringeworthy, let's talk about how I've let my mother make my life decisions. Nothing can be worse than that," he said.

They had their divorces in common. She loved his willingness to consider new things. Of course, he was attractive. More than anything, Maddy loved the way Ax made her feel. They hadn't known each other long, but he trusted her enough to ask for help with his company's picnic. When she talked about her past business ventures, he didn't judge her for not becoming a millionaire. She believed his own upbringing in New York with a political-focused family offered an understanding no one else had—not even El.

"I met Natasha my senior year of high school. We started out as friends, then one thing led to another, and we were living together my sophomore year of college. After that, the next step was engagement and marriage. My parents loved her, which shocked me since that was the same time I came out as bisexual."

"When did you figure out you were bisexual? Did you date men before your ex? How does that happen?"

To keep the mood light-hearted, she took a minute to tease him. Tracing the soft skin of his cheek with her lips, fingers, a quick dart of her tongue. With her hand on his chest she felt more than saw Ax's breathing hitch then quicken. Yeah, he was turned on as much as she was. He'd said he wouldn't kiss her without permission, but she hadn't made the same promise. Maddy licked her lips. She wouldn't kiss him right away, but she'd be surprised if they made it through the night without another attempt.

"I didn't have some kind of epiphany to come to terms with my sexuality. It just...happened. High school and college weren't my exploration years, or anything like that. When I met Nat, we clicked at first. Things got easy and I found myself on a path I didn't like, but we were already five years into marriage at that point. Mom and Dad didn't even blink an eye when I introduced her as my girlfriend. Maybe I gave off vibes. I can't say for sure, and in the end it didn't matter. They accepted me as I am. Despite the fact they'll never see me as good enough when it comes to my life aspirations, at least I've never worried they would shun me as their daughter."

She stuffed a mushroom in her mouth, loving the crunch of the breading with the softness of the mushroom. The thin-cut rosemary seasoned fries were almost as good as the mushrooms. Talking about Natasha wasn't the highlight of any day. It wasn't pain or regret. Nowadays thinking about her marriage and the fact that the reason she got married was convenience made her cringe at the laziness. It was easy to fall into the trap of "what if she'd been smarter." Paid closer attention.

The answer was always the same. It didn't matter what if. Her decision to marry Nat, to stay with the other woman, to divorce her, all led to the present. If it wasn't for all of that, then Maddy wouldn't have moved to Podunk to help her grandparents. She may not have met Elowen, and now she may have missed the chance to meet Ax. Rather than regret her decisions, Maddy would make the most of what was right in front of her.

"Play again?" Maddy bounced her legs up and down. Excitement raced through her body, making sitting still impossible.

Ax took a bite of French fry. "Let's go. I'm ready to redeem myself and ask the questions."

"How about cricket?" Maddy snatched up the axe first. She swung it back and forth next to her leg.

"What kind of lumberjack would I be if I can't even win against you in ax throwing?" He laughed.

"A crazy, sexy woodsman who knows how to win over the ladies." Maddy shook her finger at his chest. "But no complaining when I knock it out of the park again."

She squared up in the lane and let the axe fly. Maddy returned to the table and grabbed another mushroom.

"Ow." Ax wiped the back of his hand over his eyes. "Your mushroom squirted my eye."

"Are you a fan of squirters?" she asked.

"No." His brows furrowed. "Wait...you mean, like..."

His cheeks turned rosy.

"Well, I wasn't talking about mushrooms."

Ax shoved more than a few fries in his mouth. Maddy laughed. Such an easy question and he couldn't say yes or no. The man wasn't exaggerating when he said talking about sex in public made him uncomfortable.

"Oh, you'd know if you liked the squirt. It's impossible to miss. Come to my next class and I'll give some tips on how to make a woman do that."

The pink of his cheeks deepened to red. Maddy leaned up on her toes and kissed him on the cheek.

"Hmm. Now that would be worth attending. Not that your classes aren't good, but some of those tips could come in handy." He winked at her. "Pun intended."

"Have you ever had phone sex? Or sexted someone?" She tossed out the question more for reaction than his actual answer.

"That's an embarrassing answer," he mumbled around the mouthful of food.

"Why? I'm not going to judge you. It's ...you tend to shy away from sexual innuendos, yet you're open to me."

After a couple of drinks, he swallowed hard enough his Adam's apple bounced up and down.

"You entice me. I never know what's going to happen next." He went to the lane for his turn.

"Have you and El ever dated?" Ax asked as the axe stuck in the bullseye. "I know you like both genders. I've seen the two of you flirt, although El doesn't appear to be bisexual. She likes you though."

Maddy rocked onto her heels. She hadn't thought about her interactions with El or how they'd look to an outsider. Was that what made him pull back? Had he been worried that she'd pick El over him?

"One thing I've learned about myself is that I don't want to pass up on an opportunity to live because it's taboo or unknown. I married a woman because it was easy and safe. I'm thirty-five years old." The words came without thought. "El wasn't an opportunity, still isn't. When I first met her, I'll admit I harbored a crush, but that didn't last longer than me realizing she wasn't into women at all. What looks like flirting to you is nothing more than two women who are best friends. We're close because she's been my rock. When my grandfather died, El was there even though we hardly knew each other. If you're worried about having to compete with her to win my attention—don't. That's a nonissue."

It was important to Maddy that he understood how she felt when it came to El.

He massaged his jaw. She tried to read the emotion in his eyes, but they were too clouded. Relief maybe? Confusion? Maddy hoped he heard the truth in her words and believed that there wasn't a romantic connection between her and El. The crush had been just that—a crush.

"Until you asked the question, I didn't think I had a problem with your friendship. I'm not worried about competing. Even if you did have a thing, we're trying this out between us. It sounds like she's been good for you and that makes me happy. We may not have known each other long, but I care about you, Maddy. I like to know that you have trustworthy people surrounding you."

"Talking to you comes so naturally. I don't want to miss the chance that we might have more because I'm with Elowen. A relationship between us will be hard since neither of us has done this in a while. Communication will be the most important thing we can do to make it work. A month or two from now, if one of us decides we don't want to keep pursuing this relationship, then we break up."

The weight on her chest grew heavy as the man she'd come to desire more than anyone else stared in silence. Maddy chewed on her lip. Open. Honest. Personal.

"You're confident about this," Ax murmured.

"No more than you. I'm scared. Sure, I work in a sex boutique, and I teach adults how to spice up the bedroom, but that doesn't mean I'm entering this with more experience than you. It's a risk. But for you, it's a risk I want to take."

"It's your throw by the way. I scored a six," Ax said.

Maddy stepped up to the lane, grabbed the ax, and launched a one-handed throw. It rotated twice before slamming into the target with a thump and falling to the floor.

Ax went to the lane and picked up an axe. He set his stance then let the tool go. It landed to the right of the bullseye. After retrieving it, he threw four more times. Maddy stayed at their table.

"How will your family react to you dating someone who works, maybe owns, a sex shop?" Maddy asked Ax, ready to remove the spotlight from herself.

"I don't know. Right now, I don't care." Maddy started to argue, but Ax held up his hand to stop her. "Say what you want about when the time comes, I will care. There's no way for me to deny that you're right. Until then though, I'm not going to miss this chance. Marrying Daphne was a mistake. I missed out on a lot of my life making sure she was happy. Now it's my turn. You are an incredible woman. You're offering me the choice to find happiness. For now, I'd like to live in the moment."

Ax's smile made it impossible for her to argue. From him, the whole thing sounded easy. Too easy.

"What about when it's not easy? You paint this incredible picture of us being instantly happy." Maddy kept her attention on the wooden board at the end of the lane.

He took Maddy's hand and placed it on top of his. With his free hand, he rubbed the top of hers.

"Dating won't be without arguments and trials. We'll have to find a balance. There will be jealousy on my part, or yours. The key is we work together to find our way through the rocky patches. Neither of us can predict how tomorrow will go, or next year. Maybe the relationship lasts, maybe it doesn't. Like I said, all I want is to try."

Maddy swallowed the lump forming in her throat. It seared a path down to her stomach, which rolled and flipped. The man in front of her was too good to be true. Any minute now the other shoe was going to drop. Maddy bit the corner of her lower lip. The ache to kiss him grew each second.

The rough calluses on his hands left a tingle in their wake as he continued to rub the top of her hand. Comfort. Fire tinder. Irresistible. Maddy lifted onto her toes. She angled her body toward his and closed her eyes. Maddy inhaled, calming as his woodsy scent filled her senses. This was right. She hoped he'd get the hint to close the distance between them. If he didn't...

"How did you like it?" The assigned trainer's voice shocked Maddy back to reality.

Her heels landed on the ground with a thud. Her boobs bounced for added effect. She blew a strand of hair out of her eyes then cleared her throat.

"It was fun," she said.

"Yep. Harder than I thought, but we enjoyed it." Ax faced the man with a strained look in his eyes.

Maddy plastered on the best fake smile she could. "This was a great night. We should've come out sooner. It's too bad we've got plans tomorrow that start before the sun rises."

Yeah, Ax was no happier than Maddy about the interruption.

"Great. That's what we like to hear. If you'd like to extend your time, let me know. If not, when you're ready to go, I'll close out your tab at the bar."

He gathered their glasses and empty dishes before walking away without a hint of the significance of the moment he'd ruined.

"I guess we should go." Maddy pulled the strap of her purse over her shoulder.

"We don't have to rush off, you know." Ax raised one eyebrow in question.

"How do you do that? I've tried the one eyebrow thing. People tell me it makes me look like a crazy person." Maddy shook her head. "You look...intimidating."

Ax did it again and she laughed.

"Before we go, I have a question for you." Ax maneuvered until they stood side by side.

Maddy wasn't sure what to say or do.

"I would like to propose a probationary relationship." Maddy furrowed her brows. Ax continued, "We agree to try this out with no expectations of anyone. We agree to exclusivity."

His proposal made sense. Ground rules but no promises of forever. No expectations.

"Is there a timeline? Will we sit down in one month and make declarations?" she asked.

"No timeline. We should feel safe enough to speak up any time something isn't working, or if we want to celebrate what is working that's good too. At some point, when the time is right, we can make more formal declarations if we choose. All I ask is that we agree to be exclusive with each other and give this an honest chance."

"And no sex for now. Making things physical adds more layers and expectations," Maddy added.

It had been a long six weeks of forced abstinence. As much as she wanted to feel Ax's body against hers, Maddy would put those desires on hold until they were both comfortable.

Ax's grin was innocent, but the smolder in his gaze threatened Maddy's control. No doubt they would burn the sheets to ashes when the time came.

"You're in?" he asked.

With a nod and a happy dance, Maddy agreed. They were going to do this.

"One last stipulation." Maddy looked at Ax. "Every Friday is date night. There's no canceling and no rescheduling to another day unless it's an emergency and we both agree."

"I believe we need to seal this with a kiss." Ax grinned as he slipped his hand around Maddy's waist to tug her into his chest. His fingers brushed the skin of her belly.

"If you agree," he whispered against Maddy's neck.

In answer, Maddy leaned forward and pressed her lips to the skin poking out from the collar of his shirt, needing to feel his want. She brushed her fingers along his side, coming to rest on Ax's waist. Ax's fingers brushed Maddy's cheeks. Maddy soaked up the sweet sugar of the coke he'd been drinking and nipped his lower lip, pulling a moan from him.

"Mmm. A little tonight. Tomorrow, we have to be professional at the picnic." Maddy leaned her head back.

With two fingers, Ax lowered Maddy's chin so they were eye-to-eye again. He leaned down and kissed her square on the mouth. No hesitation. There was no wall between them this time. Ax said he hadn't known what the cause was, and maybe it was still there, but he'd found a way around it. Their kiss was urgent, desperate. A perfect display of how he made her skin crawl with need. Maddy's muscles twitched in anticipation until she turned and grasped the sleeves of Ax's shirt in her hands.

"Now you know how it feels. Intense. Like the heat of hell intermingling with the comfort of heaven." Maddy's breaths were shallow. There wasn't enough air in the room to compensate for the fire he ignited inside her.

Ax's chest vibrated with a chuckle. Maddy let her head fall against the wall of muscle. They were destined to find themselves kicked out of a public place if they kept going at this rate. She tugged her shirt down, straightened her hair, and took the lead to get out before they'd never be allowed back.

19

Maddy

Oil bubbled and crackled while the warm scent of fried fish permeated the air. The growl in her stomach started out quiet but grew louder with each step toward the food trucks. Fish and chips, seafood, burgers, and fries. A table sat near the drink stand full of desserts Weald families had brought. The ice cream truck parked closer to the table of desserts than the other trucks. The owner sold ice cream pops with bird and turtle character faces. Even if the kids didn't appreciate the retro options, Maddy hoped some of the parents enjoyed the nostalgia.

The crews and their families filled the space with laughter, games, and an all-around good time. Maddy's cheeks hurt from the smile she'd worn all morning.

Advertising for the bar had been more of a challenge. El and Nana helped generate subtle ideas to introduce Pinks. Jack volunteered to help El serve drinks to the families. They figured out a way to get the soda machine set up at the park, and their table had The Rustic Knob logo on the hot pink vinyl table cover. El came through with her connections and had five hundred plastic cups made with the logo on them as well. It cost some money, but the payout was worth it.

"Well, you've proven your skills as a planner. That's for sure." Stan chomped on a stick of fried food.

Heat filled Maddy's cheeks. "Thanks, but the day's not done."

"The food is the best we've had in years. Trust me, nothing could ruin the celebration."

She huffed.

"I've learned not to count my chickens before they hatch."

After she'd returned home the night before she'd gone through the list, checking and rechecking the details. Still a knot in her stomach had her on edge, waiting for the muddy shoe to drop. In the past, when she was certain everything had gone to plan, someone—namely her parents or ex-wife—would point out all the ways she'd failed. The crew members or their wives, maybe Nana or El would do the same. Maddy had more confidence in that truth than her ability to plan this event.

Stan waved at a woman with bright red curls flaring in a gust of wind blowing across the parking lot.

"Come meet my wife. Carol's been dying to talk to you."

"Oh. I...ummm...I need to get down the hill. The games start soon, and I want to make sure everyone has what they need."

Stan grabbed her hand, pulling her behind him as they made their way to the woman. A small piece of the pretzel Maddy had been snacking on lodged in her throat. Meeting new people meant clammy hands, racing heart, and a ringing in her ears. No matter the advice anyone gave her: count backwards from ten, deep breath and slow exhale, and her favorite to get over it, none of that worked. Her time at Pinks had helped but didn't cure her of the sensations.

"I'm glad to meet the girl—I mean woman—who's making my life easier."

Maddy squared her shoulders as she extended her hand.

"Meet Carol. Carol meet Maddy," Stan said.

Laugh lines carved deep into Carol's cheeks. Love radiated from her gray eyes. The older woman took Maddy's offered hand in a tight grip. Her skin was soft but thick, unlike Nana's.

"Hello," Maddy said.

"Oh, honey, you gotta own that greeting. These boys will steamroll you otherwise."

Carol's chuckle put her a little more at ease.

"Yes, ma'am."

"You've done a great job today. I can't wait for whatever else you've planned. My Stan spent the last few days talking about this. You got him excited again after that relative of his bailed."

As she began to thank the woman her tongue and brain froze. The most enticing scent of musk and spice filled the air around them. The same smell that had teased her the last couple of days lit her body on fire, flames she didn't want and couldn't ignore. Every nerve tingled. A knowing smile curled Carol's lip upward.

Maddy searched the field in front of them, to her left and right, but didn't find the owner of the intoxicating aroma.

"Ax is a looker, but that boy has a past he doesn't like to talk about. That's trouble. You don't want to take a ride on that train."

Carol lifted her chin, pointing over Maddy's shoulder.

"I can hear you, Carol." Ax's deep laugh rumbled through Maddy's chest.

Oh, she wanted to take a whole lotta rides.

"Of course, you can. It's not as much fun talking about you when you're not around. Ask my Stan. If I can't say it to his face, then there's no point." Carol chuckled.

Stan shook his head. "She's not lying. Carol will tell it how it is without hesitation. To hell with anyone who has a problem."

"Carol, you're stunning as always." Ax hugged Stan's wife, which gave Carol a chance to wink at Maddy without being caught as she wrapped her arms around his waist.

She shook her head at the older woman and laughed. "Carol, it was very nice to meet you." Maddy held out her hand again only to be yanked into a hug.

"You too, dear," she said.

Maddy turned toward the hill grinning as she'd done all day. The empty field at the bottom had been set up for the afternoon activities.

"Hope you get to join in the three-legged race," she said. "I'm going to check on the drinks and desserts before going to the field. See you there."

Stan shook his head while Carol nodded and clapped her hands. Ax winked at Maddy.

Oh no. She groaned and her heart rate kicked up another notch. Maddy needed reinforcements in the form of El. At least with the other woman at her side she'd have a distraction from the residual tension of the night before.

Sweat tickled the back of her neck as she cheered the wheelbarrow racers across the finish line. The sun beat down on the open area. A few of the teens huffed and puffed about having to spend the day playing "stupid kid games" but that was the worst.

Shouts and high fives started up when Crash set his partner's feet on the ground first. They'd won the last three events. Joshua was a lanky six-year-old boy. From what she'd figured out, Crash volunteered to bring the little guy while his mom and dad attended a funeral for the family.

It'd been more than two years since Maddy had packed up her things and moved from Upstate New York to Podunk. In that time Nana had kept her busy with Pinks and doctors' appointments and helping around the house. There hadn't been a lot of time to make friends. As she watched the employees of Weald and their families, she imagined she could belong.

"You're thinking way too hard over here." Ax's voice vibrated all the way to her core.

Maddy whipped around, her hair smacking her in the face.

"You and I have some pent-up tension that's built for a while now. Now that the doctor released me from my prison of no-sex all

I can think about is having sex in some fashion. Add in your...everything, and we ended up here." Maddy stared at the man who had them both wired for sound.

He rested against a tree, one ankle crossed over the other, his arms over his chest. His T-shirt pulled tight across his body, highlighting the obvious muscles beneath the cotton. And damn, the man filled out a pair of jeans. Her lungs struggled for air.

When he inched forward Maddy held up her hand to stop him. "Let us take all this in."

He laughed, pushed off the tree, and came to their side. "Not much to look at in comparison to you. Maddy, you look better than any dessert on that table or in the truck."

Electricity sparked between them when the tip of his finger smoothed over Maddy's arm.

She found herself leaning into his touch, hoping he'd do more. Another heated kiss, maybe. Madelyn closed her eyes.

Ax cleared his throat. "What's next?"

The scratchy hesitation in his voice pulled Maddy back to the moment. She shook her head clear of the daydream.

"Tug-of-war."

He's got a damn sexy chin tilt.

"What are the teams?" he asked.

"Kids versus adults." Of course, she didn't tell him about the secret weapon she'd arranged for the kids. It wasn't going to be a fair contest, but then again, it wasn't supposed to be.

"Don't you think the odds are in the adults' favor instead of the kids."

Maddy chuckled. "I wouldn't worry about that. Go round up your men, I'll get the kids, and we'll show you how tug-of-war is done."

Too tempting to resist, she pushed his shoulder to get him moving. Heat shot up her arm and through her body. A better reward than a hot chocolate sundae with a whole damn jar of cherries on top. She smiled at his back as he made his way down the slope to the mud pit where she'd set everything up.

"Maddy, hey. I've been looking for you." The quiver in El's voice froze Maddy in place.

"Talk to me, gorgeous." Maddy maneuvered around people until they were alone, away from anyone who might wander over and ask questions. Like Ax or Carol.

"Umm. I mean...I need to go." El's breaths quickened with each word.

It had been a long time since she'd witnessed her best friend go into full panic mode. Maddy pressed on El's shoulder until she bent over, bracing herself on her knees.

"Breathe. In. Out." El followed directions. "That's it. Keep going."

Maddy watched the group gather for tug-of-war. A flash of her and Ax holding hands watching their own children play with everyone else at a picnic shook Maddy to the core. She wasn't at all ready for kids, hadn't even considered it a possibility, but with the seed planted, she knew that was her future goal. To stave off her own panic attack, Maddy checked on El who had once again found her balance.

"Oh, goddess. I'm sorry. How embarrassing." El scrubbed her hands down her face.

"It's okay. Why are you in such a rush to go? What happened?" Maddy walked toward the gathering.

"It's work. There's an emergency I need to handle. Sorry for scaring you. I overreacted. Jack's manning the table and Lola is entertaining the families who stop by." El fluttered her hands in the air. "I know this is inconvenient and I am sorry."

Maddy held her friend's face between her hands. With her eyes locked on El's she matched the other woman's breathing once more. Panic gave way to calm.

"Whatever is going on, we can talk about it tomorrow. For now, enjoy the day. Have fun and when you're ready to tell me what kind of emergency would get you this worked up, then I'll be here to listen." Maddy took a few steps away from El, then stopped and looked over her shoulder. "Maybe you'll find a nice, single Weald employee that you can hook up with to relieve some of your stress."

El nodded. "Yep. That's great advice. Except, I don't date. Remember?"

Inwardly, Maddy groaned. It wasn't often that El became stubborn and unwilling to listen. Often, the tables were flipped, and El was the one calming Maddy. Her yoga breathing techniques came in handy.

"Today is about nothing other than the picnic. I owe you for all the help you've provided. This wouldn't have been such a success without your connections." She pulled El into a hug, needing the comfort from her touch as much as El seemed to need it to hold onto the calm.

"You don't owe me anything. This is all you." El tightened her hold around Maddy's waist. "We need to work on boosting your confidence because your talent is not something to brush off."

With a shake of her head, Maddy broke their connection. El's voice didn't waiver. Her words were sure. The moment of anxiety and panic seemed to have passed.

"Don't get me wrong, I had fun with the planning, but you're the one who hooked me up with the logoed merchandise." Maddy looked around the park and smiled.

Gratitude and compliments were difficult for her to accept. A failing she recognized but didn't know how to change.

"The great thing about planning is that you don't have to do all the things, you need to reach out to the right people who help you finalize the end game. Then you manage those people—both areas in which you excel. Maddy, if you could see that your strength lies in creating the big picture and finding the right people to help you build the small pieces, then you'd understand why all of us are in awe of your capabilities. Some days I hate your parents and your ex-wife for cutting you down the way they did."

"Don't hate them, please. I'm not making excuses for their behavior because that's not fair to myself. We all make mistakes. For me, it's better to acknowledge the mistake, figure out how to keep from repeating it myself, and move on."

El grinned at Maddy. Unshed tears burned Maddy's eyes. Becoming friends with El was one of the best ideas she'd ever had.

"For now, we'll move on. Like you said, today is about the picnic. Even though I know you're already plotting a way to help me figure out relationships, know that I'm plotting ways to prove your own self-worth to you. Today's proof that we could be dangerous in the business world if we partnered up. Consider this as your warning. I'm plotting devious things."

"The tug-of-war starts in ten minutes." A male voice boomed from a bull horn.

"Come on." Maddy snatched El's wrist and drug her back toward the open field. She'd worry about El's promise later. There was a picnic to finish. "We need to get everything set up."

With Carol's help, Madelyn managed to get fifteen dads, crew members, and friends of the families lined up on the adult side of the rope. Four teens joined in on the kid side. While the adults joked about the kids running scared Maddy picked up the tape wrapped around the middle of the rope, then circled her free hand over her head.

"On your mark." She shouted with a glance to her left. "Get set."

The adults pulled the rope taut.

"Go." Maddy screamed.

As the adults yanked the kids' side tightened. Adults slid through the mud, their heels digging in while the teens eased out of the pit, their grip loose on the thick twine.

"What? How?" Ax and Crash asked at the same time.

Maddy bent over in half, laughing until tears streamed out of the corner of her eyes. The men's expressions matched. Big eyes. Strained muscles. Creases in their foreheads from exertion. A flatbed truck rolled into view, the rope turning through the pulley. Kids cheered and jumped up and down.

"We win. You lose!" A chorus sang.

Brown, mud-soaked arms wrapped around Maddy's waist and lifted her off the ground. "You...that...amazing."

Ax swung Maddy around; his eyes lit up with joy. She wiped a streak of mud off his cheek. Time froze and the world around them went quiet. Everyone else disappeared. She tilted her chin to his until their eyes met. Maddy's lips gravitated toward his. With millimeters between them Ax turned his face to the left before lowering her to the ground.

"Best day ever," he said.

"Yes, it is." Maddy grinned.

"Maddy, I expect my Stan will be talking to you soon about next year's picnic. This was one for the memory books. Thank you for everything you've done."

Carol pat her shoulder before walking away. Maddy felt the heat rise in her cheeks. Ax nodded, a smirk spread across his lips.

"Told you so." Ax smacked her butt.

"Told me what?" she asked.

"That you're good at this." He laughed, slid one arm around her waist and gathered Maddy into his side.

They walked up to the parking lot as the sun set, arm in arm. If this was the way she'd feel every day, then she'd do whatever necessary to happen to keep Ax with her forever.

20

Maddy

Maddy glanced at herself in the bathroom mirror. Tonight was her and Ax's official first date. She didn't count the bar meetups or axe throwing as dates. They were friends getting to know each other, nothing more. Now, they were officially dating.

Her normal nights out included a quick dinner and drinking at the bar while she waited on El to finish whatever marketing gig she had going on. An actual Friday by herself meant cooking at home followed by ice cream and snuggling with her cat.

She huffed, sending a piece of hair straight up. By Wednesday she still hadn't figured out what to plan. While meeting with a potential new vendor she let it slip that she could manage finding new contacts better than dating. The vendor suggested a night learning to cook. It was practical, fun, and dinner all in one.

"Maddy, are you ready for your big date?" El's voice taunted her from the front room of the house.

"Giving her a key was a bad idea," Maddy mumbled to herself.

Of course, she'd given her best friend a key a year ago—not that it changed Maddy's current regret.

"Hmm. I think I'm underdressed." The deep rumble of Ax's voice stopped Maddy's heart for a split second.

She whipped around to find him leaning against the door, arms crossed over his chest. Her heart rushed to start again. His jeans hung low on his hips and a navy blue, long-sleeve, o-neck T-shirt fit snug around his chest and biceps. Strength that promised he'd keep her safe, secure. Confidence that he could handle her in the bedroom. He'd pushed up the sleeves, drawing her eyes to his forearms and the brightly colored flames tattooed from his wrist to his elbow. Rugged casual with a hint of bad boy.

Maddy licked her lips then smiled when he adjusted his stance and cleared his throat. Her cheeks flushed as she imagined sliding up his chest, tasting his skin along the way. What lay beneath his shirt? She wasn't sure if he had hair on his chest, or whether she wanted him to have any. If he did, would it be coarse or soft?

"Well, the tension between you two would need a butcher knife to cut through." El chuckled. "He and I met up outside. I hope you don't mind that I let him in."

Chill bumps rose on her arms. Being close to him, his scent wrapping around her like a blanket, propelled Maddy's body into chaos. Flushing one second and shivering the next. The sparks between them bombarded her from front to back. Overwhelming in the most exhilarating way possible. Maddy placed her palm on Ax's chest. His pulse raced beneath his shirt.

"Nope. Not a problem at all. Thank you. I don't mean to be rude, but why are you here?" Maddy used El as a distraction.

Her best friend laughed. "Don't worry. I won't be here much longer. I stopped by to see if you needed help getting ready. Since it's obvious you don't, then I'm not going to stick around."

"Did Maddy tell you where we're going?" Ax asked.

"I'm a little jealous. Going to a cooking class is on my bucket list of things to do before I die. Guess I should take Maddy's advice and find me a man." El winked at Maddy.

"My buddy Crash is single."

Maddy smacked Ax on the arm. If they wanted El to leave, then he needed to quit talking to her.

"All right. All right. Point taken. I'm out of here." El waved good-bye and left.

Maddy took advantage of El's momentary disruption and nipped at the curve of Ax's neck. The vibration of his low growl reached inside her chest and down to her core. She curled her fingers into his shirt. The hard staccato of his heartbeat beneath her touch gave Maddy a focal point and helped to clear her mind of the sex haze she'd brought on herself. Playing with fire and all that.

He wrapped his hand around her wrist and pulled her to him. Maddy tucked her head into Ax's shoulder.

"Mmm. I'm thinking right now if we don't stop, your plans will have to be delayed or canceled." Ax's lips brushed the top of her ear.

She squeezed her eyes closed. He was right. Maddy took a deep breath then tried to step away from him. Rather than break is hold, Ax tightened his hold of her wrist while wrapping his free arm around her waist.

"I could call and cancel our reservation then we can play a game of human Operation with fruit body parts that you have to grab with your teeth instead of hands." Maddy pressed into his chest, her hands molded around his hips. "Some cherry nipples. Strawberry belly button. I can lay banana slices along your cock and drizzle them in chocolate."

If he wasn't ready to let go, then she'd take advantage of the moment. Teasing him until he broke.

Ax groaned. "No. We made a deal. Date night is cooking class. You can plan your game of human Operation for some other time. I'll wait in the living room while you finish getting ready."

An hour later Maddy and Ax stood behind a large butcher block countertop. They were one of eight groups that evening. The chef began with a quick summary of their meal. Flavors of Provence from along the Mediterranean coastline. Maddy chose this class because of her secret admiration of Chef Julia Childs, who inspired the meal.

"We'll start the meal with gougéres," the chef said.

Ax leaned down to whisper in her ear, "What is a gorge-air-ees?"
She bit her lip to keep from laughing.

"It's a cheese puff and it's pronounced goo-shair," she answered.

"Goose hair?" Ax screeched in a way only a person with his deep voice could. "Why would we eat this?"

"Because you love cheese? This will be the most delicious cheese puff you've ever had."

Ax turned her to face him then planted his lips against hers. She couldn't breathe.

Maddy leaned forward. "I can be quite the cook when I want to be—despite what El might say to the contrary. After tonight, you'll beg me to make dinner often."

"I have no doubt." Ax winked at her.

They began making the first dish. Maddy rubbed her now cold hands together to warm them. She wasn't sure if the goosebumps were arousal, or fear of what they might end up doing.

"I'll cook for you naked." Maddy picked up the paring knife in front of her. She shook it at Ax. "But not if you don't pay attention tonight and help."

They got to work following the recipe card. Maddy did most of the actual preparing while Ax sampled ingredients. The rhythm between them came easy, and she found herself enjoying the process. The chefs came by their table a couple of times to check in. She smiled when Chef Desiree paid her a compliment.

"I need to ask a favor of sorts." Ax pulled a plastic bag of nuts from his pocket.

"What is that?" Maddy pointed to the bag.

"Almonds," he answered.

"You do realize we're cooking dinner, right?" she asked while beating eggs into the dough.

Ax nodded. "Yep. I always carry snacks with me at work. When we're out at a site it's not like I can run to the vending machine and grab something. I'm getting hungry waiting on this stuff." He shrugged. "Anyway, my favor."

"What's up?" Maddy double-checked the recipe for the next step.

"My mother called today and reminded me about a fundraiser in New York I promised to attend. After I told her I wasn't sure I could make it she spent the next fifteen minutes pointing out my faults and why I'm too immature to live by myself in the woods. You'd think being forty-five would earn me some points, but to her, I'm still eighteen or in my early twenties."

Listening to him talk about his mother grated on Maddy's nerves. Her parents weren't perfect by any means, which was why she'd made the decision years ago to set her own boundaries—something Ax didn't seem very good at. He had a huge heart, and she hated that his mother took advantage of him.

"Maybe we can help you set some rules for your parents. You know, like boundaries to keep your mom out of your business." Maddy tapped her finger against the butcher block counter.

He took a deep breath. "I would like for you to attend the fundraiser with me."

"Is this one of those black-tie dinners where everyone pays an exorbitant amount of money to say they gave a charitable donation? But it's a chance to measure the size of their pocketbooks."

"Pretty much sums it up. They're boring, pretentious, and I loathe going to them. This one, though, means something to me. It's a fundraiser for Chiari's Malformation, a medical condition my cousin has." Ax grabbed the dirty spoon she'd set to the side.

She appreciated his help with cleaning up behind her. The work after cooking was one of the main reasons she didn't do it more often. Maddy hated cleaning and some of the more complicated dishes meant an hour's worth of cleaning.

"I'll be there. I'm going to need some time to find a dress." Maddy didn't hesitate to say yes. "When is it?"

Ax pulled up his phone and clicked on the calendar. Anxiety kicked her heart rate up a notch or twenty as she took a second to consider what going with him meant. Despite saying yes, she sent a silent wish to the goddess that she could find some excuse not to go. It wasn't that she didn't want to visit New York. Going to the City felt like a big step in their relationship. Hotel rooms. Meeting the parents. Expectations.

"Three weeks. We'd fly in on Friday and come home on Sunday. Unless we decide to stay longer and make it a vacation of sorts."

"I'll need to check and see what I have scheduled. We want to start rotating our inventory more often, which means I'm working on securing new vendors. I may need to be available for them."

The excuse was lame, Maddy wouldn't deny that. If she had to be glued to her desk for a contract, it wasn't worth the energy. That was another reason she'd never enjoyed corporate America. The freedom of working for Lola and taking over some of Pink's management tasks meant she worked her own hours as long as the store was covered, and employees were happy.

Ax took the utensils from her hands and sat them on the countertop. Then he turned her by the shoulders until they were face-to-face.

"Right. Let's try this again and you can tell me the truth." Ax tilted his head to the side. His brows raised in a dare for her to argue.

Maddy clenched her jaw. When put on the spot, communicating feelings wasn't as easy as everyone made it sound—no matter how much she preached the importance.

"I haven't been back to New York since I left. My parents came for Papa's funeral, but that was more out of necessity than want." Ax stopped her from turning her head the other way.

For some reason sharing was easier when she didn't have to look the person in the eye.

"Are you worried that going back will throw you into some kind of nightmare? PTSD of sorts?"

Did he have a point? Maddy hadn't considered her sudden onset of anxiety was more related to Natasha than meeting the parents.

"Maybe. This is all pretty quick for me. Meeting the parents will be awkward. Where will we stay? In one hotel? What about our arrangement not to have sex yet? I'm not sure I can hold to that promise if we're sharing a bed."

Ax let Maddy return to the cooking process. She should've asked questions before saying yes. Now, there was no way to retract her acceptance.

Strong hands massaged the tension from her shoulders. Maddy let her head fall back onto Ax's chest. They could take a few more minutes before working on the next dish for dinner.

"Don't worry about my parents. If you're worried what they'll think, it's none of their business. As far as the room, of course we need one room and one bed—a big bed—but that goes without saying."

Maddy raised her eyebrows at Ax's mention of only one bed. The inevitability of finding love when limited to sharing a bed with an almost-stranger made her melt inside. Of course, this wasn't the same situation, but maybe if she looked at it from a different perspective it wouldn't trip as many triggers.

"All right. Let's move on to the salmon." Chef Desiree called from the front of the room.

They turned back to chefs, ready for the next dish they were supposed to cook.

Maddy leaned into Ax's side.

"I won't badger you anymore tonight, but please trust me not to throw you into something you won't enjoy."

Recently she questioned whether she even trusted herself to know what was good. Ax was an honest man. Nothing to this point made her uneasy. If it was the past invading her present, then it was time to burn those memories out with new ones.

"I think I can do that," she said. "You never answered me about the sex promise we made."

He gifted her with a smile and squeezed her hand. "Thank you. It would mean the world to me for you to be there, but I would never pressure you into something you don't want to do. How about we spend the next three weeks building up the momentum and agree that if something happens, it happens. No expectations and no let-downs."

Maddy nodded.

"Yeah. I like that plan."

They spent the rest of the night cooking, eating, and laughing. Maybe a trip where the stressors of home weren't around would be good for her. The time away could help her figure things out with Pinks and The Knob as well, give a different perspective if she looked at it from the outside.

21

Maddy

"Where are we headed today?" Maddy asked as Nana eased into the front seat.

Tuesday afternoon was Maddy's time with Nana. Each week they went out for lunch, talked about the shop and bar, then Nana headed off to one of her friends' homes for crocheting.

"The diner first, then go to the park. It's a gorgeous day and I want to enjoy the weather."

She followed her grandmother's directions. Lunch at the park sounded like a fantastic idea.

They chose a bench near the playground. One of Nana's favorite past times was talking to the moms who took their kids to the park to play. All the regulars called her nana or grandma. A few of the kids liked to call her memaw.

"Thank you." Maddy took the offered plastic silverware from Lola.

"You're welcome. Now, let's get down to business. My sources tell me you think you can't fill my shoes. I wear a size five. They aren't that big."

Maddy rolled her eyes. Lola Begay was a lot of things, but she wasn't a comedian. Even her dad jokes failed in the humor department. She wasn't certain who the "sources" were, but there was no denying the rumor since it was true.

"Who's your source? They shouldn't be telling stories like that."

Lola waved her finger at Maddy. "It doesn't matter. Now tell me what's going on? You know I'm not going to be able to keep these businesses forever. Either we need to get serious about you taking over, or I need to start considering alternatives."

For a few minutes Maddy's food became far more interesting than the turn in conversation. Of course, they talked about Pinks and The Knob, but more along the lines of performance—not Maddy's interest in ownership.

"I'm not creative like El or you. The DIY sets are genius, but I never would have thought of that." Maddy took a drink of tea.

"Maybe not, but your classes filled within a week and a waitlist long enough to fill more. You've already set up a series of classes that get more in-depth as you go along. The more classes you offer; the more repeat customers you'll have. Before you know it, you could offer them two to three times a week. It's a service this town, and our clients, need. Not to mention, those grab bags are a result of your class. We wouldn't have thought of them otherwise. Now what's your next objection?"

Wow. Viewing creativity that way gave her a whole new perspective. Maddy didn't have to think of everything. Ideas came from everyone and everywhere. She thought about working alongside El and Ax at the picnic. Collaborating and managing the project turned out to be easier than she'd expected. If the compliments from the Weald families were any indication, she'd done a fair job.

"I'm not very good at sales. How many customers have I run off because I didn't catch on that they aren't open to more adventurous toys? The best thing I can do is sell tarot cards, which aren't normal inventory for Pinks. The Knob isn't a big deal, Jack handles everything for inventory and service. What if we split the businesses? I could take one and you could give Jack the other."

When Nana hadn't responded after a few minutes, Maddy began to wonder if she'd upset her grandma.

"Sales are such a small piece of Pinks. We've already got a team to do the daily work. Count that as another problem taken care of.

I'm talking the overall ownership, not the minutiae of managing or even inventory. Maria is a great employee; you could consider using her strengths to help you."

"That's true." Maddy didn't want to push the Jack issue. If Lola didn't address it, then the obvious answer was no. "I'm better at teaching the classes and running the office. What if I get overwhelmed and flake out? It would be detrimental to the businesses."

Nana shook her head. "Madelyn, you're reaching for excuses. We both appreciate the importance of maintaining your work-life balance and managing your mental health. Your papa and I used to go on weekend excursions all the time. We loved to jump in the car on Friday night and drive until we couldn't stay awake any longer. That's where we'd find a hotel and spend the next two days. Grab El or that lumbersnack, Ax, and enjoy a weekend of happiness. That'll save your sanity."

"What if I say no?" Nana lowered her chin and shook her head. Disappointment thickened the air between them. Maddy backpedaled, not wanting Lola to get the wrong idea. "I'm not saying no, just asking what if. The facts are the facts, Nana. I'm not business savvy like my parents or you and Papa.

"When you moved in with your grandfather and me two years ago, I wasn't sure if you'd want to work at the store, much less own it. He and I talked about selling before he passed. Those two businesses are like my children. Your mother ran off to New York with you and your dad. I'm not going to sugar coat anything for you, Madelyn. Selling them would be difficult and it would hurt, but it was never our intention to pressure you into taking ownership. I had an offer from The Weedle Company. They want to tear down the buildings to build a fancy hotel. It's a last resort. I'd rather Pinks and The Knob go to someone—or you and a significant other if that's the case—who wants to keep it around. We're a town staple. The nicest boutique in fifty miles. The only good cigar bar in Oregon."

Maddy chuckled. She was as proud of the businesses as her grandmother. Acceptance sat on the tip of her tongue, but her brain refused to push the word out. Her heart cracked at the idea of letting her grandparent's legacy escape her grasp. Why couldn't she say the word?

"Mom and Dad pushed business so hard at home. Part of the reason I moved back was to get away from the corporate life they lived. I hate that lifestyle."

Lola nodded. "I hate it too. Delbert and I begged your mother not to go to New York. We told her there were ways to pursue her dreams here on the West coast. She wasn't having it though. Both of us knew the minute she and your father left Podunk we wouldn't watch you grow up."

"Why is that? Mom won't talk about it."

"I made mistakes raising your mom. Much like you resent your parents for leaving you to build their careers, your mom believed Papa and I did the same thing. I've owned these two businesses for twenty-five years, but I've been an entrepreneur for a lot longer.

"This won't come as a surprise to you, but I was never good at being a housewife. Delbert didn't want that either. He wanted a partner to do things with him, which worked out well for me. Settling down didn't come easy for either of us. At the time we found out I was pregnant; we'd been considering not having children."

Maddy stared at Lola with wide eyes. Nothing she'd said surprised her, but it was still shocking.

"Was Mom a mistake?"

"Neither your grandfather nor I had family to help. We weren't ready to change our nomadic lifestyle. I would never call your mother an accident, but our plans were to settle down first. Then, whatever would happen was going to happen. If we had a child, we'd welcome them with open hearts. A much higher power than me had other plans, though. At the time, I was old when I had your mom at twenty-five."

Maddy soaked it all in. "None of that sounds bad."

"Your grandfather and I admit to making mistakes. Until your mama turned five, we didn't stay in one place longer than six months. Our nomad life took away her chance to enjoy making friends. Maybe she wanted to explore the world on their own terms. Maybe she hated Podunk. I've tried to ask many times, but she's never shared."

"One day during the last year of my MBA, I asked her about you and Papa. We'd had this huge fight about learning how to balance family life with building a career. She wanted me to find a reputable company with advancement opportunities until I took over as CEO. I wanted to spend more time with Natasha. Mom said Nat shared her beliefs but didn't want to hurt my feelings to tell me."

Acid forced its way up Maddy's throat. She moved her fork around the plate, no longer interested in eating. Dredging up memories of her marriage continued to send Maddy into a dark place. She wanted to get past all the pain and talking was supposed to help.

"Your mother and I have differing ideas in many areas—parenting and family included. I don't think she ever intended to distance herself as much as she did. As my daughter and son-in-law's values changed, so did our relationship."

Maddy listened, took a moment to digest her grandmother's theory, then applied her own experiences to the idea. It made sense.

"It doesn't always feel like my relationship is different, but I understand what you mean. Growing up I always wanted Mom or Dad at my school stuff. By middle school I no longer expected them to show up at anything. Sheila, my nanny, went to more of my ballet recitals and soccer games than Mom or Dad combined."

Nana smiled. She twisted on the bench to face Maddy. "I didn't know you did either of those activities."

"Not for long. Like any other kid, I tried for a few months then quit. I remember telling Mom if she loved me she'd let me play soccer. Even today I feel guilty for manipulating her. I was ten and all my friends were playing." Maddy and Lola laughed at the story.

She watched the kids playing on the swing set. An older group tried to make it across the monkey bars. They'd get past one or two then fall to the ground and start over again. Maddy vowed to give her kids opportunities to fall down and get back up. They wouldn't have to be perfect. She'd make sure to teach them to follow their own path—as long as it was legal.

"I wish we'd spent more time with you when you were a kid. The blame isn't limited to your mother. Delbert and I should've made more of an effort to visit. Thinking about it now, I suppose your mother and I are not that different. We made excuses about the businesses to cover our wounded pride. I'm sorry, Maddy. Even if you choose not to take over the shop and bar, please use my experience and your mother's as a lesson in what not to do."

Maddy began gathering their trash. Her phone buzzed with a new message.

Ax: Hey, beautiful. Checking in to see how your day is going.

Maddy: Hey! I'm good. Having lunch with Nana at the park.

Ax: Do you think we could get together tonight? I'd love to see you. There's something I'd like to talk to you about.

"Is everything okay?" Nana asked when Maddy returned to the table.

Maddy startled, lost in thought, and distracted by the text from Ax.

"It's nothing. Ax wants to get together tonight, but I'm closing at Pinks. Thank you for sharing with me. Can I think about everything for a little while longer?"

"The time limit is all your doing. As long as you decide before I leave this realm for my next life as a gorgeous fairy with your grandfather at my side."

Maddy's mood lightened with her grandmother's declaration. Lola had said from the day her husband died that she'd see him again in another life as a fairy. The older woman didn't even let the idea of death bring down her spirits. Maddy sent off a text to Ax.

Maddy: I have plans at the store tonight. I'm supposed to close. The bar needs my attention too.

"You're avoiding him. When I talked to El yesterday she said you haven't talked to since Friday." Nana clutched her knitting bag. "What's going on?

A bottle of top-shelf tequila rested between balls of yarn in her bag. One of Maddy's life goals was to have a group of friends like Nana's crochet group.

"If I said I didn't want to talk about it, would you let it go?" She knew the answer but asked anyway.

"Nope. I'd rather talk about your love life than the store anyway. You owe me an update on your relationship."

Maddy drummed her fingers along the steering wheel.

"First, I'm not avoiding him. We went out Friday and we've texted since then. I haven't seen him. Anyway, have you ever experienced perfection such that you get scared because it could change overnight?" Maddy asked.

"Of course, I have. Meeting Delbert was like that. When the bank approved the loan for Pinks and The Knob, I experienced the same thing. This man has stolen your heart, hasn't he?"

A lump formed in her throat, not because Nana accepted their relationship without question, but she didn't berate Maddy for her fear. She nodded.

"Officially, we've been dating for less than two weeks. Already, my heart declared its love for him and I have to fight saying the words every time I'm around him. He asked me about El and if we've ever dated."

Nana murmured her understanding.

"What did you tell him?"

"The truth. I had a crush on her, but never acted on it. El and I are friends, and that's all we'll ever be."

Nana placed her knitting bag on the floor. She reached for Maddy's hand, cupping it between her own.

"Did he accept your answer? Doubt you in any way?" Nana squeezed their hands together.

Maddy shook her head. "That's part of the problem. He takes everything I say in stride. I've even pushed hard with the sex talk because I know it makes him uncomfortable. Please don't lecture me about testing someone to determine their worth. Every time I do, I beat myself up for days afterward. If he knew, he'd tell me it was over—at least I that's what I would do."

"What scares you more, the quick connection with Ax or that you're going to end up in another relationship like your marriage?" Nana asked.

A comfortable silence filled the car. Maddy took advantage of the time to consider her own words.

"That's a loaded question." She let her thought trail off. "Our first kiss was good, but as we were kissing this wall formed between us. The words to describe it don't exist, beyond something was off. Flirting is easy. Physical touch comes naturally. Since that first kiss, we keep getting interrupted and I can't help but wonder if it's a sign."

"He has his own set of demons to battle. Neither of you come from healthy relationships. To rebuild takes time and this situation you've found yourself in happened overnight." Nana tapped her leg with a bright orange fingernail. "Your fears are not unjustified. Your hesitation makes sense. There is no harm in slowing down. Fight your own fight and let him support you while you support him in his battle. I think, and I could be wrong, but I don't think I am, that you will both find yourselves stronger on the other side."

"Since our date on Friday I've chosen not to face my fear of scaring him away by saying the wrong thing," she murmured the truth threatening to suffocate her.

"My sweet girl, you've done everything right from what the details you've given me—even if there aren't many. As long as you both consent, then you should put your focus on building things together. Keep communication open if someone has a problem to eliminate the fear of sharing concerns. Worry about what you can control, not what you can't. Whatever you do, do not borrow disaster. That will lead you down a path of heartache for certain."

Simple words she needed to hear. A weight lifted from her chest. "Thank you, Nana."

"Enjoy these moments, sweet girl. You've been given the chance at love again, don't squander it. Now take me to my ladies. We need to start on our Christmas gifts. We're running behind this year; four months is not long."

Maddy rolled her eyes. They sold more peter heaters and crocheted pasties with tassels for Christmas than any other time of the year. She imagined the surprise on people's faces when they opened their gifts.

22

Ax

"Ax, man, we could use your help over here," Crash called to him.

They had to finish clearing out the current plot by the end of the day. As foreman, the responsibility to make sure they met their deadlines fell to him. If they didn't, worrying about Maddy would not be a valid explanation.

"Yeah. Coming. Sorry about that." Keeping an eye on the crew was his responsibility, but he couldn't stop thinking about Maddy.

As they worked to clear the land, he daydreamed of the picnic. Their cooking date. The night spent throwing axes. Maddy's ease of teaching. Her energy.

By the end of the day, he'd made up his mind. Maddy had to close that night. Once the store was empty, he'd go see her. As much as he liked the plan for a date every Friday night, the scheduled time made him restless. Ax loved unscheduled activities. He didn't want to have to plan every time they were together.

Less than two weeks in and he found a way to complain. Ax began to question his own mind. Was he pulling away to avoid hurt? Maybe he had another reason to keep finding reasons why their relationship was unstable.

"Let's go to The Knob to wind down before we call it a night." Crash took a drink from his jug of water.

"Can't. I have something I need to do," he replied as he pulled his backpack from the desk drawer.

"She can wait. Besides, if that tone of voice is any indication, the *something* is working right next door. Nothing wrong with making a stop first. Besides, you've been choosing her over me and I'm feeling left out."

Ax sighed. Crash needed more attention than any woman he'd ever dated. The man loved adventure and hated being alone. Since Ax had deserted their friendship for Maddy, some guy time wasn't such a bad idea.

"All right. Let's go. I'd have ended up there anyway before I went to the shop."

His friend smirked. "Exactly."

Jack offered the obligatory chin nod when Ax and Crash walked into the bar. The old bartender held up two fingers, but Ax shook his head.

"A Coke tonight."

"Everything okay, son?" Jack asked as he sat the drink on a napkin in front of Ax.

"I'd hoped to talk to Maddy, but her car isn't outside."

Jack made a clicking sound with his tongue. "She was here for a couple of hours then left for an appointment. If I heard right, she'll be back to lock up. You mess it up with her?"

The laser focus of his gaze warned Ax to be careful with his choice of answer.

"Not that I know of. We've been hanging out more, maybe she was catching up on missed work." Ax ran his hand through his hair.

"You're distracting her until she's too busy to sit still?" Crash jumped into the conversation.

"It's not like that. Besides, if Maddy didn't want to do something, she'd say as much."

Jack made a clicking sound with his tongue. "Maddy's a ball-buster. Gotta put up with some hard hits, but it'll be worth the trouble."

"I'm going to need more than one ice bag for the ball-busting."

Crash raised an eyebrow. "That why you've had some raging hormones? Too many shots to the manbits?"

"It's a wonder you're single. You know women don't care for a man who puts everyone in one category or another based on actions." Ax sipped his drink.

Jack stopped wiping the glass in his hand. "I'm a slow old man these days. Care to offer up the details of what you mean?"

Nope. Talking about gender roles was not at the top of his list of relaxing conversation.

Ax shook his head then shot off a text to Maddy.

Ax: Hanging out at the bar until you get back, Maddy. How was your afternoon?

It didn't take long for Maddy to reply first.

Maddy: I've had better. Had the meeting about the settlement. They did everything you said they would. We still haven't come to an agreement. I hoped this would be done today.

Ax: Sorry. We legal types can be stubborn to a fault sometimes. Want to talk about it? I could help with their counter.

"Son, I know you heard me. Quit draggin' your feet and tell me what you're hinting at." Jack set both his hands on the bar.

Ax looked the bartender in the eyes—not as a challenge, but out of respect. He loved Maddy like a daughter. But there were some things that weren't his business. Before he answered, he wanted her to know what was going on.

> *Ax: Jack wants to know about gender roles and expectations since I put my foot in my mouth with Crash.*

> *Maddy: Please don't give the old man a heart attack. I don't think Lola would appreciate it.*

She added a laughing emoji to the end of her text. Ax grinned.

> *Maddy: Pretty sure he'll be sorry he asked. *mind blown emoji* Later, I want all the details on his reaction and yeah, I'm going to take you up on the offer to help with the lawyers.*

He'd delayed long enough. Jack hadn't moved from his spot in front of them, drying glasses then setting them to the side.

"People don't believe in boy toys and girl toys nowadays. Just because I let my emotions show doesn't mean I'm acting like a girl." He put girl in air quotes. Next to him Crash rolled his eyes.

"Well now, that sounds more complicated than it's worth." Jack stopped his drying and planted his hands on the bar. "I'm glad all I have to do is serve people from behind this bar. Too many years have passed for me to care about that crud."

"Since you two are talkative tonight, I could use some advice." Ax traced the top of his glass with his fingertip.

Crash liked women—even if he wasn't the most eloquent of men when it came to his words. Lots of them. Sometimes one at a time, then multiples other times. If anyone could give him insight, he'd hoped his friend would.

"About?" Crash looked at him over his glass.

"Women. Maddy."

"Mm. I'll try, but we both know I'm not great in the relationship department. Hell, I can't even get one to spend a week with me anymore."

That was a conversation for a later date.

"What would you do if you were falling hard for a woman, but not all of the pieces clicked yet. Like you're missing something, but you can't put your finger on what it is."

Crash tilted his head to the side in question. "Talk to them?"

The answer came without hesitation, yet his stomach churned until the acid burned and he wanted to throw up.

"You make it sound easy. The whole idea of talking to Maddy about this has me tied up in knots. In such a short time, I've had more fun with her than I ever had with my ex-wife. The last thing I want is to screw it all up with my neediness and confusion." He pressed the heels of hands into his eyes. Pressure built behind his temples.

Crash swiped his finger across his phone. "I didn't take you to be such a worrier. She's got you turned inside out. By the way, is her friend single by chance? Maybe if you hook us up, I can get some insider information on Maddy for you."

Without thinking Ax reached over and smacked his friend on the back of the head. Crash had lost his mind if he thought Ax would set him up with El. The conversation took a quick nosedive into ridiculousness.

"So helpful. Talking to her seems the best option I have. Do I sit her down for a specific conversation, or wait until the time is right during a date?" He massaged his temples.

Work was stressful enough. The last thing he needed was relationship woes. Then again, they were his own doing. If he'd suck it up and communicate, he knew the problem would be solved.

"Both? I don't know." Crash looked away from his phone to Ax.

"Both what?" Elowen chimed in from behind Ax.

"And you are?" Crash looked over Ax's shoulder and gave El a full-body, head to foot and back again, inspection.

"That's Elowen." Ax chuckled.

She moved around Ax and stuck out her hand to Crash. "Maddy's best friend, becoming Ax's friend, and the most charismatic of our group."

Ax took a drink to hide the red in his cheeks.

"How do you figure the most charismatic? What if that's me?" he asked.

"I set up Maddy's Blind Love profile. She agreed to test it for me since I needed testimonials for the marketing campaign. I'm a marketing consultant and working for Blind Love right now. If it wasn't for my request, the three of us wouldn't know each other—no, that's wrong. You wouldn't have had the pleasure of meeting either of us."

Elowen smiled. Her green eyes sparkled.

Crash cleared his throat. "Any chance you're still in the market for testers?"

"Nope. I'm guessing you're more like the friends-with-benefits type. I bet you have an account on FireSpark."

The laugh that burst out of Ax caught even him off guard. Elowen didn't hold her punches. She'd surprised Crash as well, if his silence was any indication.

"Been there, tried that. Now I'm aiming for some reality show to set me up with my soulmate."

The two of them gave each other a side eye that had Ax wondering if he should leave the room.

"Good luck with the reality show. You should be a real treat with the way you get straight to the point." She flicked her hand in the air. "Don't bother with the 'if you hurt my buddy, I'll make you pay' speech."

"Jack, I need some cigars. Can you open the humidor for me?" Crash walked to the end of the bar.

The Knob had a large walk-in humidor at the end of the hallway on the Pinks side.

"Sure. What are you looking for?" Jack asked while he followed Crash.

Ax would thank Crash later for the chance to talk to El alone.

"Have you talked to Maddy, today? She said she'd be here tonight, but we haven't seen her yet." Ax turned his attention to El.

She shook her head. "It's Tuesday, which means she had lunch with Lola. Then she had the meeting with her lawyer."

"Tuesday is Lola day?" Knowing her normal routines was something he wanted to learn.

Getting the details about her day-to-day activities felt normal, like something to take them beyond the physical lust for each other. He couldn't remember being excited about the mundane things with Daphne.

"Yep. They have lunch, talk about the businesses, and then Maddy takes her to her knitting group where they drink and make obscene things like peter heaters and boobie tassels they sell online and in the store during the holidays."

He waited, studying El for any sign she was joking.

"You're serious?"

El laughed. Jack huffed.

"One hundred percent. I've been to one of her crochet nights, those old ladies are the best." El chuckled. "You should see them when they've all had some shots of tequila. It's like The Golden Girls but better."

Once more, Ax found himself speechless. He tried to imagine a group of older women sitting around crocheting boobie tassels and drinking tequila. His imagination refused to stretch that far.

"Do you think everything is okay with Maddy? I mean, we've talked since Friday, but something seems off in her texts. Distant, I guess."

Elowen didn't hesitate when she nodded. "If she had concerns about you, she'd tell me. Communication is important to her. After what she went through with her ex, Maddy will be the first to say something if there's a problem with your relationship."

Communication. Again. Like a light in the Red-Light District of Amsterdam, he should've known what she'd say.

"If I tell you something, private, think you can withhold from sharing the details with Maddy?" Ax paused. Elowen straightened on the barstool. "Nothing bad. It's me, not her, but given your friendship you may be the best person to help me figure out what to do."

"Jack, I'm going to need something harder than water." El called out to the bartender.

They waited for him to bring El a new drink. Ax gulped. His heart beat hard enough to leap out of his chest. His throat dried up like the Sahara Desert.

In New York, Ax didn't have a lot of close friends. Sure, he had his circle, but most of them were acquaintances that he went to the bar with for a drink and talked business, or a football game where they sat in the VIP box and celebrated being better than everyone else. No one had ever been open to talking about anything personal.

Maybe that was his problem. He didn't know how to break down his walls and connect with someone on a soul level.

"You're right about the importance of communication. This is more than that, though. Has she told you anything more personal about us?" Ax asked without looking at El.

The last thing he wanted to see was judgement or ridicule in her eyes.

"Maddy and I share almost everything, but one of us dating is new territory since, other than a one-off date for me, we've not had anything long-term to talk about."

"Gossip is what you two do." Jack snorted as he inched his way up and down the bar.

Pink tint colored El's cheeks. Ax bit his tongue against the urge to apologize. With Daphne he'd apologized every time he spoke, and she didn't like what he had to say. He wasn't the one who made her blush.

"Why is talking hard?" Ax looked to Jack for help, but the old man shrugged his shoulders and moved away from them. The easiest thing to do would be rip the band aid off, but Ax wasn't sure he could do that. Not with the best friend.

"Talking thing is hard for me, too. My parents didn't like to talk to each other. They yelled and then walked away. The only boyfriend I had talked, but more in dictates than joint communication." El turned to face him, more relaxed, no longer clutching her hands until her fingers turned white.

"That sounds awful. I've got some learning to do, that's for sure. I've never been in a relationship where both parties were willing to put in the work. It's kind of refreshing. Most of my experience is that everyone follows the steps without talking about anything. Step one: first date. Step two: sex. Step three: move in. No discussion until the breakup and then it's an explosion."

El chuckled. "Accurate. Hit me with your question. I can't promise I won't overreact, but I'll try not to."

Appreciative of her honesty and willingness to try, Ax gave himself a quick pep talk then dove in.

"We've had two real dates, not counting the picnic. I love hanging out with her. Flirting, touching, talking, and all the other things you do when you're getting to know someone comes easy for us. Except the first time I kissed here the spark dimmed." He stopped to take a breath.

El's brows furrowed. She tapped the side of her glass. "Because of you or her?"

"Me," Ax said. "You have no idea how much time I've spent the last couple of weeks trying to put my finger on whatever is pulling me back. I haven't had any lightbulb moments, or I wouldn't be sitting here talking to you."

Silence settled between them. Each breath came easier with the weight lifting from his chest.

"I understand what you're asking. The thing is, I don't know if I can help you. When you ask yourself what could make you hesitate to let your guard down what's the first thing that pops in your head?"

He gave El's question serious thought. "That everything is perfect and I'm going to screw it up being myself. Which is then followed by what my mother would say about me dating someone who owns a sex toy shop. Then I follow that up with an entire dialog about how I don't care what she thinks, which brings up imaginations of her comparing Maddy to Daphne and everything continues to spiral from there."

"There is a whole lot to unpack there. You weren't exaggerating when you said you've put a lot of thought into this."

Talking to El one-on-one made him feel less crazy about the whole ordeal. Like Maddy, she didn't judge or ridicule him. He understood why they were such good friends—they were alike in many ways.

"Right. What's worse is all of this happened in a matter of seconds. The kiss wasn't bad. I want to kiss her again. At this point, I'm scared of the same thing happening and Maddy won't want to put in the time to wait for me to get out of my damn head."

"You're a smart man, Ax. You thought this through. Maddy will appreciate someone who considers their words before jumping out with no worry in the world. Talk to her. Tell her how you feel. I bet if you can start to let all of this go and enjoy the moment, the kiss will come natural next time."

Maddy's quirky energy drew Ax in like a fly to honey.

"You're right. Have you ever had a crush on Maddy?" El's eyes grew wide as saucers before she burst into laughter. He didn't know where the question came from or why he asked. As much as he knew he should take it back, an apology wouldn't form.

Ax added their friendship to the unacknowledged reasons he struggled to let down his walls.

"No. Maddy is gorgeous. I can flirt with that woman all day long, but I have zero romantic feelings toward her. Maddy is the most bisexual person I know, she's attracted to people no matter their gender, but I stick to cis men. Not that I have anything against anyone else's sexual preferences, that's mine."

"Okay." He nodded but didn't get the instant relief he'd hoped for.

"You don't believe me?" El asked.

"I do. You know, I said I was waiting for the glass box around us to break. If you'd said yes, I think I would've felt better. That would've given me a reason to work through in my head and move on. Now I'm back to square one."

"Talk to Maddy, see what she says. You're getting worked up over nothing. Even though Maddy hasn't text me regaling of your sexcapades and declaring her undying love to you, it doesn't mean she's not happy." El smiled.

"I will. Thank you, El."

"Hello, lovebirds." Maddy's voice came from behind El.

"Hey, beautiful." Ax grinned at Maddy.

"It's the lady of the hour." El turned on her stool. She reached out and hugged Maddy. "Now that you're here, I'm going to head out."

"Ahh. What did I do to run you off?"

El chuckled. "Nothing. I stopped in to say hi to Jack, and you if you were around, and Ax was here. Now it's late, and I need to go home. I'll talk to you tomorrow."

She gave Maddy a quick kiss on the cheek then headed toward the door to leave, but not before she mouthed "talk to her" at Ax.

Ax resituated on the stool until Maddy stood between his legs. He had to make sure he didn't screw this up with his own insecurities. Maddy gasped when he slid his hands up the back of her thighs and over her bottom. She glanced over her shoulder right as Crash rejoined them at the bar. Ax followed her gaze and sent a telepathic thank you to his friend for not watching.

"What are you doing?" Her question came out breathless.

Ax grinned. "Saying hello."

"Umm…" She whipped her head back and forth.

"There's no one paying attention to us. Do you not like being close to me?" Ax moved his hands up her back, massaging her tense muscles with his fingers.

"No. I…" Maddy sucked in a breath. "I like it very much."

"Good. Unless you say no, I'd like to kiss you now." He licked his lips. Maddy bit the corner of her lip and nodded.

Ax leaned forward while pushing her closer to him until they met in the middle. This wasn't a quick peck on the mouth, and he didn't intend to devour her. Following El's advice, he closed his eyes and wiped his mind clean of intruding thoughts. Ax took his time savoring the soft dips of her lip. The sweet hint of chocolate. Maddy moved closer, her fingers dug into the top of his thighs to spread his legs further. She stepped closer to him, moving her hands up his legs and over his ribs until she wrapped her arms around his back, deepening their kiss. His chest expanded. She moaned into his mouth. His cock grew hard in his jeans. They were going to have to take things to next level soon or he might explode.

His mother's voice shrieked in his thoughts. Ax squeezed his eyes tighter and willed the distraction away. The one person who mattered in the moment was Maddy.

"You two need a room. The steam coming off you is making this seat a bit uncomfortable." Crash waved a piece of paper like a fan.

Ax pulled back, resting his forehead against Maddy's. This time her eyes sparkled. She licked her lips and rocked against him, teasing a little more.

"I hate him sometimes," he murmured.

"No, you don't. He's your friend, you expect it." Maddy kissed him again before backing out of his hold.

Crash slipped off his barstool and then sat his drink at the back of the bar. "You two have fun. I'm headed home since I can see our time is up."

He took Maddy's hand in his and kissed her palm. A pang of jealousy ripped through Ax at his friend's smooth move. Crash fist bumped Ax.

"You don't have to go, man."

"Don't take this the wrong way but watching you guys together makes me want to vomit. I'm lonely enough. This pours salt into a wide-open wound."

Ax wasn't sure what to say. Crash was the last man he'd ever expect to admit to feeling alone. Crash left without another word.

"I hope you don't take relationship advice from him very often." Maddy chuffed.

Ax shook his head. "He means well, he struggles to put his thoughts into words. You get used to it."

"I'm glad to see you. What were you and El talking about?" Maddy flashed a finger at Jack who answered with a quick chin nod.

"She helped me start to unravel a problem." Even though everyone told him to talk to Maddy, he wasn't ready.

Their second kiss wasn't a disaster. The air between them sparked with possibility. Ax was not going to ruin the moment by airing out his insecurities.

"Well, whatever it was, I hope she helped. Now, let's get back to kissing." Maddy jerked him off the barstool, smooshing their faces together. Ax pulled back, gasping for air before diving in for more.

El helped in more ways than one.

23

Maddy

Her desire rocketed up ten notches, which was already high after not seeing him for a couple of days. Nana's advice flooded her thoughts. She needed to enjoy the moment and not borrow worry.

"Mmm." Maddy touched her lips. "We should make it a rule to greet each other this way more often."

"I second this rule," Ax murmured against her lips. Maddy tossed her head back and laughed.

She shivered when he brushed his fingers along her back to pull her tighter. When she gasped, he deepened their kiss and slipped his tongue between her lips. Maddy wiggled, sending shocks of pleasure straight to her core. Yeah, she was falling quick for Ax.

"What brings you here?" Maddy asked.

"Came to see you." Ax answered.

"I came over to check on Jack and grab a drink. I still need to close down the store tonight." They'd texted off and on throughout the week but hadn't seen each other.

Worry coated her emotions like oil, causing everything else to slide away. She'd spent the week attempting to decipher each text for an underlying meaning and coming up empty. At least his kiss scrubbed away some of her doubt, replacing it with a tingling need for more.

"Care if I stick around?" he asked. "I could help in the shop. Even though I know nothing about the stock, I can run a register."

She smiled. It would be a lot better closing with someone else than on her own. Maybe they could talk, clear the air.

"I'd love if you did. Let's head over. Maria is ready to go home to her family." Maddy grabbed his hand to lead the way.

They didn't make it ten feet into the store before a customer called out.

"Sir?" the female customer tapped Ax on the shoulder.

Maddy had no idea how she knew he wasn't a customer himself, but she didn't step in. She wanted to see how Mr. I don't know anything about anything beyond vanilla sex did.

"Yes?"

Maddy and Ax turned to face a couple standing next to a shelf of lava lamp vibrators. Lola ordered them on a whim, but they weren't selling. They decided to put them on sale. A few customers even came back with comments about how hot the lamp got if they left it on too long.

"This is a vibrator?" The female handed Ax a box with a purple, lava lamp appearing, vibrator.

"Ummm...yes. I think so." Not the best answer.

Maddy bit her lip to keep from laughing.

"Does it warm like a lamp?" the male asked.

Ax read the back of the box. When he didn't find the answer, he glanced at Maddy. She grinned and tilted her chin in a small nod.

"Yes, it does," he answered with more confidence than when they first walked over.

"We have a limited number. What's on the shelf is what we have, and I doubt we'll restock. If you want one, I'd recommend getting it now. Before you ask, no we haven't tested that one. The reviews are okay. Most complain that it doesn't get warm enough or gets too warm when left on too long. Others have complained that the vibration isn't strong enough." Maddy jumped in to save Ax from any more questions.

The man looked at his wife with wide eyes. Maddy smiled, she knew that look of fear and insecurity.

"This might be a little more than we're looking for. What would you recommend for a couple that wants to be a bit more adventurous, but hasn't tried anything yet?"

"Oh. I can take this one." He lifted onto his toes like an excited child.

"You've done this?" the man asked, more interested in what Ax had to say than Maddy.

Even though it wasn't unusual for men to be more comfortable talking to other men, it still pulled a growl from Maddy. She was knowledgeable, even more than Ax, and wouldn't guide them in the wrong direction.

"Nope. Not yet. But this lady," Ax pointed at Maddy. "Teaches a class on how to spice up the bedroom and she has some fantastic suggestions.

Her heart expanded. Ax wasn't taking over. He was propelling her to the top of the food chain. Acknowledging her expertise and she fell a little more because of it.

"How often are the classes offered?" the lady asked.

"Every other week right now, but as we garner more interest, they'll be available more often. If you'd like, I can sign you up for the next 101 class. Or you can go on our website, there's an online registration as well." Maddy smiled. Teaching had become one of her favorite things to do.

That afternoon's conversation with Lola collided with the joy of talking about the workshops. If she took over as owner that could mean she'd have to find someone else to teach. There were multiple obligations to owning two businesses. She filed away the concern for later. She'd figure out a solution that allowed her to enjoy a career and keep her grandparents' legacy alive.

"If you don't mind, I'd love to go ahead and get into the next class. I bet they fill up fast." The woman pointed to Ax. "Can you show him what you were going to recommend?"

Ax nodded then led the man to the pre-made sample sets Maddy and Lola put together each week.

"Come with me." Maddy led the lady to the counter, excited because she'd encouraged new people to attend the classes and Ax was selling merchandise.

Maria met them at the register. "You care if I head out?"

"Don't mind at all. Ax and I will hold down the fort. Give the kids hugs for me." Maddy smiled at Maria. She'd been a regular at Pinks before Lola offered her a job seven years ago. Maddy hadn't met anyone more excited to sell sex toys than Maria. She was a perfect fit for the shop.

By the time Maddy and her customer were done with their discussion, and she'd signed the couple up for the next one, Ax and his customer joined them. They paid for their items and left with a smile.

The next hour flew by. Ax helped as much as he could and Maddy laughed when the questions made him blush more than the customers. He hadn't been exaggerating when he said he was bland as could be when it came to sex. A younger group of customers came in asking for butt plugs, lube, and some condoms. Maddy had to jump in and help when Ax spun around in circles trying to find the plugs and couldn't.

While she started counting down the drawer, Ax leaned against the counter, his arms crossed over his chest, pulling the sleeves of his shirt tight against the lean muscles. Her mouth watered. They'd agreed no sex until they were ready and had more time to develop an emotional connection. She hoped it wasn't too much longer. Maddy could've kissed him again, but her body wanted more. Lots more.

Maddy closed her eyes and dreamed of him pressing his lips to her clit and humming. It would make her body twitch with pleasure. Her fantasy continued as he moved from her clit to the inside of her thigh, pulling the tender skin with his teeth. A little pain, but not too much. Maddy shivered. His hands were big, callused, rough in the all the ways that made his touch perfect as she imagined them rubbing up and down her legs. His thumb passed over her clit. A slight touch with the right amount of pressure to ratchet up her arousal another level.

She gripped the drawer of the register and bit her lip, hoping he didn't catch on that she'd wandered off to fantasy love island. After lifting up on her arms to kiss Ax's neck, she bit down pulling a groan from him. He applied more pressure against her clit, his fingers thrust inside of her finding her g-spot with ease.

"Oh my gouda." Maddy moaned.

"Everything okay?" Ax pressed against Maddy's back.

His surprise touch, in real life not her fantasy, made Maddy jump a foot in the air. She clutched her neck. Tiny beads of sweat dotted her forehead. Her panties were soaked. The daydream blurred the lines between reality and fantasy.

"Yep. I'm great. Perfect. Fine." Maddy stammered, picking up a stack of five-dollar bills to count.

She refused to look at Ax. If she did, he'd no doubt have questions.

"Tell me about the meeting with your lawyer," he said.

With a sigh of relief, Maddy put the fives back in the drawer and pulled out the tens.

"I told them I wanted a product recall and refund to anyone who already purchased the item. Noah and I came up with a dollar amount to ask for as well."

"How much?" Ax moved to the other side of the counter where Maddy could see him.

She sighed as her heartrate returned to normal and the heat radiating through her body cooled. Frustrated that the cravings and slickness between her legs hadn't dissipated.

"Our initial request was a hundred thousand. Noah said it was a reasonable number. I'm willing to drop it some, but not a lot." Ax nodded but didn't say anything more. Maddy continued. "I guess now I wait and see what they counter with. Do you think they'll follow through with my requests?"

"Truth? No. They'll want to negotiate lower terms when it comes to requiring their product recall and refund all those who purchased. The other contingency they may argue is your amount for restitution."

"Why would they argue that? All I asked for was the total of my hospital bills and the difference in what I would have made working full-time. Some people would have asked for hundreds of thousands."

"That's true, but they're going to fight it because they don't want to accept responsibility and pay what you're owed. I would advise you not to budge on that number. Compromise in other ways to redirect from the restitution. In fact, if they push back, you could suggest a higher payment and remove the request of the recall and refunds."

The drawer clicked shut. Maddy considered Ax's opinion. It made sense. Even on TV the ones being sued never took the first offer. There were always counters and negotiations.

"What kind of law did you practice?" she asked Ax.

"Criminal. To my father's disappointment, I became a prosecuting attorney. He wanted me to work at his law firm, defending the criminals, but I had other plans. Justice has always been important to me."

Interesting, but not surprising. Ax cared about people. She'd watched him at the picnic. His coworkers loved him. Their families loved him. In the time they spent planning, talking to local businesses, Ax had been nothing but a gentleman. Yeah, the idea that he'd taken the good guy's side made sense.

"What about the people who don't see justice because they're accused of crimes they didn't commit?" She decided to play devil's advocate for a minute.

"They are half the reason I wanted to prosecute. Some people get the wrong end of the stick when it comes to crime. As a prosecuting attorney, I made it my job to ensure the bad guys were put away, but if there was someone wrongfully accused, I did my best to help them as well."

It shouldn't have surprised her that Ax attempted to do right on both sides of the law.

"How does that work? Do you try and find the right person?" she asked.

"Nope. Can't do that. I didn't throw the cases either. It was important to me to provide the right evidence to the jury, so they could make informed decisions. While I'm sure I didn't stop every wrong conviction, I figured if I was honest about the evidence I presented and the questions asked, if I didn't try to manipulate things to my favor, then I did the best for both sides of the case."

The man was perfect, and his ex-wife was the worst kind of sort to have taken advantage of that. Maddy cringed.

"El may have mentioned you wanted to talk to me." She hoped changing their conversation would help her mind calm down.

"Yeah, I did. I've been thinking."

Maddy's body tensed. If he'd talked to El and there were decisions to make, then her worry hadn't been for nothing.

"Are you unhappy?" she asked.

Ax shot up from his spot where he leaned on the counter. He waved his hands in the air. "No. Not at all. I'm beyond happy with us. This is better than I ever imagined."

"All right. What's up?" Maddy chewed on her nails.

She watched his throat move when he swallowed. Once. Twice. Ax looked at her then at the case in front of him. A need to reassure him grew, but she waited. Ax would say what he needed to say on his own time.

"First, I should apologize for an awful first kiss. You deserve better and, in my head, it was better...until it wasn't." He dragged his hand through his hair. "The kiss tonight is what our first kiss should've been.

"Don't beat yourself up too much. I wasn't complaining." She grinned and winked at him.

Ax was one of the few men she knew who were willing to apologize and own up to their mistakes—although that wasn't a mistake where Maddy was concerned. She breathed a sigh of relief. If this was all that he'd talked to El about, they were fine. She left the security of the register and moved to his side.

"After talking to El, I accepted a reality I wasn't ready to see. You're the first person that I've been with who I chose. Our relationship is different than any I've been in before because it's more meaningful to me. The connection we have is stronger than any I've experienced. If I'm being honest, that scares me. If you feel me pull away or put up a wall, please don't run. I'm trying to figure this out as we go."

"What do you mean, I'm the first person you've chosen to be with?" Asking the question did something inside Maddy.

The idea that he chose her should've given her confidence, made her stand up straighter. Instead, Maddy curled her shoulders forward, afraid of what he meant. It wasn't a feeling she liked but didn't know how to avoid it either. Natasha had enjoyed threatening Maddy with breaking up or divorce to get her way. As much as Maddy wanted to say she'd healed from the emotional abuse she'd experienced, that wasn't true.

Ax ran his hand down his beard. One of his ticks had to be playing with his hair—on his head or facial. He'd done it more than once while they talked.

"I'm not sure how to say this without sounding needy. As a teen and in college I dated a few women but stuck to one-night stands because it was easier. If I brought someone home, my parents had questions." He stopped to take a few breaths.

Maddy watched as he rolled his head to one side then the other. So far, her panic hadn't faded. She understood about the one-night stands, but it didn't explain his ex-wife, or his choice to date Maddy.

"After the first couple of girlfriends, I stopped dating. Mother orchestrated that fateful reunion between Daphne and me, and we ended up married," he continued.

"Okay, but you could've said no. In essence, you still chose Daphne. I don't understand how I'm any different?"

"Setting up a profile on Blind Love wasn't an urging of my mother's. There is nothing about our relationship that will get me into a better law firm or help me become the frontrunner of a political campaign. Dating you was my choice with no ulterior motive."

Anger began to replace panic. Maddy wasn't sure if it was warranted, but she didn't want to deny her feelings either.

"Are you happy with us? Are you okay that you won't get anywhere by dating me?" Maddy emphasized not getting anywhere. "I know you said this is more meaningful, but I'm trying to figure out why. If I'm overreacting, I'm sorry."

Ax cupped her face between his hands. He wiped away wetness from the corner of her eye.

"I'm over-the-moon happy with us. The whole point of what I said was that I don't want to date to climb some ladder of advancement. That's what makes you special. You are the most amazing woman I've met. Because of you, I want to be better. I want to own my mistakes, tell my mother to fuck off, and bring meaning to my life with something I enjoy, not what others have planned out for me." He leaned forward and kissed her.

This was slow. Deliberate. The love in his touch made her knees weak. Maddy gripped his forearms to keep herself standing.

"While I still don't understand how you feel, I don't want to lessen anything. Part of my quick reaction is a result of my ex-wife. You make me want to be better as well. Thank you."

He tilted his head to the side while still holding her face in his hands. "Why thank you?"

"Being with you is making me face some hard truths about my relationship with Natasha. Not in a bad way. Just hard."

He chuckled. "I think we've proven that's true for both of us. It's crazy what happens when you meet people who understand you and connect with you on a level you didn't know what possible."

"I lo—" Maddy froze. She'd almost said she loved him. "I like to think you're right and we're going to learn more about each other. Connect on a deeper level."

"Yes, we are. Now, let's finish up here and head home." Ax kissed her once more, then let go.

Immediately she missed his touch and wanted it back. He was right, they needed to close up shop and go home.

24

Maddy

Ax: I'd like to take you to a dinner theater _for our date this week._

Dinner theater didn't sound fun at all. She wondered if that was something he had done in New York with his family. Portland had dinner theaters that catered to the elder population—all the more reason not to go. Maddy did Broadway when forced to. Not dinner theater.

Maddy: Nope. Pick something with more spunk. I prefer enjoying the show, not sleeping through it.

Ax: Ouch. Is there somewhere specific you'd like to go?

Maddy: There's a cabaret in Portland I've wanted to go to for a while now. I'm not sure how you feel about a sophisticated strip show, but I say let's expand our horizons and see what it's all about.

The plan was perfect. She'd get to visit a cabaret and Ax would get the joy of watching women stri—maybe.

Ax: When's the show? I'll make dinner plans if you get tickets. I know it's my date and I'll pay you back, I can't get away from work right now to order them.

Maddy: You're in luck. It's tonight, and why did you wait until now to plan our date? I checked and there are tickets *available. It starts at 9 pm. Can you get dinner reservations? I can meet you at The Knob by 6.*

With her fingers crossed, Maddy pulled up the show's website and started the order to purchase tickets. As she finished putting in her card information her phone dinged with a new notification.

Ax: All right. Arrangements are made. I'm picking you up at 6.
Maddy: Can't wait to see you. What should I wear for dinner?
Ax: Anything you wear will be perfect. The restaurant isn't super fancy.

Maddy grinned. She had the perfect outfit that she'd been waiting to wear. A blue satin, off-the-shoulder top paired with a high-waisted skirt in pale yellow flowy fabric covered in cute Polynesian designs. Her red low-heeled sandals rounded out the look. The outfit was perfect for the Copacabana show they were going to see.

After Tuesday night, they'd text a few times, but work kept them too busy to see each other again. She hoped both of them could set their fears aside for the night and enjoy their date.

Maddy stepped out from behind the door of Pinks. Ax sat at the bar talking to Jack, providing her the opportunity to enjoy the view. He'd worn the darkest blue jeans with a blue plaid shirt and navy-blue vest. Maddy's mouth watered. He'd rolled up his sleeves to his elbows. The flame tattoo on his arm on full display.

"Good evening. You look stunning." Ax whistled. He ogled her in from head to toe.

He swept his hand in an arc toward the door of the bar. Maddy's smile deepened with her happiness.

"Night, Jack," Ax called over his shoulder.

"Take care of her." Maddy didn't turn to look at the older man, but she knew he'd watch them all the way out the door.

"Not to be rude, but can we take my car?" she asked. "I know this is supposed to be a surprise, I'll even let you drive, but getting in and out of your truck in dresses isn't always the easiest thing to do. Besides, my car looks better."

She snickered and winked at Ax.

"You're going to trust me to drive your baby?" he asked.

"Yep. You get to drive this beauty and walk into wherever we're going with me on your arm. Are you going to complain?"

The man would've been an idiot to say yes. Maddy wasn't ashamed to admit she looked good.

"Hmm Jack and Dean might have a few words for me if I try to argue." He took the offered keys from the tip of her finger, then pressed his lips to the top of her hand. "Let's go."

They climbed into the car. Since Maddy's 1967 GTO was a true beast, she lifted the center console and slid all the way across to sit right next to Ax. Twenty minutes into the drive, she began to fidget. Ax rested his hand on her leg.

"What's wrong?" he asked.

"Nothing." She huffed. "That's not true. I'm anxious. Tonight could be a lot of fun, and I guess I'm hoping neither of us let's our past or our heads get in the way."

Ax squeezed her leg. "Thank you for saying something. My stomach has been tied up in knots worrying about how the night will go. How about we both agree to smack some sense into the other person if we go off the rails?"

Silence filled the car while Maddy gathered her thoughts. She played with Ax's fingers, tracing her own up and down their length.

"I can go with that. We also have to promise not to get mad if we don't agree with their assessment." The second part was more for Maddy than Ax.

At least she was trying to be more conscious of her own actions and emotions.

"Deal." Ax laced their fingers together then squeezed her hand.

Maddy breathed a sigh of relief. They were going to have a great time. Copacabana and dinner with a hot guy who wasn't afraid of sharing his feelings and willing to work on putting their relationship first.

"Where are we going to dinner?" she asked.

He pulled off the interstate toward downtown.

"I decided to go somewhere different, at least for me. They have Swiss specialties like goulash, escargot, and a dish called Emince Zurichoise."

"Emince Zurichoise? What is that?" She butchered the name of the dish.

"I believe the online menu said it was pork sautéed in a mushroom cream sauce. Also, they can adjust most of their menu items if anyone needs to. I hope it's as good as the reviews say."

Warmth filled her chest. A few weeks back her greatest worry was getting to know Ax. One thing she'd learned was that he paid attention. He cared about her likes and dislikes.

"This place sounds adventurous. I like it," Maddy said.

The rest of the evening passed without more joy-dampening conversation. They ate more food than she'd had in months. She threatened Ax that he'd have to carry her out of the restaurant if they didn't skip dessert.

The show turned out to be better than a spruced-up strip tease like she'd expected.

"That show was not at all what I expected." Maddy hadn't stopped moving since they got in the car to head back to Podunk. She kept shifting in her seat, bouncing up and down.

After the lights went down and the show started, Ax had moved his chair right next to Maddy. The man teased her with his wicked fingers all the way through the first act. During intermission Maddy thought she'd have to go to the bathroom to take care of her overwhelming need for an orgasm, but he wouldn't let her leave the table.

They spent the half hour talking about nonsense things like how penguins mated for life. She debated between laughing at him and hating him. His knowing winks and deliberate lack of touch made her lean toward hate for the moment.

"I had no idea a 1970's gender-bent comedy about showgirl relationship drama could be that damn sexy." Ax chuckled.

"Lola was my favorite. The music and dancing were professional quality, which surprised me. I've never been to anything like this before." Ax nodded, his focus on driving more than looking at them.

She wished they'd go home together for the night. Waking in the morning, sharing a bed, brought on happy butterflies in her stomach. The first time for sex was always nerve wracking. If that was anything like the rest of this relationship, it would turn out to be better than she'd imagined and a lot less stressful.

Maddy leaned her head against the back of the seat. Her arm fell across Ax's lap.

Cold air brushed over the top of Maddy's breast, which peeked out from the blue satin shirt. From the corner of her vision, Maddy watched Ax lick his lips.

25

AX

Maddy's skin looked soft, lickable. On a whim, he reached over and traced along the edge of her top with the tip of his finger. Rather than smack him for being brazen she ran her fingers through his hair, grasping the ends and holding on.

"Is this okay?" Ax's voice dropped an octave.

His muscles clenched as he waited for her permission to do more. All of their talk about not being physical, and he'd been the one to make the first real move. Then again, ever since Maddy brought up sex at their cooking night that was all he could think of—not that it was an excuse. More a sign of his weakness when it came to his attraction to her.

"Yes." The huskiness of her voice made his cock swell.

"Touch yourself, Maddy. Show me what you like."

Handing out orders wasn't something Ax did in the bedroom. During the first class he attended that Maddy taught, she mentioned how some people liked being directed when it came to sex. The thrill of testing her theory set his body on high alert.

From the corner of his eye, he watched her follow his instructions, first unbuttoning her top then pulling her breasts from beneath the cups of her bra. Ax inhaled too fast, which led to a coughing fit as he choked on air.

"Everything okay?" she asked.

"Yep. Keep going."

Maddy took her nipple between her fingers and tugged. Her head lulled against the seat. Ax glanced over. He had to pull the car over before they caused an accident. Maddy groaned. She reached over and cupped her hand over the bulge in his jeans.

"Ax." His name fell from her lips.

"Son of a bitch." Ax jerked the car back into their lane. Maddy fell against him, her breasts pressed against his arm. "Sorry about that."

Maddy giggled. The click click click of the blinker as the car slowed and turned offered a distraction for Ax as he exited off the highway.

"Where are you going?"

Ax growled. "Keep up with the boob lesson. I'm going to get us somewhere safe so I can watch and then take care of you."

"What if I want to take care of you?" She reached for him once more, this time rubbing her hand up and down his cock.

The seat dipped as she shifted onto her knees, facing Ax.

"If you have the energy after I'm done with you, then I will be at your mercy." He pulled into the furthest parking spot of a highway rest stop.

"That sounds like a challenge." Maddy popped the clasp of her bra.

Ax leaned forward and took her nipple into his mouth. Maddy ground her knees into the seat. He ran his hand across Maddy's stomach, up her ribs, to massage the breast his mouth wasn't on. Maddy's breathing turned erratic while his cock throbbed between his legs. Maddy reached between them to pull her dress up.

"No panties." Ax groaned.

"I'm surprised you didn't figure that out with all the teasing you did during the show." Maddy spread her legs to reach her core.

At first Ax considered stopping her, but he'd wanted to know what she liked.

"Mmm. I suspected but wasn't sure. Why don't you lean back and give yourself more room." Ax bit the soft inside part of Maddy's breast, next to the breastbone where she'd find more pleasure than pain.

"That mouth of yours is torture." Maddy didn't do as he said. She leaned back on her hands, offering her chest to him.

"Tortured? Is that what I'm doing? I thought you were enjoying this."

Bantering back and forth during foreplay was new to him. Missionary position with the lights off didn't invite talking or having any kind of fun if he considered his past experiences. Ax found that he appreciated the change.

Being with Maddy was as close to having sex for the first time again would ever be, like he was a virgin all over again.

"Enjoying isn't a strong enough word for the way my body is screaming for your attention right now. It's torture because I'm on the edge of coming, but not there yet." Ax started to apologize, but Maddy shook her head. "Don't apologize or change anything. This is perfect. Remember, it's been more than six weeks since I've had an orgasm. The first time was never going to take long. Now that you found a semi-secluded spot, we can have some fun."

Maddy leaned forward and pulled Ax to her. She kissed him on the forehead, along his jawline, then started a path down Ax's neck to his shoulder where she bit and sucked with more force than he expected. Ax swallowed. He gripped Maddy's hips hard enough he worried about bruising her.

The seat dipped when Maddy moved once more. This time leaning back like he'd proposed earlier. The pull between them was too hard to let go, so Ax followed. His breathing ragged. His cock hard enough to hurt. He feared the simple act of unbuttoning his pants would make him come.

"Now who's being tortured?" he whispered. Laughter filled the car. "Six weeks is way too long for someone to suffer without some type of pleasure. We're going to remedy that right now. Pull your skirt back up."

"Are you comfortable?" he asked Maddy.

"Minus the fact that I can feel my clit throbbing. The door doesn't make a great pillow, but I'm not going to complain if you have plans to take my mind off where we're at. Is now a good time to tell you I've never had sex in a car?"

Ax slid his hands under Maddy's skirt, lifting it as he made his way over her thighs. A smile turned his lips up at her declaration. Despite his limited experience, he would be the first to give her an orgasm in a car. His new challenge wasn't to wipe away the sabbatical, but Ax vowed to make it the best orgasm she'd ever had.

Every brush of Maddy's skin took Ax closer and closer to his own climax. The heat coming from the woman lying beneath him. The look of adoration in her gaze. Ax teased his hands up and down Maddy's legs. Closer to her core then further away. He rocked his hips with each pass.

"Do not get off in your pants. No matter how drained you make me, I'm going to take care of you tonight." Maddy scolded.

"Be careful. I wouldn't want you to make a promise you can't keep. Like you said, it's been a minute since you've found pleasure." Ax lowered himself between Maddy's legs.

Maddy sat up as much as she could to give him more room.

"You don't have to do that, Ax. It's too tight a fit," Maddy said.

He ignored her. It didn't matter that his knees were pressed against the door. The pain in the morning would be worth the sound of her reaching ecstasy from his mouth. He lifted her legs over his shoulders then pressed his mouth to her core. Maddy's head fell against the window.

"Okay. I'll shut up. You can stay down there as long as you want." Maddy moaned.

He moved his tongue along the split between Maddy's lips, dipping the tip in and out as he went. Maddy lifted her hips against his mouth. Rocking faster against him. Her groans grew louder. Maddy dragged one of his hands up to her breast. With their fingers laced together, she massaged one side then the other. She guided him to her nipple. He pinched the bud between his fingers, tugging the way she showed him.

"Close," she hissed. Maddy rolled her head to the side.

Ax never let up. He worked one finger into Maddy, then another. He rotated his wrist around, pushed in and pulled out. He lifted his head and pressed his lips to the inside of Maddy's thigh.

"Give it to me, Maddy. Come for me," Ax commanded.

Maddy's muscles tightened against his fingers. She thrust her hips high then brought them down with enough force to rock the car. Over and over as she rode her orgasm. Ax covered her scream with his mouth. They may have been hidden at the back of the parking lot, but there was no need to increase the risk of them getting caught.

"Holy macaroni," she said as soon as she came back to earth. "That was...wow. Give me a couple of minutes to recover. That deserves a second round with you as the recipient."

"I could watch you orgasm all day long. In fact, when we go to New York I believe I'm going to make sure that happens. A whole day of sex and orgasms. That's my plan."

They'd agreed to wait the three weeks to make any decisions. Once again, he'd jumped the gun. Ax was batting a thousand with his patience. The woman did things that turned him inside out and his brain needed a jumpstart to keep up.

Maddy brushed her finger over his brows. "Stop worrying. You didn't upset me. After tonight, a day of sex and orgasms sounds like heaven. If you can repeat this in New York, then I won't argue."

"In this, I'm happy to oblige." Ax kissed her. Reveling in the joy of achieving his goal.

Maddy's eyes drifted close. Her hair fell in waves down her shoulders. Even though he was still hard, he wouldn't make her give anything in return. As promised, he'd worn her out and that was enough for Ax. Later, at home in his shower, he'd recall what they'd done. Wrap his hand around his dick and imagine hearing her scream once again. His hand would tighten around his cock the same way she'd tightened around his fingers before reaching the pinnacle.

Ax straightened Maddy's skirt. He found a blanket in her back seat and laid it over the top of her then adjusted himself and settled in behind the wheel once more. They had a long drive home to Podunk.

Dinner. Cabaret. Orgasm. The recipe for a perfect date.

<h1 style="text-align:center">26</h1>

Maddy

As it had been every other Saturday for the last six months, the library parking lot was full of cars and buses dropping off the seniors for "Dance, Dance, Saturday." Nana flipped the cover down on the mirror in the sun visor and made a smacking sound with her lips.

"All right, I'm ready to swing my hips and show those men how I brought sexy back."

Maddy rolled her eyes. "You have got to stop with the videos, Nana."

"Those are the greatest thing since the television. They give me plenty of ideas for the shop. You should watch more instead of condemning me. In fact, you might have learned how poor of a product that dildo was if you'd done more reading. Maybe then you wouldn't have all those damn stitches to keep you abstinent for the next six months." Nana crossed herself as though she were Catholic, even though she claimed not to like organized religion at all. "Rest in peace."

Madelyn scrunched her nose. "Rest in peace?"

"Yes, of course. Your poor vagina's dead. Aww hell, Madelyn, you'll have cobwebs for the doctor to clear out before they remove the abstinence rule."

"Nana! The doctor gave me the all clear. No more denying myself pleasure."

"Thank goodness for that." Nana clicked her tongue.

After rolling up the windows, she opened her door. "Can we go inside and annoy the old men rather than me?"

Maddy walked around the car and opened the door for Nana.

The older woman laughed. "Oh honey, I don't annoy them. They all love me. The thing that annoys them is the rejection when they try to come home with me. Your grandfather may be dead, but I sure don't plan to let any other man in my bed."

Once Nana eased herself out of the car Maddy took her arm in hand and guided her into the library. "You know Papa wouldn't be upset if you did find another man spend time with."

"No, he wouldn't, but I sure would." Nana patted the top of her hand. "Close your mouth. Tell me how things are with that sexy lumber hunk."

"Nana. His name is Ax. You could use it occasionally. I'm sure he'd prefer that over lumber hunk."

"Yes, yes. Maybe he would, but I like lumber hunk. Did you get over your concerns?"

Maddy shook her head. Lola did whatever she wanted regardless of what others said. "Yes, we did. Last night we went to the cabaret in Portland."

Her cheeks warmed as she recalled what happened on their way home.

"That explains the post-orgasm glow. Excellent news. Now let's dance."

The local library was one of the largest Maddy had visited. Back in New York she'd spent some time working in a library, and while it was large in size, it didn't have anywhere close to the number of books as this one. The place was one big open rectangle with shelves and shelves of books. In the middle of the room was a help desk with six computer stations that were always staffed by a library worker.

Considering the size of the town, it had shocked her to find a library big enough to hold almost everyone in town for special events.

Madelyn smiled when they turned left to the event area. Two rows of five long tables had been set up with at least fifteen chairs along each side.

"What's going on, Nana?"

A wide smile made wrinkles bunch under her eyelids. Her eyes glowed with excitement.

"You didn't check the calendar, did you? It's taco Saturday. The staff loves us enough to have food catered in, then we're salsa dancing the hour away." Nana waved to a few of the library workers as they inched their way to the tables, stopping to hug and say hello to all of her friends.

Maddy took the purse from her grandmother's arm and pulled out a chair for her. "Well, you have fun. I'll be back in a couple of hours. Call me if you need anything."

Her grandmother's skinny fingers wrapped around Maddy's forearm. "You should stay. At least eat with me. It'll be fun. I'd love some of my friends to meet you."

"Nana, I've got things to do."

"Pshaw. What could you need to do? It's eleven-thirty in the morning. Pinks is closed for inventory and the bar doesn't open until two. I'm guessing your boyfriend is sound asleep in bed recovering from the excitement of last night."

"Nana, do you know how to salsa?"

"Of course, I know how to salsa. How do you think I snagged your grandfather?"

"With your good looks and witty banter at the bar?" Maddy shrugged. Papa loved to talk about how he stole Nana from men at the bar.

"Aww that's because Delbert never liked to admit how much he loved ballroom dancing." She put lettuce and tomatoes on her tacos. Nana's gaze wandered across the room; a smile made the creases at the corner of her mouth more pronounced. "Our families grew up together, but your grandfather courted me in secret. We used to go to these restaurants and bars with live bands and dance floors. We had to be careful. Got thrown out of more than one place. But he loved to dance, making his happiness worth the risk. No way would I have turned him down."

A rock caught in Maddy's throat. The love her grandparents shared came through in Nana's memories. The wisp of romance when she said his name. A twinkle of mischief as she no doubt recalled their escapades.

Not for the first time, Maddy regretted spending years away from them. Even if her parents took her to New York. She couldn't blame them for everything. At thirty-five Maddy'd had plenty of time to return on her own.

The two of them ate in silence while people shuffled into the library and made their way to the food. The octogenarians had more friends than she did. As for the romance her nana had lived...well, Maddy came to peace with her limited possibilities a few years ago. Love in Nana's younger days was a lot different than now.

"Lola, you're lovely as ever."

When Maddy glanced up at the newcomer she bit the inside of her cheek. Hard. The man rested his palms on the table, a cheesy grin lit up a face full of wrinkles highlighting his years. He winked at Nana.

"Why thank you, Dean. The rainbow is a nice choice."

By rainbow she meant the long strands of hair dyed the colors of a rainbow and shellacked until they stood straight out from the crown of his head like a unicorn horn.

"Ahh, yes. The kids call me extra. But they don't argue anymore." He smoothed his weathered hands over the sides of his bald head. "Who's the beauty you brought along today."

Maddy held out her hand. "I'm Madelyn. Lola's—"

"My granddaughter." Nana interrupted.

"I should introduce my grandson to you. He could use a woman as pretty as you to keep him in line."

Her cheeks warmed at his compliment. Dean. Ax said his adopted grandfather's name was Dean.

She stood from her chair and tucked her purse under her arm. "Nana, I gotta get my errands done. I'll be back at two to pick you up. Dean, it was nice to meet you."

Errands was her nice way of bowing out of the day. While it was fun watching everyone on the dance floor, Maddy was still riding the high of the night before and wasn't in the mood to sit around in the library all day.

Nana took Maddy's hand in hers. "All right. I guess I won't be able to convince you to stay. Dean is a great partner, you know. I'm sure he'd be happy to teach you a few moves."

She guffawed and covered her laugh. "I'm sure he could, but I need to get stuff done if I'm going to work at the shop tonight."

"Have fun. I know we will."

With a quick kiss on the cheek, Maddy headed to the front of the library. Dean stepped in her path before she made it out the door

"You can't resist my charm." He grinned. "One dance. Then you can put in a good word to your nana for me. I've been trying to convince her to go to dinner with me for months. She always has excuses."

It didn't surprise Maddy that Nana had turned him down. The older woman enjoyed flirting but refused to spend time with another man. She'd said "death do us part" meant the separation was temporary and she wouldn't disrespect the love of her life that way. They'd agreed to disagree on that theory.

"One dance." Maddy conceded and placed her hand in his after setting her purse and keys on the table next to them.

Dean offered a quick nod before tugging her onto the makeshift dance floor.

A few turns across the floor confirmed his abilities. They glided around almost as if dancing on air. She giggled, recalling a bittersweet memory of her papa. He loved to let her stand on his feet and sweep her across the living room as Nana leaned against the door jamb to the kitchen, swaying her hips to the music.

"This is how it should be when you're in the arms of someone who loves and cares for you. When you find the right man, Madelyn, he'll carry you through this world. Not because you can't, but because he will do everything in his power to protect you."

Her papa's voice in her thoughts brought a tear to her eyes. Dean gave her a knowing smile.

"Thank you," Maddy said.

"You're like your grandmother. A strong, independent soul. It's an honor to dance with you," Dean replied.

They continued to soar across the space, small as it was. Maddy relaxed into the music and lost herself in the moment. When it ended, she bent to give Dean a kiss of appreciation on the cheek. They stopped next to Lola, who'd found her own partner.

His back faced her, giving Maddy a chance to ogle his lean build and sculpture-perfect ass. Her fingers curled at her side, a desire to dig into all that muscle made her insides tingle.

"Leave it to my grandson to find the second most beautiful woman here to twirl around the room with." Dean gave Maddy a wink.

Nana's dance partner glanced over his shoulder. Maddy's breath caught in her throat causing her to choke. A sudden coughing fit had her doubling over.

"This is your adopted grandfather?" she asked between coughs.

Warm, callused fingers wrapped around her arm. "Yep. In the flesh. He talks about Lola all the time. I can't believe I didn't make the connection."

"Maddy," Ax said a few seconds later. His whisper rumbled all the way to her core.

"I should have known you were my Maddy's lumber hunk. Dean, you didn't know he and Maddy were dating?"

"That's a shame." Dean clicked his tongue. "Guess I won't be using my famous line on you."

"More like infamous," Ax muttered.

Maddy didn't want to ask. No doubt it would've been better not to ask. When it came to willpower, she had none.

"What line?"

Ax shook his head. Nana rolled her eyes. Dean went to Maddy's side, leaned in and with a sultry voice said, "You wanna wrestle?" He paused and winked. "Naked?"

Heat infused Maddy's face until she was certain anyone in the vicinity would recognize her embarrassment.

"Umm. I'm not...that's not...well—"

Dean burst out laughing. Ax rushed to his side, taking the older man's arm in his hand to keep him standing upright.

"For chrissakes, Dean. That's a new shade of red for her. You're not right, old man. Not at all."

Ax followed Dean back to the table. Maddy didn't know if she should run while she had the chance or stick around. Ax was supposed to be at home sleeping off the night before, not at the library for Dance, Dance Saturday. The question she couldn't answer—why seeing him made her nervous. Her stomach had first date jitters. The palms of her hands sweat like her wedding day.

"Maddy, why don't you sit with me, and we'll let the lovebirds do some dancing." Ax waved her over.

"Not lovebirds. Dean would prefer it be that way, but I promised my heart to Delbert. I intend to keep it that way until the day I pass, and we find each other again. I'll be a fairy of course, but he'll know me when he sees me."

"Aww, as sweet as that is and as much as I respect your marriage, I'm going to soften you up. I lost my love twenty years ago. Doesn't mean I don't enjoy a quick roll in the hay."

"Ax is right. The two of you should go on and dance. I mean, you don't want to waste the time away, right?" Maddy's limit of hearing about octogenarians hitting the sack together had been reached.

She was open to sex, but there were some things she didn't need details for. Nana's stories of old were enough. While the Lola and Delbert walked each other to the middle of the dancing area, Maddy pulled out a chair next to Ax.

"I'm glad you're here." Ax kissed the top of her hand.

"I'm surprised you're here. I figured you'd want to sleep in. We got back into to town late last night and it's the weekend after all."

"This is more important than sleeping in. Dean means the world to me. Like I said, he's my adopted grandfather. If I'm his way out of the home, then I'll be there for him. Although, admittedly, you wore me the hell out last night. Not to be crass, but my dick was raw from the number of times I came."

Maddy tossed her head back and laughed. The flurries in her stomach eased. "Should I apologize?"

In all her history, she'd never been sorry when the guy didn't get off. In her mind, it wasn't always tit for tat. Sometimes she didn't get off and he did, and other times it was the other way around. There was no need to discriminate based on gender either. For Maddy, it was all about the moment. Even though she'd said she would finish him off last night, Ax held true to his word. She'd been too tired to even move away from the hard pillow of a door.

"Do you want to?" Ax asked.

She shook her head. "Not even in the least. I mean, we could've taken care of you, too."

"Could have, sure. You fell asleep before I finished kissing you, which I'm not complaining about. Besides, you can make it up to me in New York."

He smooshed his lips together. "We made it through the evening without letting our heads get the best of us."

His observation hit Maddy square in the chest. Maddy held her head in her head. "You're right. You did a pretty good job of keeping me distracted. Is that why you spent most of the show touching my legs?"

Ax took her hand in his. "Would you believe me if I said I didn't realize what I was doing? After one touch of your soft skirt, I didn't want to stop. Blame it on the hormones and lack of physical intimacy I suppose."

Maddy shook her head. She believed him. After what they'd done in the car, even as tired as she was, leaving him once they got to the bar had not been high on her list. More than anything, Maddy wanted to go home with him. Crawl in bed and wake up wrapped in his arms.

"Yeah, let's use the hormones excuse. I mean, I'd say we acted like horny teenagers, but it's good to let go of adulthood expectations every once in a while, right?"

They spent the rest of the dance class watching the seniors as they made their way around the dance floor. Some of them stopped to eat more tacos. Maddy ate until her stomach ached. Turning down delicious tacos was like begging for a curse or bad luck or something.

After they went their separate ways, Maddy admitted most of her worries were without cause. Ax cared about her and the more time she spent with him, the more she realized she was falling in love. Nana told her to enjoy the moment. Doing that helped her see how many more moments like this she wanted to have.

"Ax is a wonderful man. Dean loves him like a son." Lola started her commentary before Maddy pulled out of the library parking lot.

"He loves Dean. Talks about him all the time. Respects his advice. I had no idea he was such a player. Why don't you and him spend more time together?" When Maddy grew old she wanted what her grandparents had.

Lola and Delbert shared so much love. There wasn't a scenario where Maddy could imagine her grandmother wasn't lonely. Her continued rejections didn't make sense.

"I'm too old for relationship drama." Nana waved her off. "A man wouldn't appreciate the time I spend crocheting or working at Pinks."

She laughed. Nana didn't admit very often that she no longer worked at Pinks. When she was up there, it was more to socialize and check-in than do actual work.

"Who said anything about a relationship? Maybe you'd enjoy going to play darts with Dean."

"That's not my style. You may be my chauffeur, but other people take me places when you're working. I go to Dean's place at least a couple of times a week. How do you think we know each other so well?"

Maddy wasn't surprised by Lola's visits to the nursing home. She had plenty of friends who lived there.

"All right. I won't bother you about it anymore."

"Thank you. Now, did you have fun today?" Nana pulled a ball of yarn from her bag to roll it back into the right shape.

"Yes, I did. Ax and I enjoyed watching you and Dean dance. It was entertaining. If you hadn't made me stay, I wouldn't have spent the afternoon with him."

Nana winked at Maddy. She should've expected the unexpected.

27

AX

Sunlight filtered through the curtains of his bedroom. Without thinking, Ax jerked his arm to cover his eyes, bumping into a soft, warm body in the process. Ax cracked open one eye and smiled when Maddy looked up at him with a sleepy gaze. To Ax's delight, she'd text him after Dance, Dance Saturday for a game of putt-putt. The ache in his chest from missing her lessened when he knew it wouldn't be a week before they saw each other again.

The cherry on top came when she agreed to join him at the cabin. They'd spent the evening watching movies and talking about nothing and everything all at once. Rather than risk her safety driving home, he offered for her to stay with him for the evening without any expectation of something happening.

"Morning." Maddy ducked her head into the curve of his neck.

"Morning, beautiful. How did you sleep?" he asked.

"Better than I expected. Your bed is huge. Is this some kind of custom mega king? I'm kind of impressed." Maddy traced her nails across Ax's chest.

"Sorry to disappoint. It's nothing more than a standard California King."

"Oh, I'm not disappointed. This is still the biggest bed I've slept in. Hope you're not upset when I don't go back to my place." Maddy bounced out of bed. "Be right back."

When she walked back into the room she had her hair pulled into a ponytail and his apron hanging from her neck.

"It's six o'clock on Sunday morning. Where do you find this kind of energy?" Ax yawned.

"Lazy mornings aren't my thing. I thought I'd make breakfast e." She crawled back into bed and snuggled next to him.

Excitement charged the air around them.

"Breakfast in bed? I like the sound of that." Ax stretched his arms over his head.

She smacked him on the chest. "Too messy. Maybe one day I'll serve you in bed, but that is not today. If you can find the strength, we could go for a hike after breakfast. Maybe take a picnic lunch with us." Maddy moved to a cross-legged sitting position.

Ax's eyes fought to close again. The woman had more energy than most everyone he knew. A morning person he was not.

"You want to go for a hike before ten a.m.? You are too much. I'm struggling to keep my eyes open." He yawned a second time.

"Would you be more willing if I said I'd fix whatever you want?" Maddy asked.

"Anything I want?" he asked.

"Of course. I can't promise it will all taste good, or be edible, but I'll do my best." Maddy smiled.

Despite his stomach's deep rumble, what he wanted was a cup of coffee. Black. Hot. Extra caffeinated.

"A good pancake or waffle doesn't disappoint, but I'm afraid I don't have anything you'd want. My cabinets are full of oatmeal, breakfast bars, and milk."

"It's okay. I'll go to the store to get everything I need. You stay here and wake up some more. Have some coffee. Shower. Do whatever you do on Sunday morning." Maddy leaned over and kissed him on the forehead.

He sat against the headboard, his hands behind his head, watching Maddy. This was a great way to wake up. One he'd be happy to repeat over and over again.

"All right. If I'm asleep when you get back, wake me up when the food is ready." He laughed when she skipped out of the room.

A couple of hours later, Maddy returned to the house with arms full of groceries. The menu consisted of almond raspberry French toast, eggs, slices of honey ham, bacon, and bowls of blueberries, raspberries, blackberries, and huckleberries. Ax hadn't gone back to sleep, too curious to see what she'd return with. He helped set the table and make sure everything was ready, including fresh coffee.

"Breakfast is almost ready. I hope you're hungry." Maddy called out when he went to his room to freshen up.

On the way back to the kitchen, Ax turned off the TV. He hated eating meals with the TV on. Unless his family had company over, they never ate at a kitchen table when he was kid. Then his mother would make sure it was set to perfection. His father at the head of the table with everyone else spread out on both sides.

Maddy leaned against the wall thT separated the small living room from the kitchen, her arms crossed over her chest. Ax smiled.

"Gotta say, I wasn't disappointed that you don't have dad bod under the plaid shirt and well-fit jeans you like to wear." Maddy went to him. She hugged him around the waist.

He buried his head in the curve of her neck. She smelled of spiced apples and cinnamon.

"You know, the myth about hip indentions I've read about in romance books and seen in the movies. The ones that peek out over a man's loose-fitting jeans?" Maddy licked her lips. "That's not a myth. You proved that last night."

"Smells delicious." Ax adjusted the waist of his pants.

"Thank you. Coffee refill?" Maddy grabbed a full mug of coffee off the counter and held it out to him.

Ax took a sip and groaned.

"This is incredible. You're a goddess, Madelyn Begay. I could get use to coffee made by you every morning."

Her cheeks pinkened, making Ax even harder. He wasn't sure he'd make it through breakfast at this rate.

"Let's eat. Hold off on the goddess talk until you've tasted the food. You may change your mind." Maddy winked. "Your house is incredible. I love how small it is. Cozy."

The cabin was a perfect example of a tiny house. The front door opened into a great room with a breakfast nook and kitchen to the right. Ax's bedroom was down a short hallway with a bathroom across the way. The entire house could be viewed from the front door.

He wiped the corner of his mouth after taking a bite of French toast.

"This is good. Where did you learn how to cook? I mean, the eggs are fluffy and creamy all at the same time. This toast melts in my mouth and these berries...please don't tell me you picked these fresh. Because they taste like they are."

Maddy chuckled.

"No, I didn't pick them. You're close. The farmer's market is open on Sunday, which is why I stopped to get the berries from there. I love fresh over store-bought. Also, I prefer to support local vendors when product is available."

"Well, it's delicious. My cabin is my haven. Daphne's father was a smart man. Nine hundred and fifty square feet of pure peace and solitude. No city sounds or lights to bother me."

"Is there an upstairs?" she asked.

It was an A-frame house with a small, round window near the apex of the roof.

"Mm. Yeah. There's a loft up there, but I don't use it. It's got a desk and a large open area if I wanted another living room or game room. The ceiling is pretty short though. I thought about putting a Christmas tree up there this year that lights up the window."

"You decorate? I wouldn't have guessed that." Maddy took a large bite of her meal.

"It's one of my favorite holidays. In New York we used the finest decorations, but no one was allowed to touch them. Daphne spent hundreds of dollars every year buying new decorations. I asked her once why we couldn't reuse the ones we bought the year before, and she told me it would be frowned upon."

She shook her head. "That's ridiculous. Part of the fun is the tradition of decorating with the old and adding new memories. As bad as my parents fought, Christmas was the one holiday we got to enjoy without the arguing."

"We argued over tradition versus society expectations. I hated it. Grew to hate Daphne for it. Even my parents had traditions. At least we hung ornaments on the tree. She and I never even had a celebratory ornament for our first house or first anniversary. I'm thankful we didn't have kids."

At the mention of kids, Maddy stiffened. "Do you want kids?"

He didn't miss the sigh when he shook his head.

"Don't sound so relived," he laughed. "It's okay. I don't want them either. Kids are incredible, I love spending time with my friends' children, but to have my own...yeah, I'm not at all interested. There are far better parents than me."

"It's not that I don't want kids. With two engaged parents the workload would be easier to handle. My future plan hasn't included kids. When Natasha and I got married my family gave up hope. Then we divorced and the hope returned. Mom's first question when I talk to her is if I've met a young man who will give me babies."

Ax spit out his coffee.

"Wow. I've heard stories of women dealing with those kinds of things. Never imagined they were true."

Maddy nodded. "True and not an exaggeration."

They finished their breakfast with more childhood stories and annoying tidbits about their families. Their conversation was as easy that morning as the night before. When they finished Ax volunteered to help clean up.

As they washed dishes, Ax's mind conjured images of weekend breakfasts together. The two of them could take turns cooking and cleaning. A future.

"Dean mentioned something yesterday. He said you still haven't made a decision about Pinks and The Knob." Ax put a plate away.

He didn't want to pressure Maddy, but he wasn't going to let her off the hook without a solid reason why she didn't want to take over for her grandmother. Dean filled him in on Lola's concerns. It seemed she hadn't shared with Maddy how hard it was for Lola to go to the store and not work anymore. She wanted to hand it off before it was too late. Lola needed to know that her babies were in good hands.

Maddy's eyebrows furrowed. "Nana's been talking to Dean?"

"Yeah. She's concerned. He told me not to talk to you or pressure you, but I'm not sure your grandmother's being honest. She doesn't want you to feel bullied into make a decision." Ax drank from his mug. He had to tread lightly or risk overstepping and upsetting Maddy.

"I see." Maddy turned in on herself. "Bullying would get faster results than what I'm giving her. Since I can't seem to make up my mind, it may be better to let her sell them. At least it would be a decision and she could get to work finding the right person for the task."

He didn't like seeing her defeated without understanding why.

"Pretty sure that's not what she wants. Will you talk to me about the hesitation?"

"Sure." Maddy stretched on her toes to kiss him on the forehead. "Fair warning, there's no big secret that I'm harboring."

Ax didn't say anything. It wasn't that he didn't believe her, but Maddy had talked about her failed businesses before. He remembered how she mentioned wanting to carry on the legacy but not knowing how since she wasn't any good at sales. Instead of talking, he listened.

"Sometimes when I doubt my own decisions, talking them out helps. If it makes it easier, imagine I'm not here and you're voicing everything in your head to solve the puzzle."

They finished drying the dishes before moving back to the table. Maddy sat across from him with her head in her hands. He waited.

"Ninety percent of the time I'd say my confidence is not great at best. The remaining ten percent, it's non-existent. Teaching is something I'm good at. Standing in front of the classroom I believe in myself. Even though my education is in business, and I don't have any mentors in the sex industry, I've discovered that I'm good at research and delivering everyday knowledge for those who can't find it, or don't know how to."

Ax nodded. He'd sat in on enough of her classes to understand what she meant. Talking about sex came naturally for Maddy. As a result of her confidence in delivering information, those who attended didn't question her background or how she came into the knowledge of what she taught.

"You know what you're good at and what you're not. What's the next step to make the best decision for you?" He wanted to help guide her to the answer rather than tell her what to do.

"I get hung up on the next step. What I'm good at won't help me as the owner of Pinks and The Knob. If I give up teaching because I don't have the time, then I'm afraid I won't have anything to bring to the table and both businesses will fail."

The pieces clicked together for Ax. Maddy's problem wasn't that she didn't know what she was doing, but that she didn't have the right skills to be successful.

"What if you make a list of the things you think you're good at. Then make a list of ideas to improve the store, which, by the way, is a skill all on its own. Identifying strengths and weaknesses of businesses are qualities most people don't have. They are the skills that make business owners the best." He drank the last of his coffee while Maddy processed his suggestion.

"That's not a bad idea," she said. "What about a list of areas I'm not good in?"

The chairs at his kitchen table weren't the most comfortable. Ax went to the couch to finish their conversation. Maddy commandeered the recliner. She popped the footrest up, pushed back, then laced her fingers behind her head. "This is comfortable. I should get one."

Ax chuckled.

"Look at it as areas of opportunity, not things you're not good at. If your skills in sales aren't strong, then think of ways to work around your own limitations. Owning a company doesn't have to mean that you do everything. You have contacts, like El, who would be great to collaborate with." Inwardly, he cringed. He hadn't talked like this since New York.

Even though it made him seem less intelligent, Ax liked that his crew didn't expect much from him in creativity, innovative thinking, or his ability to debate a topic. The last year had given his brain a much-needed rest.

"I'm impressed. You've got some solid suggestions. Thank you." Maddy leaned forward to sit up. "This is more comfortable."

He had more suggestions but held off on giving them. So far, his plan worked. There was no reason to ruin her progress or make her think that it was all his idea. A light lit behind Maddy's eyes.

"One more, then I'll let this go. With the success of your classes, what would you say to starting a podcast? Weekly episodes, or maybe monthly. Keep them to thirty minutes with teasers for what's coming. With enough followers you could start making money off of it. Then there's the return off customers who come in for the shop, or order items online because of the podcast."

"A podcast sounds like fun. While I love the idea, how do you even start a podcast? I'm not bad with generic social media, but that kind of stuff and videos, yeah, not good at those." Maddy chewed on her nails.

Ax found himself grinning. Ideas twirled through his thoughts. Since he'd attended two of Maddy's classes, there was no doubt a podcast would work well for Pinks.

"Talk to El. Let her help you," Ax said.

"Yes." Maddy leaped out of the recliner. "I could produce the content and El would produce the actual show. Using the notes and prep work I do for class she should be able to guide the conversation. We could even throw in my toy reviews—if I ever get to do another one."

Ax grabbed her and pulled her down next to him.

"TV?" Maddy asked.

"Remote is on the table next to you. We can watch whatever you want, as long as it isn't some sappy love story." She slapped his stomach but didn't deny his claim.

Ax absently rubbed his thumb over her hand. He relaxed to watch the movie she'd settled on. Yeah, he could handle waking up with her in his bed, eating breakfast together, and spending a lazy Sunday watching TV before they got ready for the next week.

28

Maddy

She'd never been scared of sex. Standing in the middle of their lavish hotel room while Ax retrieved the rest of the bags, Maddy's hands shook, and her body tensed at the idea that she'd share a room with him. A few weeks ago, they had a fun night in the car. Emotions pressed in on her chest as the fight or flight instinct kicked in—she didn't know why.

Maddy drooled over the window seat overlooking Central Park. Their hotel wasn't the swanky Carlyle. Ax had surprised her with a room at One Hotel Central Park. She loved the cozy, rustic furniture. She wasn't afraid to break a thousand-dollar lampshade or get marks on the bright white carpet. Instead, they provided a blanket and pillow for her to curl up in the window and stare down on the park where she'd spent a lot of time in the City. A place she could go with a book and blanket to find an hour or two of peace. Even at night, with the lights brightening the sky, so different than Podunk, Maddy's aura calmed as she centered her focus on the open space.

The click of the door pulled her from her thoughts, but she didn't move. Ax brushed her neck with his lips. Goosebumps spread across her arms.

"You're happy," he whispered against her skin.

She snuggled into him, asking for more. Now that he was there, sharing the space with her, everything settled. Her body, heart, and mind came to the same decision. Ax was her person.

"Yeah, I am." Maddy chuckled.

Ax wrapped one arm around her shoulder then slid the other under her knees. With ease, he lifted her off the bench seat and carried her to the bedroom. Maddy tucked her head into the crook of his neck, placing kisses across the sliver of skin peeking out from under his T-shirt. She loved the way his muscles rippled under her touch. Not tensed, but not quite relaxed.

"Mmm, you can do that some more," he grumbled. "How about I show you how happy I am."

Ax shifted his arms, pulling her closer to him. Before he walked into the bedroom, he nipped the tip of her nose.

"Weirdo," she joked.

"Yep. I may not be as well-versed in these things as you, but I can still deliver an A+ performance." Ax gently sat Maddy on the edge of the bed.

She toed off her shoes.

"Strip," he ordered.

"You need a bit more authority in your tone to make me follow commands." Maddy rolled her eyes and leaned back on her hands. "You could strip then let me devour that gorgeous body you've honed to near perfection."

"Near?" He crossed his arms over his chest.

She tapped her chin. Ax uncrossed his arms to flex his muscles. He grinned at her inspection, then offered a few of his left side.

"The butt muscles could use some more definition." Maddy crooked a finger at him. "Come over here and let me double-check my evaluation."

Ax turned and stepped backward to the bed. Maddy reached out and squeezed a butt cheek.

"Hmm. That wasn't much of a test," he joked.

"This feels firm to me. You still haven't stripped. For the sight test, I need an uninhibited view."

"Tease." His mega-watt smile dampened Maddy's panties.

The gleaming promise of debauchery was one she'd hold him to. Maddy pulled her T-shirt over her head before tossing it to the floor.

She inched her way to the head of the bed, her arms outstretched to either side. "Show me the goods, lumber hunk."

Ax shook his head and laughed. "You have too many clothes on. If I'm showing off my ass, then we're going to make this fair."

"I expected you to finish taking them off." Maddy stretched her arms over her head. "I'm kind of tired from the flight."

He cocked his head to the side before reaching for the top button on his jeans. Ax didn't do a slow striptease. In one swift move, he undid the button fly and kicked his shoes to the side of the room. Maddy covered her eyes with her hand.

The foot of the bed lowered. She peaked out from between a small opening in her fingers. Ax placed one knee on the bed, his hands braced on either side. The man sported muscles upon muscles. His skin was tanned from the sun, but he didn't have short sleeve tan lines. Everywhere was gorgeous bronze. She wanted to taste him. To smother him in kisses.

Maddy purred. Her fingers ached with the need to touch him.

He turned away once more, lifted up on his knees, locked his fingers behind his head, and shimmied his waist. The muscles of his back flexed, but his butt was solid as steel. Too turned on to care, Maddy ran her finger along the edge of her panties.

"Keep up the show, I'll just take care of myself back here."

"That's not much of a threat. The night in the car taught me a lesson. I like watching you find your own pleasure."

Maddy rolled onto her hip horizontally across the bed. She bent one knee with the other leg straight out. The devil on her shoulder convinced her to slide her hand down the front of her panties. Ax grabbed her ankle to jerk her toward him.

"Eek," she squealed.

He slid himself along Maddy's body. As he neared her knee, he rotated his fingers until they brushed the inside of her leg. With his free hand, he slid off her panties and then added them to the pile of clothes on the floor.

Maddy brushed her free hand up and over his hip before bending over to taste the smooth skin of his stomach, nipping the skin to leave little red marks. In the past she'd dated a few men and women with kinks, but none of them stirred her blood the way Ax managed. Foreplay had been a quick lead in to the big show at the end. With Ax, she wanted to take her time working him into a frenzy—herself too.

Ax pulled away from her touch.

"What's wrong? Do you want me to stop?" She reached for Ax.

"Never, sweetheart." One finger slid between her folds, followed by a gentle press of his lips. "If you play too much then you're not going to find pleasure before I come. That's pretty much unacceptable in my playbook."

Maddy's body reacted to each kiss, lick, and touch of his lips and fingers. Like a ratchet, her muscles tightened.

"That...wow."

"Mmm." The word vibrated against her skin, sending her arousal near its peak. "Yes, yes it does."

Ax eased one finger in, he brushed over her g-spot for a split second. His lips surrounded her clit while he added a second finger to her pussy. The man was incredible. Slow, methodical, perfect.

"Ax. Holy hell. That's good."

He sucked hard on her clit while pressing against her g-spot at the same time. Maddy's ass launched off the bed as she reached climax and screamed. Her hips rocked back and forth, pushing his fingers deeper. Ax held her down with his free arm across her waist and obliterated her senses with his tongue.

"Oh. You're killing me." She panted. "It's too much..."

Her heart exploded at the same time as the orgasm. Ax cooed and whispered sweetness in her ear.

"Ride it through, beautiful. Focus on my hands."

"Want you," she begged and reached for him, found his hard length and gripped him hard.

Two more orgasms later, he came up for air. Maddy's chest heaved and her lungs burned.

"Your classes have taught me a lot about paying attention to your body's reactions. I should thank you for that."

She smiled. "One thing's for certain, I won't need cucumbers anytime soon with you around."

"Let's hope not." Ax slid his way up her chest. Their kiss was hot, hard, and fast.

Maddy wrapped her hand around his dick. He was hard and smooth like a worn piece of slate. His skin warmed beneath her fingers. She stroked him up and down. The kiss turned more intense along with her grip. Ax spun them to situate her on his lap.

The velvety skin of his cock pressed into her ass, a promise for what was to come. She stroked the shadow of the beard framing his chin.

"Not going to take long, sweetheart." He gasped.

"Good. Then we can take time with round two."

Maddy trusted Ax to pay attention to her body. She owed him at least one orgasm before they tried anything else. Ax slid down, never breaking their kiss or her hold, until he was flat on his back. She rested on her heels, her fist wrapped around his dick, her legs tucked against his thighs.

"Do what you want. I'm just enjoying the moment." He put his hands behind his back and closed his eyes.

Maddy grinned, sure he expected nothing more than a hand job. Without letting go, she lifted up and angled her hips forward. They lined up like they were meant for each other. She rubbed up and down on him, but not letting him enter. Maddy lifted on her knees, waited a few seconds, then lowered down until the tip of his cock split her open. The wetness from her earlier orgasms made it easy for him to fit all the way in, filling her to the max. Ax's eyes popped open.

"You sure?" he asked.

The most they'd done up to that point was oral and some finger play. Once more, he surprised her by making sure she consented to everything they did. This was the first time he let her take the reins, and there was no chance she'd back down.

"This is what I want. Before you ask, I'm on birth control." His hips rose just a touch, sending Maddy into the first level of ecstasy once more. "Yep. Exactly what I want."

When he rocked a second time her head fell back. She rolled forward, placing her hands on his chest to use for leverage. Maddy rode him hard, her thighs gripping his side. Her core muscles clamping on his cock. She bit her lip, holding off the first flutters of another orgasm.

"I don't think I can wait, Maddy."

He wasn't wrong, three more strokes up and down and she felt the pulse of his impending release. One more slow lift off, and an even slower slide back down and she was right there with him.

"Oh yeah," she whispered.

Ax's body tightened, his cock pulsed deep inside Maddy. Together they came with a groan. Maddy fell onto his chest.

"A marathon of sex is guaranteed." He wrapped his arms around her back. "How do you feel?"

She laid on top of him for a few minutes without answering. Drifting down from the haze of sex, Maddy smiled. "Like I could fall asleep with you buried deep inside me."

"I don't know any other women who would make that proposal." The rumble of his laughter vibrated against her chest. "As much as I love that idea, I need some water, and you could use some too. We need to stay hydrated for our next round."

Maddy chuckled. She rolled off to the side. Ax left the room without putting any clothes on. She took full advantage of his nudity, admiring the dips and curves of his muscles as he walked. If there was a reason to slow down time, it was this. The pure bliss of finding the man she loved was something she wanted to experience for as long as possible.

29

Maddy

She turned in front of the mirror once more. Ax had reserved an afternoon at the salon for a massage, manicure, pedicure, and updo. He'd even arranged to have her outfit for the evening delivered from the hotel. As planned, he still hadn't seen hers. The evening was going to be perfect because they were together.

Maddy couldn't wait to watch Ax's expression when she walked into the lobby in a few minutes.

"I don't know where you found this, but it is gorgeous," the stylist said.

"I got lucky. The local tailor in Podunk came across a retro pattern and wanted to try it out. When we showed up to talk to her, she'd just finished. It fit like it was designed for me."

The black mermaid dress was floor-length, off-the-shoulder, embellished with gold sequined leaf and flourish print. A thin layer of black mesh fit over the dress from the waist down. Maddy adored the retro styling mixed with sophistication. Simple and elegant with enough stretch she could still move. She'd chosen a pair of gold leather slingbacks that peaked out from the hem of the dress to add a little more sparkle.

The stylist decided to leave her hair half up and half down. Since Maddy had always wanted a waterfall braid, the stylist obliged. She took the time to spiral curl her hair as well.

From head to toe, her look was perfect.

"Thank you, Zena. This is..." Maddy carefully wiped the corner of her eyes.

"No way. Do not cry and mess up my masterpiece. Your makeup took longer than your hair. You're magnificent, Maddy. Go blow them away."

She gathered her things and left for the hotel with enough time to run up to the room and put everything away before joining Ax in the lobby.

"Wow." Ax's shock rang through the word.

Maddy had just opened the door to their room when he spoke.

The man standing in front of her was different than the one she'd fallen for in Podunk. Gone was the plaid-wearing logger, and in his place was the cleaned-up socialite Ax had once been. He wore black tuxedo pants with a deep purple velvet tuxedo jacket and crisp white shirt. A black satin bowtie completed the outfit.

"I never asked, but should I call you Easton or Ax tonight?"

"Considering you're one of the few who know me as Ax, you may be more comfortable calling me Easton. In truth, I prefer Ax, but I answer to both."

Maddy smiled. "Good because—and don't take this the wrong way—I much prefer Ax over Easton. It fits you better. At least the Ax I know. Easton is...pretentious."

"Yes, it is. Enough about me. I'm the luckiest man on earth right now. I have a breathtaking woman to show off to the world." His eyes appraised her from head to toe. "My mom's going to have a hard time holding on to the spotlight tonight once we arrive."

He took her hand and lifted her arm into the air for a spin.

Maddy preened.

"Oh yeah. I approve and then some. Please tell me it will be okay to rip this off tonight."

"There will be a lot of clothes ripping when we get back here. An evening spent next to you and unable to lose control will have me on edge." Maddy lifted on her toes to kiss Ax.

The barely-there touch of Ax's lips against hers made Maddy question if she'd imagined the kiss.

"Good. Because I'm going to want you out of it quickly." He winked at her.

"Do you think your family will approve? I know it's not a ball gown, but those are uncomfortable. This is elegance and comfort in one very nice package."

"Whether or not they approve doesn't matter. Your confidence in that outfit is the most important thing. Let me ask, are you invincible?"

"More than. I feel like I could take on a horde of nasty socialites of the female variety." Ax extended his arm to Maddy.

"That is all that I care about."

They walked out of their room arm-in-arm ready to take on the world. In all the balls, award shows, and fundraisers she'd attended, none of the dresses she'd ever worn felt as beautiful and desired as she did with Ax.

In the last couple of years Maddy had found herself again. She didn't need Natasha or her parents. Or even Ax's family to give her their seal of approval. As he'd said, all that mattered was how she felt. Right then, Maddy could take on the world.

Once they arrived at the hall where the fundraiser was taking place everything she'd known and lived for years came flooding back. It was like riding a bike. The handshakes and the fake smiles. The quiet elevator music paired with whispers from the attendees, no doubt discussing the who's who list of those who'd been invited.

More than once, she caught a gasp when Ax walked by someone then murmurs of speculation about where he'd been and how horrible his divorce had been. Many times they followed with questions about who she was and why she looked familiar.

Unsure how to reply, Maddy nodded and kept moving. Ax led her through the maze of people. Each new person he introduced was another name she soon forgot. They'd been there less than an hour and met at least fifty people.

The family table had been set at the front of the room beneath the podium. Later Ax's cousin would give a speech, and his mother would announce the winners of the silent auction. First, they had a five-course dinner with the main course choice of shitake fried rice or pan-roasted filet. Maddy chose the filet. With her luck fried rice would end up down the front of her dress and they'd find it later.

Nothing like a midnight sex snack. She snickered at the idea. Ax gave her a side-eye that said he'd ask questions later.

By the halfway point of the meal, Maddy's anxiety reached its peak. The night was too smooth. No one questioned her or asked them how they met. Ax's ex-wife was in attendance, but she hadn't approached either of them. Ax and Maddy interlocked fingers and shared stolen kisses. Nothing was secret. Socialites were nosy people, as usual, Maddy waited for the other shoe to drop.

"Easton, we're glad you made it home for the event." Eve's smile was sickeningly sweet.

Maddy's stomach clenched. She gripped her fork in anticipation.

"I wouldn't miss this. It's for a cause I support, and the funds are needed. Everything is perfect. You've outdone yourself this year, Mother."

Eve Sutherland thrived on compliments and Ax laid it on thick. His abundance of praise didn't sit well with Maddy. Each word dripped with fakeness. Under the table Ax reached for Maddy's hand. The simple touch helped her focus. She needed to heed Ax's advice and try not to borrow trouble.

"Madelyn, how did you and Easton meet?" Eve turned her attention to Maddy.

"It's funny, my best friend El set us up in a way. She's a marketing consultant and asked me to test an application for a new client. I swiped right and matched with Ax."

At the mention of his nickname, Eve grimaced. She cleared her throat and rested her fork on the plate. Maddy's foot tapped against the floor. Her gut screamed for her to run, warning her the night was about to take a turn she wanted to avoid.

"Well, that's interesting. What is it that you do for a living? Daphne, his ex-wife, is very active in the community. She loves raising money to help those who need it. In fact, she's the one who planned this year's event."

"Is that so? She did a fine job. It's funny, I'm quite active in the community as well. Of course, Podunk is smaller than New York City, but I feel my work is just as important." If the woman wanted to play games, Maddy was more than willing.

She squared her shoulders in anticipation of the next question.

"Oh. Do you plan events for Portland or Seattle? Easton hasn't talked about your activities too much."

No, she imagined he hadn't. Maddy smiled. Ax started to speak up, but she cut him a glare warning him to stay quiet. This was between her and his mom.

"I teach sex-positivity and other educational classes in a boutique sex toy shop and help run the whiskey bar next door. Recently I dipped my toe into party planning at Ax's suggestion."

Maddy took pride in her ability to maintain some semblance of control.

"Maddy," Ax whisper-scolded her.

Maddy leaned over to whisper, "It's not like I shared the topics of my classes. If you're not going to stand up for me then sit back and chill. I've got this under control."

The reality of his spineless reaction hadn't set in yet, and she was grateful for the reprieve.

"That is an interesting story. I can't help but ask why Easton would be interested in someone open about sex? That's such a private activity and my Easton is not that kind of person. I'm curious what kind of lifestyle he's found himself coerced into."

She didn't miss the way his mother emphasized my. As though she had any control over a grown man.

"Mother," Ax ground out. "Now is not the place. I haven't been coerced into anything."

Eve patted her son's hand. A silent reprimand that he cowed to by sitting back in his chair with a huff.

"Mrs. Sutherland, you're very astute and yet not at all in tune with your son. Podunk is not New York. We don't do things the same way out there as you do here. Our goals don't center around who we need to impress in order to make it up the next rung on the social ladder."

"You would tarnish my son's reputation?" Eve's hands flailed in the air. She turned on Ax. "Why would you do this to me?"

Heat rushed up through her toes. Her body flushed vibrant red. Maddy shoved her chair back and stood. This woman was worse than she would've thought possible.

"With all due respect, Eve. We're not doing anything to *you*. He and I willingly entered this relationship and have no intention of following a fad." Maddy placed her napkin on the table and pushed back her chair. "In fact, I'm inclined to say I'm falling in love with your son. You may not like that, but lucky for us, you don't get to have an opinion in our lives."

It was time for them to leave. Eve would never accept their relationship and Maddy didn't care. The fundraiser, as far as she was concerned, was over. She glanced down at Ax hoping he would join her, but he hadn't made a move to leave. A few seconds passed before Ax placed his napkin on the table.

"Easton, if you walk out of here, I will take personal offense. This family does not behave in this manner. You will be cut off if that's the choice you make."

After everything they'd been through, Maddy thought her threat wouldn't touch him. In fact, he'd followed his mother's directions and stayed in his seat.

"Maddy, come on. Don't cause a scene," he whispered.

"Unbelievable. You're no better than the rest of them. I guess I'm the fool in this situation." With nothing left to say, Maddy turned and exited the building—alone.

30

AX

"Maddy stop," he yelled across the ballroom.

She didn't stop. Ax tossed his napkin in his chair and went after her, ignoring his mother's reprimands. Her threat had frozen him in his seat. It was the biggest mistake he'd made.

"Madelyn," he called to her again when he made it to the foyer. His voice hitched.

Ax watched as Maddy paused, looked over her shoulder, then pushed open the door to leave. He didn't miss the shimmer of a tear falling down her cheek. His knees buckled, making him stumble and nearly face-plant in the hotel lobby. He'd made her cry.

If he'd stood up for her. Told his mom to shove off, left with her when she looked at him for help, then she wouldn't be running away without him.

As fast as he could in dress shoes that weren't made for running, Ax chased after the woman who held his heart in their hands. If she crushed it without guilt, he wouldn't blame her. He didn't think for a second that he could call El and ask for help. She would never take his side or try to get Maddy to give him another chance.

Maddy stopped at the curb to hail a cab. Ax lifted his head to the sky and thanked the gods.

"Go back to dinner, Easton." Maddy's words were flat.

Another punch to his gut. She never called him Easton. He cringed at the name leaving her lips. That stung more than pouring salt in a wound.

"I'm not leaving you alone. I'm sorry for what my family did to you. For what I did. We're in this together and I should have stood up to her."

"How could you sit there? To make it worse you treated me like a child."

The hitch in her voice tightened his throat. He'd never cried in front of anyone, but her pain hit him so hard he wasn't sure he'd be able to hold back right then. Ax raised his shaking hand to touch Maddy. More than anything he needed the contact to know they'd be okay. Maddy stepped away from him.

"Does your mother's approval mean that much to you?" she asked.

"No. It doesn't. I froze. Forty-five years old and I froze like a child. There aren't words to explain how sorry I am right now. You deserve better than I gave you tonight." His eyes burned with unshed tears. A lead weight of guilt pressed on his chest until each breath was shallower than the last.

The battle he'd been fighting was over. He'd lost. His head got in the way and Maddy wasn't able to smack sense into him.

"Yes, I do. I've lived the socialite lifestyle, Ax. We've talked about how much we both hate the way they treat people. One day back in town and you slide right back into the role. That hurts more than everything else."

He shook his head, pleading with his eyes that she'd understand his momentary lapse of judgement. She'd known him without all the glitz and glamor of New York.

The glare he received froze the blood racing through his veins. Ax shivered.

Maddy shook her head. Her hair fell down the sides of her face. Ax wanted to brush it out of her eyes but couldn't stand for her to pull away from him again. His nails sliced the inside of his palm.

"You've turned me inside out, made me a better man. I can't lose you. Please, give me a chance to make this right."

"I've worked hard to get where I am. No, I don't have the ideal job. I can't say that I'm a part of the community in the same way as Daphne. That's okay with me, though, because that's not me. This is me. Sex. Love. Experimentation. If you can't handle that, then why ask for the chance." Maddy pulled her shoulders back.

Even with hurt deepening the brown of Maddy's eyes, she was the embodiment of fierceness. Confidence. Determination.

His chest ached. He should've been protecting her. Providing her with the safety she deserved. Maddy was right. He was a coward.

A taxi came to stop at the curb and Maddy climbed in without another word. Ax stood, motionless, watching the yellow car drive away with his heart in the backseat.

He didn't follow. He said he'd be by her side, but when faced with the choice of his family or her, he'd chosen his family.

"Well, at least you avoided too much heartache. Can you imagine if you'd married that girl?" Eve's voice shrieked from behind him. "How do you think a relationship with a sex worker would play out? She's using you for your status."

"Don't start, Mother." He clenched his hands at his sides. Anger lit a match inside of him, melting the ice left by Maddy.

Doubt and questions fought for attention in his head.

"There's no reason to be rude, Easton. This is a blessing. You can move home now and sell that godforsaken cabin."

Ax ground his teeth hard enough his jaw spasmed with pain then turned to face his mother.

"Enough. Because of my stupidity the woman who's made me realize how much joy there is in life left without me. I don't want to sell my home. I don't want to come back to New York. Go back to your dinner. We wouldn't want you to ruin your precious reputation."

One scolding from his mother and Ax lashed out at the last person he should have taken it out on. Maddy had been nothing but supportive without the expectation of receiving anything in return. She'd both put up with his mother's silent, and not-so-silent, judgment.

He'd repaid her with a scolding and let her leave without having her back. Sure, he'd tried, but not very hard. At the end of the evening his mother still manipulated his decisions. One glare, one raise of the eyebrow and he became a coward.

He'd make it right between the two of them, but he had some work ahead of him.

31

Maddy

It took her half an hour to get to the Old Owl Club. A speakeasy in Greenwich Village that had been around for years, but few tourists knew about it. Locals came for the craft beer. She'd been in a booth at the back of the place for an hour. Maddy watched patrons come and go. Most newcomers greeted the bartender like regulars. The scene would've been relaxing if a constant replay of the evening didn't fill her thoughts.

The whole dinner turned into one big clusterfuck.

A half-empty bottle of beer balanced between her thumb and forefinger. Maddy rolled it back and forth across the table. A half-empty glass of amber liquid sat in front of her.

"Are we going to talk about what happened?" El's voice came through the phone.

She'd called her best friend ten minutes after entering the bar. She'd sat in the booth silent except for ordering rounds. Even then, Maddy preferred to hold up a finger in the server's direction rather than verbalize the request. El didn't push her to talk. When she answered, Maddy told her she'd left the dinner alone and just needed to know someone was there for her. She didn't want to talk.

It seemed El was done with the silent treatment.

"What's there to say? Ax chose his mother over me. The relationship is over." Maddy took a long draw from her drink.

"Are you going to walk away without a fight? Just like that. His mom steps in, says some awful things and you run. That doesn't sound like the Maddy that I know." Voices came through the phone.

"Am I interrupting a night out?" Maddy hoped El said no. Guilt would've made the evening worse.

"Nope. I went to the bar to drink with you." El sent pictures of the bar to Maddy.

This was why she called her best friend. El would always know what to do to help her.

"We agreed that it was all or none. If I beg him to come back or he apologizes and I take him back, what was the point in promising more? A relationship that carries on despite broken promises means nothing more than we didn't mean what we said when we decided to do this." Maddy studied the label on her bottle, picking at the corner.

"No. Your arrangement was a promise to make everything more than just sex. What's your real hesitation, Maddy? This wasn't just about helping me. Ax asked me once if I had feelings for you. At that time, I thought the question ridiculous, but now I'm going to ask—are you refusing to give him a chance because you think I'll be here when you get home as a rebound?"

Her stomach turned with disgust. In the cab on the way over the thought had crossed her mind that El might be interested. Of course, in reality it wasn't possible. She may have had her faults, but manipulation wasn't one of them and El wouldn't consider a relationship otherwise. There was also the fact that El was straight.

To her friend's question, she didn't have an answer.

The fact was, El had seen her parents manipulate each other for years to get what they felt they were owed. As a result, she defaulted to the worst expectation of people. Just another reason why relationships were a bad idea for her. Maddy wasn't setting a great example for her friend. If she wanted to help El find her own happiness, Maddy had to do better.

"You're right, we did agree to conditions. You should have heard his mother. The woman was horrible and he didn't say anything. Ax let her go on." The quiver in her voice wouldn't go away.

The lump wouldn't either. She'd gone to the bar to drink away her hurt, but that was getting her nowhere.

Couples and groups came in laughing, holding hands, sharing kisses. A pang of longing sucked the air from her chest. The room wavered when a dizzy spell hit. Her hands shook against her glass. For the first time, Maddy admitted to herself how much she wanted the affection. Love. Acceptance. Except she wasn't going to get it. Not after tonight. She pulled herself together and willed her hands to still. Shook her head clear of the new wants.

"You still haven't answered my question. Why did you run? Did you give him a chance to explain why he didn't do anything?"

"Besides being hurt, I don't know why I ran. Maybe I should've stayed to keep her from the satisfaction of winning. The dinner would've been miserable, though. No one deserves to be ridiculed throughout an entire meal. I've done that too much in my lifetime."

"That's fair. You're right, you've experienced that more than anyone should. Leaving was the right decision. Did you tell Ax?"

"Don't you see, that's part of the problem. For the last few months he's told me to have confidence. Face things head-on. I did that tonight, but he didn't. When push came to shove he turned into a coward in the corner. I run and he avoids. Neither of us handle things very well." The need to apologize for her whininess didn't even cross her mind.

A few of the bar patrons turned to look at her. Maddy mouthed an apology since she hadn't planned to raise her voice enough everyone heard her problems. El was her best friend, she'd let Maddy have a pity party then make her pull her big girl pants up and deal with the problem.

"Every time you evade my question, I going to assume it's because you don't want to tell me the truth. That means you didn't tell Ax how you felt, and you considered—although I don't know why—that maybe you would try and hook up with me. Both actions mean you're deep into your head right now, there's no chance you would see the light at the end of the tunnel. The train is headed straight for you, and you're not going to get off the track."

Her best friend said it better than Maddy. The truth and the fact that Maddy wasn't able to see the end of the tunnel.

"Fine, yes, I ran because I considered we might give it a shot. I understand there is no reality where this would happen. An apology for losing my mind momentarily isn't enough." Maddy released a long breath then tipped the bottle back and waited for the last drops to hit the back of her throat.

The lump that made it hard to breathe, talk, and think slid down with the alcohol.

"I didn't tell him because my stomach flutters the minute he walks into a room. My heart spasms every time I think about him—in the best way possible. While he held me outside, I almost gave in. He didn't want me to leave. The tears running down his cheeks were almost enough for me to turn around go back inside."

An exasperated growl came through the speaker.

"For chirp's sake, Madelyn. Why did you leave that man? Everything you say about him just solidifies the fact that you're in love. I know you told him communication was important. You preach that in all of your classes. You tell me every time I even consider going on a date. Then you do this? I want to have your back. I'm supposed to as your best friend, but it's becoming more difficult."

Maddy pushed her glass to the edge of the table. She turned to rest against the high back of the corner bench she'd chosen, pulling her leg legs up and wrapping her arms around her shins. Thankful that her dress wasn't a stiff material.

"About the time I was going to tell him we could figure everything out later his mother showed up at the door of the venue. Ax didn't see her. He didn't know that she waved me away or motioned for two security guards to join her."

They should've been back at the hotel. Ax should've been peeling Maddy's dress off her to worship the woman the way she deserved. Instead, she had to figure out how to get through the night without running into him again. Maddy didn't know what she'd do if they saw each other. One part of her heart wanted to crawl into his arms and never leave. She wanted him to tell her it was going to be okay and they'd work through this together. The other half of her heart put up a twenty-foot tall, solid metal fence with barbwire at the top. There was no way Ax or anyone would break through that barrier.

Ax supported her in a way no one else had. He planted a seed and let her nurture the idea. The podcasts were genius. It hadn't taken long for Maddy to figure out what he'd done. His direction didn't upset her either, neither did the fact that he let her take credit for everything. That connection they shared was the reason she didn't want their relationship to be over. For too long she let someone else chip away at her soul. Cut down her confidence. It took Maddy two years to feel comfortable enough to even consider dating and five minutes to find herself back in the black hole she was in when she left her ex-wife.

"Everything is different now. I'm not in this for a trial. The all or none he wanted to start with, is where I've been for the last couple of weeks. Before you get all high and mighty and tell me I should've said something, I wasn't ready. Doubt and uncertainty held me back. We shared our fears and agreed to push them out of the way rather than facing them head on."

Maddy laid her head on her arms. The phone sat next to her on the table. She waited for El to say something. Anything. This was the first time she'd voiced so many emotions about Ax. The talking helped even if El wasn't there to provide physical comfort. Maddy would acknowledge she may have blown everything out of proportion. She had a hand in the debacle of the evening.

"Do you want to keep him around?" El asked.

"More than anything. To experience the way my heart explodes knowing that I get to be with someone as incredible as him is a feeling I can't resist. I won't. Ax gives me the strength to find myself. Natasha and my family destroyed my self-esteem. I have that back. I have the confidence to know that I can run two successful businesses. I will one day love fully." Maddy wiped her eyes.

The shattered pieces of her heart began to merge back together. They'd need some glue to hold on, but for the time being she thought it would work.

"Can you come home tonight? Get some space. Think about how you want to make this right again." El's voice hitched. Maddy made her best friend cry and she didn't know how to make it stop. "Find a way to talk to him. Apologize for bailing when it got hard."

Maddy grabbed her phone to look up the airline. Since there was a three-hour time difference, it wasn't late enough that all the flights would be grounded. She glanced at the time, it was nine o'clock her time, which meant it was six o'clock in Podunk. Now she just had to hope the flights weren't full and it wouldn't break her bank account to make the change.

"There are available flights, but it will cost me five hundred dollars to get one tonight instead of in the morning. I don't have that kind of money."

With the flight out of the question, Maddy searched a reservation for their hotel. Maybe she could stay in a different room for the night. Of course, they didn't have a room available.

"Text me the information. I'll pay for it, and you can pay me back. That way you don't have to worry about running into him and you'll have time to make an apology plan. Take some time to figure things out with Lola and the businesses too. I have a feeling if you get that stress off your plate, the rest will fall into place."

She didn't want to cry anymore, but there was no holding back the tears. El didn't care that Maddy was as much at fault for the evening as Ax. Her best friend helped her when she needed it most.

"Thank you, El. I don't know what I'd do without you. I'll send it now and then go pack."

"You're welcome. Tell him that you're leaving. Don't ghost him and make the situation harder on yourself."

While Maddy wouldn't ghost Ax, she wasn't going to text him or see him face-to-face. Instead, she'd do the worst choice of all. She'd leave him a letter.

32

AX

The damn keycard refused to work. Ax's fingers shook. He needed to find Maddy to apologize. Damn his mother for doing what she did. The door lock clicked. Ax's heart jumped. He shoved open the door and sucked in a breath. The front sitting room was empty. Ax ran into the suite's bedroom. Everything was the same as when they'd left hours before, except Maddy wasn't there.

"Please don't be gone," he mumbled.

Ax yanked open the closet door. His body crumpled to the floor. "Fuck."

Both of her suitcases were gone. Maddy's clothes no longer hung next to his. Ax pounded the top of his thighs with his fists. The night went from one of his top ten to bottom five. With tears blurring his vision, Ax dug his phone out of his pocket and tried Maddy again. It went straight to voicemail.

"Maddy, I'm sorry. Please call me. Let me make this right. I fucked up. Call me. If nothing else, text me to let me know you're safe. If you don't want to talk to me, then reach out to El and have her do it." He paused, not ready to end the call. "I know you're not okay. I understand why. Call or text me, please."

Once he hit the red button to disconnect, Ax slumped forward. He'd messed everything up. Lost the woman who'd come to mean everything to him. Forty-five years old and he still asked how high when his mother said jump. Why would anyone want to be with someone who couldn't make decisions for himself?

"This is why I left New York. Except, it wasn't leaving. I ran away like a coward."

Ax stood from the floor. It was time for him to grow up. Be an adult. Make his own rules. In front of the hotel dresser, he wiped his eyes. He was going to get his woman back in his bed. Out of the corner of his eye, Ax noticed an envelope with the hotel emblem in the corner. Two letters were carefully printed in the middle. Ax. With his heart in his throat Ax opened the envelope and pulled out the letter.

Dear Ax,

I know this isn't the right way to do this. I should've waited for you to get back, but I need some space to think. I went to the airport. I'm changing my flight and heading home tonight. I'm sorry for the way the weekend ended. This is as much my fault as anyone's. Thinking we could push our past behind us was naive. In my head I thought if we agreed it wouldn't be as hard as everyone made it seem. Our connection solidified quickly. It was going so well. Guess I should've known the other shoe would drop—that's the way of life in my experience.

Now, I see what others were saying. This is hard. It takes work. Our relationship was too easy. Tonight was a wake-up call. Even though I used to be in the same circle as your family, that's not true anymore. Like your mom said, I'm a sex worker. You're a socialite.

Ax clenched his jaw. Maddy was one of the few women who had the ability to make him cry. For once, he wasn't overwhelmed with shame for the tears streaming down his face. With one bad decision—an epically bad decision—he'd lost the first woman he'd experienced true love with. Ax continued reading.

This isn't a Dear John letter where I tell you we're breaking up. That's not what I want at all. After tonight I figured out how fast we're progressing. Over the last few months, you have been my life, my everything. If I'm being honest, that scares me.

He paused reading again. Fast didn't begin to explain how his feelings transformed from strangers to a woman he could spend the rest of his life with. Given Maddy's opinion of their relationship, Ax would have to wait to tell her how he felt. The risk of scaring her into leaving was too great. His feelings would take a backseat to giving Maddy time to adjust.

I'm asking for some time to think. Find myself. You need to do the same. We have families, friends, and jobs. It's safe to say we're leaving the honeymoon phase.

"I don't care." Ax clutched a bottle of water.

Right now, you're grinding your teeth and saying you don't care. But that's not true. You do care. When forced into a corner, you didn't come out to me. You stayed in the corner and did what your mother wanted. You chose her. I'm not angry. No. I'm mad at her. At you. At the whole situation but I'm also hurt.

He didn't finish reading the letter. First, he had something else to take care of. Ax checked the time. Everyone had time to return home following the dinner. Ax changed into jeans and a gray Henley. He folded Maddy's letter before tucking it into his wallet. He threw on a hat and left for his parents' house. They needed to have a chat. Ax would prove Maddy wrong. Then he'd figure out a way to get home and start fixing the best relationship he'd ever experienced.

Ax walked through the front door without knocking.

"Mother. Dad. Please come downstairs," he yelled from the base of the staircase. He didn't care if he woke anyone else up.

Edward, his dad, came down the stairs rubbing his eyes. He tugged on the tie of his robe. They'd been in bed, even though the lights were still on. Eve followed.

"What on earth are you doing here at this time of night?" his father asked.

"There's something I need to say to both of you and I don't want to spend all night here."

"Easton, this is ridiculous. Can't you wait until in the morning?"

He shook his head. If he waited until the morning, he'd either forget what he'd wanted to say, or the effect would not be the same. There were some things that needed to be said right away because people needed to hear them in the moment. Ax had learned that with Daphne. He'd made a promise to himself not to let others walk all over him. Then he turned around and did just that at dinner.

Maddy had been right. He was part of the problem. To start fixing their relationship he had to fix himself. Or at least begin the process.

"Sure, it could wait, but I don't want to. You need to hear it now. Tonight, was an embarrassment. The way you treated Maddy was uncalled for, and I don't appreciate it. Saying I dodged a bullet was wrong. You're manipulative, degrading, and all around someone to avoid. Threatening to remove me from the family because you disagree with my choices was unimaginable. I'm a grown adult capable of making my own decisions."

"Easton, that is uncalled for. I don't know what this girl has done to you that you're blindsided to reality, but you should rethink your relationship. It's not healthy." His mother lifted her glasses to the top of her head.

"That's where you're wrong. I see clearer now than I ever have. Moving to Podunk was the best decision I've made in a very long time."

"Son, are you certain about this?" his father asked.

Ax nodded. "Yes."

"Then I'll support you, and I hope you'll let me come visit. I don't know what happened tonight, but given the lack of companions at your side, I presume it wasn't good. For that, I apologize."

"Thank you, Dad."

One down. One to go. His mother would be more difficult.

"Oh, Edward, you've always been soft toward Easton. Do not give him a pass for the disrespect he showed this evening. His cousin had been looking forward to dinner and the auction, but Easton ruined it with his sudden departure."

"How?" Ax focused on his mother. "I didn't cause a scene or bother anyone when I left."

He'd been awed by Maddy's ability to handle his mother without raising voices and causing unnecessary drama.

"Everyone saw what happened. Our table was at the front of the room. When you left and didn't return, they all knew something had happened."

"Well, it's not my fault that other people can't mind their own business. I guess that's par for the course with the crowd you've come to call your own. Those are the type of people I'm not okay socializing with anymore. I need you to hear what I'm saying, Mother."

"Yes, of course I do. Tomorrow, once you've had time to think about everything, you'll remember how much those people have helped you. You wouldn't be where you are without them."

Ax threw his hands in the air with an exasperated sigh. She was clueless. Blinded by the societal expectations he hated.

"Where I am without them? I live in a cabin in the woods of Podunk, Oregon. I'm the foreman of a logging crew—a job I got on my own without anyone's help. No one in Podunk, minus Maddy, knows about my past or that I grew up as part of the social elite. The people here did nothing for me. When Daphne and I split, they took her side. Those people never even considered that she may have been the problem. You say I have blinders on when the truth of the matter is you wear the blinders."

Sadness engulfed him when he thought of the damage he had done to their relationship. Tears rushed from his eyes. A headache started in his right temple. His body tremored. But he didn't hold back. The release of emotion freed him. Ax turned to his father.

"Dad, I hope you'll come visit. Mother, however, is not invited. Not until she wakes up and understands why I can't be around her anymore. Tonight, I made a mistake that I have no intentions of repeating. This family is toxic, something I'm ashamed to admit I didn't recognize before now."

"Oh, you are acting like a child." Eve's put-out tone broke the dam.

"Enough," he shouted. "I've tried to be respectful and follow your damn rules. No yelling. No name calling. Be on your best behavior. 'We never know who's watching.'" Ax glared at the woman who had raised him. He was acting childish, but he'd bottled everything inside for years. "The mistakes I've made are mine. I've listened to you and done what you've asked, for what? I don't even know how to stand up for myself and I'm forty-five fucking years old. Tonight, that changes."

Edward put his hand on his son's shoulder.

"While I understand why you felt that way this evening, do not ask me to do something I cannot do. I hope that when your mother and I come to see you, you'll have forgiven her for what she's done. Ignoring or pushing her out of your life is not the path to overcoming the problem."

Ax didn't argue. Instead, he hugged his dad and then left the house. Halfway to the hotel his phone buzzed with a text notification.

Maddy: I'm safe. I'm at the airport and have a ticket to head home first thing in the morning.

Ax: Thank you. I'll fix everything, Maddy. Please don't think this is over.

Ax held his breath. She'd said they weren't through. She wanted space to figure out life outside of their bubble. He respected that but wouldn't let it go on for too long. If they were going to make their relationship work, they'd need to find a balance together.

Maddy: I don't think it's over. I don't want it to be over. Sleep well, Ax.

She added a heart eye emoji to the end of her text. At least he knew the woman who'd wormed her way into his soul was safe. Once he got back to Podunk, he'd figure out the mess he'd caused.

33

Maddy

The weight on Maddy's chest hadn't eased in the three days since she'd returned from New York. Alone. She didn't expect Ax to reach out first. Not after the letter she'd left. Maddy text El the next day to see if she was around to commiserate in Maddy's misery, but she hadn't heard from her best friend either. Because heartbreak wasn't enough by itself, she stared at a contract Nana had drawn up. Maddy held her head in her hands, her elbows propped on top of the desk in the Pink's office. An offer for her to take over as sole owner of Pinks and Pearls and The Rustic Knob. No more helping from the background or learning the ropes. It was time to decide. She'd told Ax she needed time to figure out her life, this was the first step.

Nana was on the floor chatting with customers, inventorying their stock. The older woman may have a cane, but it didn't slow her down. Lola would never admit it, but Maddy knew the toll her grandfather's death had taken. She'd watched Nana replace her time at Pinks and The Knob with more group activities. Knitting. Dancing. Volunteering at the homeless shelter in the next town over.

Maddy needed someone to talk to, but her boyfriend and best friend weren't talking to her for the time being—something she'd requested from one of them. The loss cut deeper than the day her divorce to Natasha finalized. On a whim she called her mom.

"Hello, Madelyn." Her mother's voice triggered the flood gates open.

Tears fell down her cheeks. Maddy didn't try to dry them. She didn't hide the sobs. They hadn't talked in over a month. She didn't know about Ax. Right then, it didn't matter.

"Hi, Mom," Maddy pushed out between hiccups.

"Did something happen to Mom?" Her mother's voice turned frantic.

Maddy sucked in a breath and brushed her hand across her eyes.

"What? No. Nana's good. Great even." Maddy chided herself.

Of course, her mom would've jumped to the conclusion that something was wrong with Lola. Maddy rarely called and when she did, she didn't have a habit of bursting into tears.

"Then why are you crying?" Straight to the point.

"Personal stuff. Nothing to worry about." Maddy chewed on the inside of her cheek to keep more tears from flowing. Her breath hitched while she tried to regain some composure.

Her mother wasn't one to deal with tears. She didn't like to draw out conversations, and given the tears were unrelated to the reason for Maddy's call, Tina would skip the emotional questions to keep on topic.

"How are things in Podunk? Does my mother continue to run that bar and retail business?" Tina's voice dripped with disdain.

Maddy imagined the scowl wrinkling her mom's brow. How the tip of her lip would turn up in a snarl when she referenced Pinks—the retail business.

Despite not liking her grandmother's choices, her parents had never argued Lola and Delbert's success with Pinks and The Knob.

"That's why I called. Nana is ready to retire. She's offered both businesses to me."

Her mom huffed. "Oh, Madelyn, that's great. My mother is too old to keep running those businesses. Do you think you can handle them?"

The words were like salt poured into an open wound. Her parents asked a variation of that question every time she went to them with a new business idea. Natasha asked it two or three times a day when she owned the bookshop. None had faith in Maddy's management capabilities. Not in life or business. Not since she turned twenty-one and hadn't earned her degree. Even though she had her master's two years later. Or when she married at twenty-seven without a solid career. Certainly not at thirty-five, divorced and working a retail job with minimum wage pay.

Tina may have meant well. She loved her daughter in her own way. Maddy had never questioned that. Love didn't equate pride, or belief in her abilities though.

"Yes...I'm pretty—" Thoughts of El and Ax derailed her train of thought.

Elowen was thirty-seven and while she was still growing her business, she wasn't solidified as a marketing consultant. Yet, Maddy would say her best friend was successful. Ax was forty-five and divorced, working as a logging foreman, making half what he would've made in politics. Maybe he wasn't successful in a traditional way, but he'd found happiness. Just like El.

"Madelyn, you can't even answer my question. That tells me—"

"Nothing, Mom. It tells you nothing. Yes, I can handle them. I will carry on Nana and Papa's legacy, and I'll be great at it." Maddy sat up straighter in her chair.

Success didn't have to come in the form of money. It wasn't decided based on the balance in her bank account. Maddy didn't know why it took her so long to figure it out, or what made her come to the realization right then. Now that she had, there was no decision to make. She didn't need her parents' approval. Even though she pretended that wasn't what she called for, Maddy couldn't deny the truth. For the first time in her life, she realized the person who needed to be proud of her was herself.

"Old, yet naïve. I've been in business long enough to know when a person will be profitable. I'm sorry, dear, but I don't see that in you."

The sincerity in her mom's words came through the phone, but they didn't change Maddy's mind. Nor did they hit her like they had before. The words didn't send a flurry of doubt through her mind.

"Mom, I love you, and I respect your experience. This time, you're wrong. Our definition of success is not the same. Until now, I didn't realize how different we see things. I called to tell you in hopes that you'd celebrate with me, not question whether or not I could handle it. There may be some things I have questions about but picking up where Nana is leaving off is not one of them. I've been here, learned the ropes of the store and bar, gained the trust of the employees. Pinks and Pearls and The Knob will continue to be profitable. I have plans to expand and those plans will work, too. Nana believes in me enough to offer me the businesses she and Papa gave their lives to. It's my job now to make sure I show them my appreciation for that confidence." Maddy smiled.

"We'll agree to disagree. I do wish you the best of luck. Despite what you may think, I don't want to see you fail. Your father and I will help if you have questions."

Yes. They would help. They'd point out all the mistakes in her decisions. No, they didn't want her to fail. Another failure would mean another blemish on their reputation. Except this time, Maddy wasn't in New York. Anything that went south would be swept under the rug. Maddy released a long sigh. The weight to prove her worthiness lifted.

"Thank you. Is everything else okay with you and dad? Maddy bounced her feet beneath the desk, ready to end the call but out of kindness carried on with small talk.

After another fifteen minutes of small talk, Maddy ended the call. As if on cue, Lola walked into the office. A smile pulled the older lady's wrinkles tight. Maddy gave a silent plea—not for the first time—to look as good as her grandmother at that age. The magenta peacock feather gypsy skirt she wore flared around her as she danced her way into the office.

"How is your mother?" Nana asked.

"She's good. Dad got a new job and starts the six-month transition next month." Maddy traced circles all over the contract as she spoke.

Asking how Lola knew she'd called her mother would've been pointless. That fell under the category of "Nana just knows things."

Her thoughts swirled like her finger. Marketing ideas. Classes. Party planning. Podcast. Management.

"I suppose that means we won't hear from them for the rest of the year."

"Mom will say she's supporting him. Dad will say he needs to focus on closing out one business and preparing the new one. Either way, they won't have time for us." She looked at Lola who settled into the chair across the desk. "I don't care. Their life is in New York. Ours is here."

Nana slapped her thin, age-wizened hands against the arms of the chair.

"That's my girl. Have you had a chance to read over the deal? Are you ready to officially take over?"

"Yes, but I have a few changes I'd like to discuss. Ultimately, I will sign the change of ownership, but I want to make sure you're okay with the path I intend to take." Maddy held her breath as she waited for Nana to respond.

She wanted her grandmother's advice. She didn't want to fail like she had before or give up too soon.

"This is what I like to hear. My girl taking control and making my dream hers. Tell me how you're going to take the businesses to the next level." Lola smiled and relaxed against the back of the seat.

Maddy cleared her throat. She pulled her notebook from under a pile of purchase orders. Before talking she silently read each bullet point again.

"I want to hire Maria as the store manager and two more full-time people to fill the schedule. For The Knob, I want to hire another bartender and pull back on Jack's hours. He should be training the new people who will keep the bar running at his standards after he retires."

Nana held up her hand. Maddy stopped. Jack would never agree to retirement. The old man was pushing seventy years old. They had to prepare for the future.

"Jack won't like that. Since I do won't advise against it. How are you going to get his cooperation?"

"That's an area where I need your help. You know Jack better than any of us. Retirement isn't my goal. More like I want him to become manager and trainer. The Knob is as much his as ours, it's fair—in my opinion—that he has a say in operations. I'd also like to set up a pension, or retirement, of some sort for him. Jack doesn't have a lot of family around here, so I want to help him after he can't work the bar anymore."

Lola smiled. "Yes, you'll do fine. Your grandfather and I started a retirement for Jack ten years ago. The decision is yours on how you want to continue forward with the fund. Let's finish with your list, then we'll plan the details."

Maddy read through the remainder of items. Her classes were a must, and Nana agreed that they needed to remodel the classroom to make it more inviting and permanent. Lola suggested renaming them to Spice It Up with the class topic as the sub header for marketing. While her grandmother hesitated on the expansion into party-planning, she understood Maddy's reasoning. They agreed to table that for later, after Maddy had a chance to settle in a bit more.

Tears filled her eyes, and her tongue stuck to the roof of her mouth when she tried to talk about her last idea. Thinking about the podcast and working with El paralyzed Maddy—Ax's idea. He supported her taking over as owner. Ax didn't want a piece of the businesses. He didn't want any thanks for helping her unravel the confusion surrounding the change. Walking away from Ax in New York had been one of the hardest things she'd ever done. Maddy wanted to repair the damage but didn't know how to take the first step.

Picking up the phone was easy but impersonal. Going to Ax's house scared Maddy. If the man rejected her, Maddy wasn't sure how she'd recover—not that it wouldn't be warranted. Leaving him a note had been a cowardly move.

"Now, you're going to tell me how things went bad with Ax. Then we're going to brainstorm how to make it right. Call that Italian restaurant I like. We'll pick up dinner on our way home. I have a bottle of wine to keep us company through the night. None of this will work with Pinks or The Knob if your heart is in need of repair."

Maddy once again sobbed until her body shook. Pressure built behind her eyes and in her cheeks. It became difficult to breathe through her clogged nose. Nana came to her side. She rubbed Maddy's back until the tears lessened and Maddy found a small amount of calm.

"Thank you, Nana." Maddy sniffed while she reached for a tissue. "I don't know what I would do without you."

"Oh, my sweet girl, you would figure it out. I'm not magic. I don't have all the answers. The strength to get through this comes from inside. All I'm going to do is help you find that strength—with a little wine and a lot of awful sex jokes."

Maddy laughed, dried her eyes, and called in their order. By the end of the night, she'd have a plan to get everything she never knew she wanted.

34

AX

Ax rubbed his eyes. He was too old to keep staying up until three or four in the morning playing video games like he had the night before. Since getting home from New York, a week ago, he hadn't had a good night's sleep. He had a standing night out with Dean. Even though he didn't feel like throwing darts, maybe his adopted grandfather could give him some advice. He missed Maddy and hoped spending time with his adopted grandfather would ease the pain that had taken up residence in his chest over the last week.

"Evening, Ax. Dean's waiting for you. He's been in the common area for the last hour telling everyone about the tournament tonight." Susie, a staff nurse, greeted him at the front desk.

Ax shook his head. "That man loves darts almost as much as he loves women."

Susie laughed and nodded. "Come on, let's go get him."

Sure enough, Dean sat at the largest table in the common room, surrounded by six other residents. He waved his hands in the air, telling some story of his past, or how he'd tried to seduce a new student nurse.

"Hey, Pops, you ready to go?" Ax asked from behind the group.

Dean eased himself around in the chair. "You're late."

"Sorry, had to fix some stuff at the site before I could get out of there." Ax yawned.

"You look like a dump truck ran over you. Spend the night with a lady who kept you up too late?" Dean stood then lifted his bag onto his shoulder.

Well into his eighties, he moved around like a sixty-year-old. No walkers or wheelchairs for him. If it weren't for the home's rules, Dean would still be driving.

"Yep. We talked well into the wee hours of the morning until I found the weapon she needed to shove through my heart. I won the game though." He wished Dean's suggestion was the correct one.

Dean clicked his tongue and shook his head. "Those video games. Don't you know at your age they will rot your brain? What happened to your lady? The one who will keep you on your toes and make you forget your name before you fall into a deep slumber curled around her back, protecting her even in her dreams."

Dean was an old-school romantic. Knight-in-shining armor.

"Maddy is...umm...she's busy." Ax couldn't look Dean in the eyes.

"What did you do to screw things up? Last time we talked about her you looked like a man in love instead of a man fighting heartbreak." Dean asked as they made their way out to his truck.

The older man needed help getting into Ax's truck. It was the one regret Ax had about buying a truck that required side rails to get into it.

"I acted like a damn child jumping at my mother's every command." There was no reason to lie about what happened. With the gossip mill around the elder community, Dean would find out soon enough.

"Maddy is Lola Begay's granddaughter, right?" Dean asked.

"Yes, sir. That's one woman I would hate to get on the wrong side of."

"A smart man will remember that when things get rough. Did you handle the situation with your mother? You don't like to talk about her, but what little you've told me she's an emotional leech. Did you pull her off and toss her back in the river?"

Ax nodded. There was nothing else to say. They made the remainder of the twenty-minute drive in relative silence. Dean made small talk about his week and told Ax of his plan for the tournament. He wanted to speed through and wipe everyone out to get as many rounds in as possible before getting back home by ten. If anyone had the skills it was Dean.

"Because you take me out every week I don't have to suffer in that place. Ever since they moved to Seattle it's too much of a chore for my kids and grandkids to visit. You're my family, Easton. I want to know that when I leave this earth you won't be alone. Whatever you need to do to win Maddy back, you better do it."

Ax did his best not to groan. Dean tended to believe he wasn't going to stick around much longer. Ax refused to get on board.

"You're not going anywhere anytime soon. I won't be alone, and I'm working on things. I'll figure it out. I promise."

Inside The Watering Hole they found a table near the boards, and by eight o'clock he'd taken out five guys and held the top spot. Ax nursed a beer and watched.

Between matches Dean would return to the table and grill Ax some more about getting out and doing things. When boredom settled in, he texted Crash. The voices in his head were quiet for the moment and he wanted to keep it that way as long as possible.

Ax: Plans this weekend?

"Hey, I haven't seen you here before." A skinny blonde with too much makeup took Dean's seat across from Ax.

He checked his phone. Crash still hadn't text back.

"Then you must not come on Thursdays very often. I'm here every week with Dean." Ax turned his attention to Dean's second throw.

"Ahh. Well, how's it going tonight?" she asked.

"Sweetheart, this is not the man you want to try and take home. His heart's taken and he's not at all interested." Dean sidled up next to the woman. "Now, if you don't mind someone with a bit more experience..." He winked and the woman shivered.

Ax spit his drink out when her eyes went wide, and her face paled despite the layers of makeup.

"Dean, you're scaring the poor lady." He shook his head.

His phone buzzed with a notification. Dean laughed at the blonde then went back to the tournament.

Crash: I'm a lonely bachelor. Do you think I have any plans?
Ax: Looks like that makes two of us.

His heart clenched at the reminder of being a bachelor again. Despite her letter saying they weren't breaking up, and the text that later followed, the radio silence he experienced gave a different impression. Ax knew better than anyone how actions spoke louder than words.

Crash: What the hell did you do to lose Maddy?
Ax: Too long to text.

"I'm ready to go. Tonight's a bust. There's no way we can finish before curfew." Dean tapped his fist on the table.

Ax didn't ask questions, there wasn't a reason to. When Dean was ready to go, it was time to pack up.

Before heading back toward Podunk, Ax sent off another text to Crash.

Ax: Meet me at The Knob if you want the details.

Maybe they could come up with a plan together to convince Maddy she didn't need space to figure out life. It was a longshot, but Crash had a good idea once in a while.

Crash: What if she's there? If you broke her heart, you think Jack will let you in?

He hadn't considered not being allowed back in The Knob. Ax said a silent prayer that Maddy hadn't shared everything with Jack. The Knob had become a safe haven for him over the past year. If he lost that and Maddy, his mom was right, he should just move back to New York.

Ax: See you in 45. I won't know about Jack until I get there.

"I'm such an idiot." He slapped his hand to his forehead. "Maddy and I had a great thing going, and I fucked it all up."

"That why Maddy's been moping around here the last week?" Jack guffawed.

Ax groaned. He hadn't realized Jack joined him at the bar. For the first time since Ax had been coming to The Knob Jack wasn't behind the bar.

"You working tonight?" Ax wasn't ready for the old man's inquisition.

He was like a grandfather to Maddy. Protective vibes radiated off of him.

"Nope. Maddy and Lola decided I'm too old to be behind the bar all the time. They put me to work training new staff. Those two women have it in their head that I'm going to retire soon."

Ax laughed. That sounded like something they would do. It was a pretty good plan, too. Jack wouldn't have that many years left. The fact that he still spent forty plus hours standing, pouring drinks, and keeping the place spotless was more than impressive.

"I bet you don't know what to do with all your free time." Ax signaled to the new bartender.

He was younger, mid-twenties. Tattoos up and down both arms. Ax was pretty sure he saw some ink on the kid's neck, too. Surprising considering Jack's age.

"Apple bourbon for Ax. Bring me a water please," Jack barked their order.

"Yes, sir." The kid grinned at Jack's groan.

Ax shook his head.

"That boy keeps calling me sir when I've told him a thousand times I'm not his commanding officer." A weathered hand clutched his shoulder. "Want a piece of advice about Madelyn?"

He nodded and hoped the old man's words weren't, "You hurt our girl and we'll make life a living hell for you."

"She's not shy. Madelyn doesn't hold back from what she wants. Right now, what she wants is to prove she can handle life on her own without your help. We all know she doesn't need someone to help her, but Madelyn fell for you hard and fast. I reckon whatever happened, she's the one who left."

Jack's assumption wasn't too far from the truth. The problem was, Ax had made his own mess of everything. He needed to know how to get her attention. She deserved an explanation and apology. The explanation was simple...he lied to himself about cutting his mother's control. It was true now, but the night of the dinner he saw firsthand how much he'd tucked away to dela with later.

"I'll keep that in mind."

"Bring me a blood and sand." Crash jumped onto the barstool next to Ax. "Let's see if this one is worth the money you're paying him."

He leaned forward to shake Jack's hand.

"If that boy knows what a blood and sand is, then I'll give him a raise."

Ax didn't have a clue what the drink was. Since Jack didn't balk at Crash's order, he assumed there was some kind of hard liquor involved.

"You want advice on how to make amends?" Crash asked.

"Pretty much. I've dug myself a ditch I can't find a way out of. A simple apology isn't enough."

"Gotta tell us what you did. The short version, please. It's been a long day, and I left the comfort of my couch for you."

That was the part that scared him the most. Judgement sucked when it was warranted. Of all his friends, Crash would be the most understanding. Jack would read him the riot act until Ax told him how much he wanted to fix his wrongs.

As luck would have it, the bartender came over with Crash's drink. He'd make sure to tip the guy in thanks of the reprieve from answering right away.

"A blood and sand. Scotch, Cherry heering, sweet vermouth, and orange juice." The kid garnished it with an orange twist. He wiped the bar clean before moving onto another patron.

Crash nodded. He swirled the drink. Smelled it. Then sipped. After a minute or two he looked at Jack and smiled. "The kid gets a raise. Maybe a promotion. Either you've done well training him, or he has experience bartending."

"All right. You had time to gather your thoughts. What did you do?" Jack asked.

He took a deep breath then released it.

"My mother made a rather harsh introduction at the fundraiser dinner. She said some things to Maddy that were uncalled for and unwarranted. My dumbass didn't stand up for Maddy. In fact, when Mom told me to sit down to avoid causing a scene, I did just that."

Crash whistled.

"Son, the number one lesson when it comes to relationships is that you always have your partner's back. If you don't agree with what they're doing, then you discuss it later. In front of people—especially your mother—you should've been there for Maddy."

Ax leaned his elbows on the bar. He held his head in his hands. "I know that."

"I'm trying to decide how much shit I should give you for this move. We could go all night, or we could get down to the problem and solution."

One of the reasons Crash was Ax's best friend was his practicality. For most people he came across as a ladies' man who didn't know much of anything. It took them a few months to get past the posturing. Ax had no doubt the guy was smart. He looked at problems from different angles. Crash was his right-hand-man at Weald.

"Have you told your mom to go suck a duck?" Jack asked.

Ax nodded. "She's judgmental and thinks everyone not a part of her circle is beneath her. It's a large part of the reason I had to leave New York after my divorce. I couldn't stand the idea of being around their lifestyle anymore. Oregon brought change. Newness. I had a chance to remake myself how I wanted to."

"Right. What have you considered doing?" Crash signaled for the bartender. "Another one please. Refill his too."

"I'm good." Ax put his hand over the top of his glass. "My expertise is nil in this area. I married a woman who made all of our decisions. Before her, my mother did the same thing. Hell, even now my mom's manipulated me into her decisions. That's why I need help."

"He has a point. An apology is good, but you need to show you mean it. Words aren't as important as actions."

His phone dinged with a notification. While Ax opened up the email, Crash and Jack brainstormed how to help him.

Impromptu Course Offering: How to Talk to Your Partner. Maddy was holding a new class.

"What?" Crash asked.

"Maddy's newsletter. She's teaching a surprise class and sent out an email to encourage people to sign up." Ax held his phone up for Crash to read.

"That's perfect, bro. She's giving you the perfect opportunity. We can go to the class, and you can tell her how much you want her back. If you want to add some flair, get down on one knee and ask her to forgive you for losing your backbone and not being there when she needed you."

Ax covered a yawn with the back of his hand. Like Crash, he'd had a long day.

"Genius. This is why I text you. When is the class?" He scrolled through the email. "Saturday. That's two days from now. Good. I'll be done with the late hours at work and can get some sleep."

"Well, that was easy enough. Looks like Maddy's taking care of you without realizing it." Jack turned to face Ax. "This isn't a chance you're going to get again. Before you grovel, you need to make sure she's the woman you want. I'm not talking marriage. Commitment. Communication. Consent. Those are the three c's that I value. Take my advice...be smart."

Ax nodded. He wouldn't argue with Jack on this point. The man was right. He had one chance.

"You're right. I'm too tired to think right now. I've got a couple of days to figure out what to say."

Crash downed the rest of his drink. "Great. Can we go now?"

Everyone agreed they'd done all they could do. Everything else was Ax's responsibility.

35

Maddy

Crash: I hope you know what you're doing. This is my broth-er we're setting up.

Maddy read Crash's text for the fifth time. She hoped she knew what she was doing too. It was her heart she was setting up. After working out the details for her takeover a few days ago, Nana brainstormed ideas on how to get Ax back.

It was Thursday night. Tomorrow was supposed to be date night—if everything went to plan. With Lola and Crash's help Ax would show up for her impromptu class right on time. It was Nana's idea to hold a class on communication. Of course, that was after she lectured Maddy about her behavior in New York. Maddy knew better than Ax how important communication was.

Within minutes of hitting send on the newsletter, the class filled to capacity.

She sat at the front of the remodeled classroom. They'd added coat racks on one of the walls to hold the toys she introduced. It gave people the chance to touch or try them out on their own time. Rather than a basic classroom set-up with metal chairs in rows and a podium front and center, she'd purchased a few round rugs to cover the floor with extra-large, fluffy pillows near the front for sitting. In the middle were couches and settees with a handful of plush chairs scattered throughout.

Jack helped her get a refrigerator installed, which she'd stocked with drinks and cold snacks like fruits and vegetables—not used for demonstration. At the back of the room were high-top tables and stools. They'd increased the cost per person to cover the new décor. No one complained or refused to pay.

Maddy brushed her sweaty palms down the front of her black, pencil jumper dress she'd paired with a blue short-sleeved cotton shirt. The outfit boosted her confidence, which she needed to win back the man she loved.

A few minutes later Crash entered the room followed by Ax. Maddy sucked in a breath. Her knees knocked together loud enough for the class to hear. The two men found stools at the same high-top as El, who'd agreed to come for moral support. Nana sat in one of the plush armchairs in front of El's table.

Ax had succeeded in taking control of her heart and soul. She'd been impulsive and walked away, hurting everyone in the process. Maddy smiled when they sat together. If her best friend wasn't upset with Ax, which she wasn't, then everything would be okay. Of all the things she'd done wrong when she left, Maddy was grateful she told Ax she didn't want to break up.

The watch on her wrist vibrated an alert to start the class in five minutes. Maddy cleared her throat.

"Good evening," she whispered. She took a drink of water and tried again. "Good evening."

Those standing found open seats around the room. The din of voices quieted. Everyone's attention turned to Maddy. Boulders rested in the pit of her stomach. She glanced at El who gave her a discreet thumbs up before checking to see what Ax was doing. His body language didn't give her any hints to how he felt about being in the same room with her. She hadn't returned any of his texts or calls since returning from New York. There was a need for groveling, which she planned to do for most of the evening—in a subtle way.

Seconds passed that felt more like hours. Maddy steadied her breathing, pulled back her shoulders, and started class.

"For those who've attended a few of my sessions before, you know the number one rule is communication. You must be open to listening and talking to your partner, or partners." She pointedly turned toward Ax. Her next sentence was meant for him. "That's the way to build trust."

"Communication is harder than it sounds," one of the regulars spoke up.

"Yes, it is. Often times we don't know how difficult until we find ourselves in an uncomfortable position. My usual classes are about toys and how to use them in the bedroom. Tonight, we're talking about talking. If you want to spice things up you need to be able to have real, honest conversations with your partners. We're going with a roundtable format. Please chime in whenever you want. Or don't. The choice is yours."

Maddy pulled her stool from behind the podium and sat with the group. Lola said she got on their level, became one of them instead of the teacher, more people would open up. For her plan to work she needed everyone to feel safe to speak.

The first few minutes started slow. A few newcomers asked questions or gave examples of times they needed to communicate better. Maddy appreciated the advice everyone offered—some of it good in her opinion, but not all.

"I had to learn the hard way that communication sometimes means slowing down to listen. Also, people's actions can communicate more than words." El winked at Maddy. "Situations can make us question our assumptions and points of view."

Maddy held her breath. Her nails dug into her palms from clenching her fingers into fists. They hadn't planned on El being one of the first to get the conversation rolling. Maddy wasn't sure if she should thank her best friend or scold her later.

"That's a good point. After a recent argument I caused, I admitted that I was a big part of our problem. To begin fixing things within our relationship I spoke to my parents and explained that I didn't appreciate the way they treated my girlfriend." Ax stared at the table rather than making eye contact with anyone in the room. Maddy held her breath, unsure what he would say next. "When they tried to tell me that I was making a bad decision, I explained that I no longer cared about their opinions. If they couldn't accept me for who I was and at least be cordial to my chosen partner, then I didn't want them in my life."

The room gasped. Maddy heaved out the breath she'd held. She recalled the evening of the dinner. Remembered standing on the curb talking to Ax. Like El pointed out, Maddy didn't take time to listen. When fight or flight mode kicked in, Maddy fled.

"I'm sorry," Maddy whispered.

She lowered her chin to her chest. Lola told her she'd made a mistake. Ax proved her grandmother's statement with no more than a sentence or two. Her plan for a grand gesture withered away in the moment. Maddy didn't want the classic romance book ending. She just wanted a hug.

"Me too." Ax lifted her chin with his finger.

He hadn't made a sound leaving his seat and coming to stand in front of her. Ax got down on one knee and took one of Maddy's hands in his. Her heart stopped beating. While she was ready to admit her feelings had transformed into love, she was not at all ready for a proposal. Her eyes went wide. Behind him, El covered her mouth with her hand. Lola grinned from ear to ear. They were happy for her, but if he did ask her to marry him she'd have to say no.

They weren't ready for that step. There was more they needed to learn about each other. When her heart restarted it beat three times as hard.

"I want us to keep trying. To work through this snafu. Like you said, it's not easy. Listening is as important as talking and actions do speak much louder." Ax kissed Maddy. A short peck on the lips. "I don't want the promises and negotiations hanging over our heads. In my opinion, those offered us too much freedom to just give up. Can we please make this an all or nothing, exclusive relationship?"

Maddy hesitated to smile. Hope sprouted that she didn't screw up their relationship. Ax squeezed her hand.

"You're not asking me to marry you?" Maddy whispered.

The man in front of sucked in a breath. She'd surprised him as much as he had her. She shouldn't have been as relieved as she was to see him caught of guard.

"I'm falling in love with the most amazing woman I've ever met. We've got areas to work on to become better people, better partners, and better lovers. But we knew that going into this. Marriage isn't something I'm quite ready for, though. What do you say we give it a few more months, or even years, maybe we just make this a long-term thing without the legal complications of marriage."

Maddy squealed. Hope rushed through every muscle and nerve in her body.

"Of course. Long-term sounds good. No marriage. I'm okay with that. The last week has been miserable for me. Lola and I signed the contract, and I was too scared to call you because I didn't want to be rejected. How can you forgive me?"

A chuckle broke the moment. Maddy had forgotten they were in the middle of a class. Everyone around them smiled.

"Please answer. This is the best example of communication I've seen. In fact, I'm taking notes."

The two of them laughed.

Ax turned to face the group. "I'm forgiving Maddy because she may not have communicated vocally, but she left me a letter explaining why she ran from us." He looked over his shoulder at her. "All is not forgiven. I'm going to need reassurance that you won't do that again. Almost Dear John letters are not my preferred method of communication."

Maddy nodded. Her heart swelled. She squeezed Ax's hand. She hadn't forgiven him for his actions either. They would need to talk. This wasn't the time or place. Like El said, this was the first step to forever. A step she was more than willing to take.

"Forgiveness can come in stages. For me, if I don't forgive enough that I can sit and talk to you. Figure out what happened and why the road shifted the way it did, then what's the point in even trying? Like Ax, all is not forgiven, but this is the first stage to finding our forever path."

The people in the room nodded. A few clapped. Some started quiet conversations with whomever they arrived with. Maddy stood with Ax next to her.

"Exclusive. No easy way out. All or none." She glanced at Ax. "I'm in. I love you more than words will ever be able to express."

Acknowledgments

No book is written without help. This one has been a long time coming. With each draft, with each new joke, with each new version came someone else that helped me get through this process. I'm going to miss someone, so I want to start by saying thank you to everyone who helped me with this story, even if you didn't realize you were helping.

Thank you to my husband for encouraging me to keep going, even when I didn't have confidence that this book was going to be any good. This book wouldn't have been a book without the crazy brainstorming session with K.J. Harrowick, Megan Van Dyke, Melody Caraballo, Laura Hazan, Abby Glen, and Talynn. This is what happens when a dildo explodes while you're giving it a try.

Cass Scotka, I owe you so much thanks. For choosing me for Kiss Pitch and for helping me see the good in this story. Your motivation kept me going when I was ready to sideline this project.

Kiddo, thank you for the art. Thank you for being you. Thank you for showing me what it means to keep going to achieve dreams.

Also by Jen Davenport

Evanoir Witches
The Coven's Apprentice
Secrets and Sacrifices

Standalone
Love Vibes

Watch for more at https://www.authorjendavenport.com.

About the Author

By day Jen spends her time behind a computer reading regulatory documents (also known as bland writing with no excitement). By night she can be found reading, working on edits for critique partners, writing her next great story, or chilling with her family. Jen's been reading and telling stories since she could talk.

A Texan at heart, it doesn't matter that she transplanted to the Midwest nearly 20 years ago. Rain or shine, humidity or snow, she's happiest with a book in hand. There's nothing better than a good love story no matter if it takes place in space, has dragons, or just a good 'ol small-town hero and heroine.

Read more at https://www.authorjendavenport.com.